MICHELANGELO'S NOTEBOOK

A man appeared out of nowhere like a soundless black shadow. A light flashed briefly in Finn's face and she lifted one arm to cover her eyes, her heart pounding in her chest as fear clutched at her throat.

"What the hell?" was all Peter had time to say.

There was a brief rustling sound from directly in front of them and Finn caught a quick scent of cheap aftershave before something hit her on the side of the head hard enough to take her to her knees. The flashlight? Maybe, because everything was dark now.

She heard Peter rush forward to help her, and in the last split second before the blackness swallowed her, she heard a distant terrible cry cut short by a drawn-out gurgling sigh and she wondered who it was making that awful noise.

MICHELANGELO'S NOTEBOOK

Paul Christopher

AN ONYX BOOK

ONYX
Published by New American Library, a division of
Penguin Group (USA) Inc., 375 Hudson Street,
New York, New York 10014, USA
Penguin Group (Canada), 90 Eglinton Avenue East, Suite 700, Toronto,
Ontario M4P 2Y3, Canada (a division of Pearson Penguin Canada Inc.)
Penguin Books Ltd., 80 Strand, London WC2R 0RL, England
Penguin Ireland, 25 St. Stephen's Green, Dublin 2,
Ireland (a division of Penguin Books Ltd.)
Penguin Group (Australia), 250 Camberwell Road, Camberwell, Victoria 3124,
Australia (a division of Pearson Australia Group Pty. Ltd.)
Penguin Books India Pvt. Ltd., 11 Community Centre, Panchsheel Park,
New Delhi - 110 017, India
Penguin Group (NZ), 67 Apollo Drive, Mairangi Bay,
Auckland 1311, New Zealand (a division of Pearson New Zealand Ltd.)
Penguin Books (South Africa) (Pty.) Ltd., 24 Sturdee Avenue,
Rosebank, Johannesburg 2196, South Africa

Penguin Books Ltd., Registered Offices:
80 Strand, London WC2R 0RL, England

First published by Onyx, an imprint of New American Library,
a division of Penguin Group (USA) Inc.

First Printing, June 2005
20 19 18 17 16 15 14 13 12 11

Prologue

July 22, 1942, La Spezia,
The Ligurian Coast,
Northern Italy

Maggiore Tiberio Bertoglio, wearing the uniform of one of the Mussolini Black Brigades—complete with ebony shoulder boards, bloodred-and-silver double-M collar tabs and a silver-and-black skull-and-crossbones insignia on the forepeak of his regulation bustina—sat in the backseat of the dusty Lancia staff car, arms crossed over his chest Il Duce–style, not feeling half as grand as he looked. The uniform was a fraud. He was not in the army at all but in the much reviled OVRA, the Organizzazione di Vigilanza Repressione dell'Antifascismo—the Organization for Vigilance Against Anti-Fascism: Mussolini's secret police, the Italian gestapo.

He'd flown up from Rome in a cranky old Savoia-Marchetti SM.75 that morning, the old bluebird insignia of Ala Littoria still faintly visible just behind the triple black axe fasces of the Italian air force on the tail. After four bumpy hours in the air he'd arrived at the La Spezia naval base, borrowed the staff car and a driver and was now almost at the end of his journey.

The driver took them through the narrow, winding streets of Portovenere, working their way down to the fishing port at La Grazie. The immense bulk of the twelfth-century Castello Doria was at his back, built eight hundred years before to guard the approaches to the Gulf of Spezia and still doing its job. In the protected gulf itself Bertoglio could see half the Italian navy at anchor, including the huge battleship *Andrea Doria* and its sister ship, the *Giulio Cesare*. Battered and blackened but still afloat.

The staff car finally reached the crumbling old dock and Bertoglio stepped out of the oversized, sand-colored jeep and gave the driver a quick, boot-snapping Fascisti salute.

"Be back in half an hour, no more," Bertoglio ordered.

"Certainly, Maggiore. Half an hour."

The driver nodded, put the battered Lancia in gear and drove off. On the heavily treed island of Palmaria, half a mile away across the bay that marked the harbor for the fishing village, he could see the long low building that marked the convent of San Giovanni All' Orfenio. It stood almost on the shore with a small cement dock of its own, a large, ancient dory tied up to an old black iron bollard. Bertoglio looked around and finally spotted a small fishing boat tied up a few yards away, its owner smoking and talking to another man.

"How much to take me across to the convent?" Bertoglio asked stiffly. The fisherman looked him up and down, eyeing the major's curling single stripe on his arm and the Mussolini brigade tabs.

"Why do you want to go over there?" the old man asked. His brown rheumy eyes took in the black forage cap and the death's-head insignia. He didn't appear to be impressed.

"I have business there, old man. Now, how much to take me in your boat?"

"To take you, or to take you there and back?"

"There and back," Bertoglio snapped. "You will wait at the dock. I will have a passenger."

"That will be extra."

"Why am I not surprised, old man?"

The other man smiled and spoke for the first time. "Every time you call him 'old man' the price goes up. He thinks he is as young as a goat, this one. All the nuns want to fuck him, he is sure of it."

"I leave the fucking of nuns to that priest Bertole," said the old man, laughing, showing the stumps of half a dozen brown teeth. "He may like screwing old women with mustaches, but I prefer the young little *ostrica* you find on the promenade."

"As though they would prefer you!"

"How much," Bertoglio interrupted.

"That depends on how much you have."

"It is only two hundred yards."

"You are the Christ, Maggiore. You can walk on water?"

Bertoglio reached into the pocket of his jacket and took out a wad of lire, peeling off half a dozen notes. The old man cocked an eyebrow and Bertoglio peeled off half a dozen more.

"Good enough," said the old man. He made a sweeping gesture with one gnarled hand. "Step into my princely gondola and I will guide you across the waters to the convent."

Bertoglio made his way into the boat awkwardly and eased down onto the rear thwart. The old man climbed in after him and unshipped the long oars. He used one to push away from the dock, put both into their locks and began stroking strongly away from the pier. Bertoglio sat stiffly in the rear of the boat, his hands gripping the gunwales, feeling slightly queasy as they went farther out into the bay. There was a large bucket close by with something brown and gelatinous floating in it. The contents of the bucket stank and Bertoglio's already nervous stomach began to heave.

"Squid heads," the old man explained. "You trap them when they start to copulate and rise to the surface in their passion. You behead them before they have a chance to spray their sperm and then keep them in the sun for a day or two. Better bait that way."

Bertoglio said nothing. Ahead of them the convent drew closer. It was a long, low building, built with an odd step in it to conform to its rocky setting. There was a steep meadow behind, and within what he took to be a white-painted wrought iron fence there was a small cemetery plot, shaded by several stunted olive trees and sparsely planted with a few simple stones and crosses.

The old man hauled on his starboard oar, sliding around the slim uprights marking sardine and herring weirs built to catch the meandering schools on the incoming tide, then pulled straight for the small dock in front of the convent. As they approached the pier a thin, elderly woman in a dark blue habit and with a white wimple framing her narrow face came out of the front door of the building and walked down to the dock, hands tucked into her sleeves. She stood there waiting calmly as Bertoglio approached. For a moment he felt frightened and ashamed as he had been as a child when creatures like these were the center of his universe and ruled it with a hawthorn switch. That, combined with the roiling of his stomach, made him feel distinctly uneasy as he stepped up out of the fisherman's small boat and onto the dock. The woman stared at him, then turned without a word. She walked back up to the convent, Bertoglio close behind. A moment later he followed her into the coolness of the stone building. It was dark; there appeared to be no artificial light. Bertoglio blinked. The old nun crossed a plain vestibule unmarked by any ornament then turned into what appeared to be some kind of common room outfitted with several shelves of books, a large plank table, a few chairs and a fieldstone fireplace. There was a single window, its shutters closed, and through the broad louvers Bertoglio could see down to the narrow beach and the dock. The old fisherman had disappeared and could be seen halfway across the bay.

Bertoglio cursed. *"Caccati in mano e prenditi a schiaffi!"* He pounded one fist into his palm.

"Did you say something, Major?"

A short, pleasant-faced nun in her forties stepped out of the shadows on the far side of the fireplace. Unlike the elderly sister who had led him here, this nun wore a heavy circlet of carved wooden beads around her ample waist and a large metal cross hung on a chain around her neck, cutting down between her large, pendulous breasts.

"I said nothing," said Bertoglio. "Who might you be?" he asked rudely, sticking his chin out in an unintentional mockery of Il Duce.

"I am the mother superior, Sister Benedetta. You presumably are the man they said would be coming."

"I am Maggiore Tiberio Bertoglio, Sixth MVSN Division Tevere," Bertoglio snapped.

"I was expecting someone from the secret police," said Sister Benedetta.

"There is no secret police in Italy," said Bertoglio.

"And you are not really here, Maggiore. You are a figment of my imagination." The woman smiled wearily. "I suppose the tedeshi Gestapo is enough for both countries."

"I have come for the child," said Bertoglio. He reached into the pocket of his blouse and took out a small packet sealed with the crossed-key and triple-crown imprimatur of the Vatican.

"You have friends in high places," said Sister Benedetta. She put her stubby forefinger under the seal and ripped the packet open. It contained a birth certificate and a travel pass counterstamped by the Vatican, the Swiss government and the Nazi Immigration Authority. There was a second set of travel documents for an unnamed adult. "These documents are in the name of Frederico Botte," she said.

"That is the child's name."

"No, it is not, and you know it, Maggiore."

"It is now. Fetch him."

"And if I told you there was no Frederico Botte in this convent?"

"I would prefer not to answer that, Mother Superior. It can do neither one of us any good. If you hide the child or fail to present him there will be repercussions of a serious nature." He paused.

"I am only doing as I was instructed, Mother. This is no pleasure for me, I can assure you."

"All right."

Sister Benedetta picked up a small bell from the mantel of the fireplace and rang it. The sound was harsh in the room. A few moments later a very young woman appeared, looking uncomfortable in a skirt, blouse and sweater. She was holding the hand of a young boy of about three. He was wearing short pants, a white shirt and a narrow tie. His dark hair had been slicked back with water. He looked very frightened.

"Here is the boy. This is Sister Filomena. She will take care of his needs. She speaks both German and Italian so there will be no problem in understanding her requirements for herself and the child." She stepped forward, kissed the young woman on both cheeks and handed her the travel documents and the birth certificate. Sister Filomena tucked the papers in the deep pocket of her plain cardigan. She looked as terrified as the child. Bertoglio understood her fear; he'd be frightened if he were going where she was headed.

"The boat I came in has gone. How will we return to the mainland?"

"We have our own transportation," said Sister Benedetta. "Go with Sister Filomena. She will show you."

Bertoglio nodded, then snapped his heels together. His arm began to move stiffly upward in the Fascisti salute and then he thought better of it;

he nodded sharply instead. "Thank you for your cooperation, Reverend Mother."

"I do it only for the child; he is innocent of all this madness . . . unlike the rest of us. Good-bye."

Without another word, Bertoglio turned on his heel and headed out of the room. Sister Filomena and the child followed meekly after him. In the doorway the child paused and looked silently back over his shoulder.

"Good-bye, Eugenio," Sister Benedetta whispered, and then he was gone.

She moved across to the window and peered through the louvers, watching as the three figures moved down to the dock. Dominic, the young boy from the village who helped with the chores, was waiting by the dock. He helped the child into the convent's dory, then helped Filomena to her seat as well. The maggiore sat in the bow like some ridiculously uniformed Washington crossing the Delaware. Dominic scrambled aboard and unshipped the oars. A few seconds later they were moving out into the narrow bay between the island and the mainland.

Sister Benedetta watched until she could no longer make out the figure of the child. Then she made her way out of the common room and down a long corridor between the individual cells, finally reaching an exit door in the lower section of the building behind the baths and toilets. She stepped outside into the failing late-afternoon sunlight and followed a narrow cinder path up the hill to the cemetery. Bypassing it, she went farther, into the dark trees, finally reaching a small dell filled with flowers and the dark scent of the surrounding pines.

She followed the path down into the saucerlike enclosure, listening to the sighing wind high above her and the distant weathering roar of the sea. If Katherine had loved anything she had loved this place; her only peace in a bruised life of fear and apprehension. The priest from Portovenere would not sanction her burial on sanctified ground, and in the end Sister Benedetta had not argued. There was no doubt in her mind that this place was closer to God than any other and that Katherine would have preferred it.

She found the simple marble cross without difficulty, even though ivy had grown up around it. She dropped to her knees, taking the time to pull the creeping tendrils away from the stone, revealing the inscription:

Katherine Maria Teresa Annunzio

26	5	1914
22	10	1939

PACEM

Slowly Sister Benedetta unwound the rosary she kept on her right wrist and clutched it in both clasped hands. She stared at the stone and whispered the old prayer of the popes that had amounted to the young woman's last words before she threw herself into the sea:

"It is sweet music to the ear to say:
I honor you, O Mother!
It is a sweet song to repeat:
I honor you, O holy Mother!
You are my delight, dear hope, and chaste love,
my strength in all adversities.
If my spirit
that is troubled
and stricken by passions
suffers from the painful burden
of sadness and weeping,
if you see your child overwhelmed by misfortune,
O gracious Virgin Mary,
let me find rest in your motherly embrace.
But alas,
already the last day is quickly approaching.
Banish the demon to the infernal depths,
and stay closer, dear Mother,
to your aged and erring child.
With a gentle touch,
cover the wary pupils
and kindly consign to God
the soul that is returning to him.
Amen."

The wind grew louder as it swept through the trees, answering her, and for a single moment of peace, the faith of her childhood returned and she felt the joy of God once more. Then it faded with the rolling gust and the tears flowed down her cheeks unchecked. She thought of Bertoglio, of Filomena and the child. She thought of Katherine, and she thought of the man, the arrogant unholy man who had done this to Katherine and brought her to this end. No prayer of popes for him, only a curse she'd once heard her mother speak so many years ago.

"May you rot in your tomb, may you burst with maggots as you lie dead, may your soul rot into corruption before the eyes of your family and the world. May you be damned for all dark eternity and find no grace except in the cold fires of hell."

1

Her hair was the color of copper, polished and shining, hanging straight from the top of her head for the first few inches before turning into a mass of wild natural curls that flowed down around her pale shoulders, long enough to partially cover her breasts. The breasts themselves were perfectly shaped and not too large, round and smooth-skinned with only a small scattering of freckles on the upper surface of each mound, the nipples a pale translucent shade of pink usually seen only on the hidden inner surfaces of some exotic sea-shells. Her arms were long and stronger-looking than you might expect from a woman who was barely five foot six. Her hands were delicate, the fingers thin as a child's, the nails neatly clipped and short.

Her rib cage was high and arched beneath the breasts, the stomach flat, pierced by a teardrop-shaped navel above her pubis. The hair delicately covering her there was an even brighter shade of hot copper, and in the way of most redheaded women, it grew in a naturally trimmed and finely shaped wedge that only just sheltered the soft secret flesh between her thighs.

Her back was smooth, sweeping down from the long neck that was hidden beneath the flowing hair. At the base of her spine there was a single, pale red dime-sized birthmark in the shape of a horn, resting just above the cleft of the small, muscular buttocks. Her legs were long, the calves strong, her well-shaped ankles turning down into a pair of small, high-arched and delicate feet.

The face framed by the cascading copper hair was almost as perfect as the body. The forehead was broad and clear, the cheekbones high, the mouth full without any artificial puffiness, the chin curving a little widely to give a trace of strength to the overall sense of innocence that seemed to radiate from her. Her nose was a little too long and narrow for true classical beauty, topped by a sprinkling of a dozen freckles across the bridge. The eyes were stunning: large and almost frighteningly intelligent, a deep jade green.

"All right, time's up, ladies and gentlemen." Dennis, the life drawing instructor at the New York Studio School, clapped his hands sharply and smiled up at the slightly raised posing dais. "Thanks, Finn, that's it for today." He smiled at her pleasantly and she smiled back. The dozen others in the studio put down an assortment of drawing instruments on the ledges of their easels and the room began to fill with chatter.

The young woman bent down to retrieve the old black-and-white flowered kimono she always brought to her sessions. She slipped it on, knotted the belt around her narrow waist then stepped down off the little platform and ducked behind the high Chinese screen standing at the far side of the room. Her name was Fiona Katherine Ryan, called Finn by her friends. She was twenty-four years old. She'd lived most of her life in Columbus, Ohio, but she'd been going to school and working in New York for the past year and a half, and she was loving every minute of it.

Finn started taking her clothes off the folding chair behind the screen and changed quickly, tossing the kimono into her backpack. A few minutes later, dressed in her worn Levi's, her favorite sneakers and a neon yellow T-shirt to warn the drivers as she headed through Midtown, she waved a general good-bye to the life drawing class, who waved a general good-bye back. She picked up a check from Dennis on her way out, and then she was in the bright noon sun, unchaining the old fat-tired Schwinn Lightweight delivery bike from its lamppost.

She dumped her backpack into the big tube steel basket with its Chiquita banana box insert, then pushed the chain and the lock into one of the side pockets of the pack. She gathered her hair into a frizzy ponytail, captured it with a black nylon scrunchie, then pulled a crushed, no-name green baseball cap out of the pack and slipped it onto her head, pulling the ponytail through the opening at the back. She stepped over the bike frame, grabbed the handlebars and pulled out onto Eighth Street. She rode two blocks, then turned onto Sixth Avenue, heading north.

2

The Parker-Hale Museum of Art was located on Fifth Avenue between Sixty-fourth and Sixty-fifth Streets, facing the Central Park Zoo. Originally designed as a mansion for Jonas Parker—who made his money in Old Mother's Liver Tablets and died of an unidentified respiratory problem before he could take up residence—it was converted into a museum by his business partner, William Whitehead Hale. After seeing to the livers of the nation, both men had spent a great time in Europe indulging their passion for art. The result was the Parker-Hale, heavily endowed so that both men would be remembered for their art collection rather than as the inventors of Old Mother's. The paintings were an eclectic mix from Braque and Constable to Goya and Monet.

Run as a trust, it had a board that was gold-plated, from the mayor and the police commissioner through to the secretary to the cardinal of

New York. It wasn't the largest museum in New York but it was definitely one of the most prestigious. For Finn to get a job interning in their prints and drawings department was an unquestionable coup. It was the kind of thing that got you a slightly better curatorial job at a museum than the next person in line with their master's in art history. It was also a help in overcoming whatever stigma there was in having your first degree from someplace like Ohio State.

Not that she'd had any choice; her mom was on the Ohio State archaeology faculty so she had attended free of charge. On the other hand she wasn't living in New York for free and she had to do anything and everything she could to supplement her meager college fund and her scholarship, which was why she worked as an artists' model, did hand and foot modeling for catalogs whenever the agency called, taught English as a second language to an assortment of new immigrants and even babysat faculty kids, house-sat, plant- and pet-sat to boot. Sometimes it seemed as though the hectic pace of her life was never going to settle down into anything like normalcy.

Half an hour after leaving the life drawing class she pulled up in front of the Parker-Hale, chained her bike to another lamppost and ran up the steps to the immense doorway capped by a classical relief of a modestly draped reclining nude. Just before she pulled open the brass-bound door, Finn winked up at the relief, one nude model to another. She pulled off her hat, slipped off the scrunchie and shook her hair free, stuffing hat and scrunchie into her pack. She gave a smile to old Willie the gray-haired security guard, then went running up the wide, pink marble staircase, pausing on the landing to briefly stare at the Renoir there, *Bathers in the Forest*.

She drank in the rich graceful lines and the cool blue-greens of the forest scene that gave the painting its extraordinary, almost secretive atmosphere and wondered, not for the first time, if this had been one of Renoir's recurring fantasies or dreams: to accidentally come upon a languorous, beautiful group of women in some out-of-the-way place. It was the kind of thing you could write an entire thesis about, but no matter what she thought about it, it was simply a beautiful painting.

Finn gave the painting a full five minutes, then turned and jogged up the second flight. She went through the small Braque gallery, then went down a short corridor to an unmarked door and went inside. As in most galleries and museums, the paintings or artifacts were shown within an inset core of artificial rooms while the work of the museum actually took place behind those walls. The "hidden" area she had just entered contained the Parker-Hale's prints and drawings department. P&D was really a single long room running along the north side of the building, the cramped curators' offices getting the windows, the outer collections areas lit artificially with full-spectrum overheads.

The collections were held in a seemingly endless number of acid-free paper storage drawers ranged along the inner wall. In between the shoulder-high storage cabinets were niches fitted with a desk, chair and a large flat light table for examining individual items. The light tables were made of a sheet of opaque white glass lit from beneath and held in strong wooden frames. Each table was fitted with a photographer's copy stand for taking inventory slides of each print or drawing, and every second niche contained a computer terminal with the entire inventory of the collection entered on its database, complete with a photographic image, documents relating to the acquisition of the object and a record of the works' origins or provenance.

Finn's job for the entire summer consisted of checking that the inventory number, slide number and provenance number all matched. Grunt work certainly, but the kind of thing a twenty-four-year-old wet-behind-the-ears junior curator would have to get used to. What was it her mother was always saying? "You're a scientist dear, even if the science is art, and everything is grist to your mill."

Grist to your mill. She grinned at that, picked up a stenographer's notebook and a pencil from the stationery cupboard and went down the row of paper storage units to where she'd been working yesterday. After getting her degree, she'd spent a year in Florence, studying in Michelangelo's birthplace, walking where he'd walked and learning the language as well. Now *that* was grist to her mill, even if it did involve getting her butt pinched black-and-blue by everyone from the guy in the archives office to the goofy old priest in the library at Santo Spirito.

She wouldn't be mounting seminal shows of the works of Renaissance Florentine painters her first day on the job. Besides, she'd been promised that if she did well as an intern she'd be given a paid position next year. She wanted to be able to live in New York while getting her master's, but it was expensive, even when renting an Alphabet City dump like she did.

Willie appeared again, going on his rounds, fitting his key into the watchman's box and moving on. Other than that, the whole department seemed empty, which was just the way she liked it. She found the drawer she'd been working on yesterday, slipped on a pair of regulation white cotton gloves and started to work, jotting down numbers from the acetate covers on the drawings and then taking the numbers and sometimes the drawing itself to the niche to be compared to the information on the computer database.

After two hours she was yawning and seeing double but she kept at it. She finished one drawer and then started on the next, this one so low she had to drop down into a squat to get the drawer

open. From that angle, she saw that one of the
drawings had slipped into a small crack at the
back of the drawer and was almost invisible. Unless the drawer was completely open it would be
easy to overlook.

Finn carefully pulled open the drawer as far as
she could, then reached in blindly, feeling for the
small edge of acetate she'd seen. It took a while,
but she finally got her thumb and forefinger on it
and gently pulled. Eventually it came free and
Finn brought it into the light. She lifted it up to
the top of the paper storer and used her toe to
push the drawer closed while she took a closer
look at the drawing. She almost fainted.

The drawing was approximately six inches by
eight inches, rough cut at the left side or perhaps
torn. Even through the acetate cover she could see
that the paper was in fact high-quality parchment,
probably lambskin, rubbed with chalk and
pumice. At one time or another it had been part
of a notebook, because at the bottom corner she
could see evidence of stitching.

The illustration was done in a sepia ink, so old
the lines had faded to spidery near-invisibility.
The quality of the work was masterful, clearly dat-
ing from the Renaissance. It was a woman; the
large breasts were clearly visible. She was wide
hipped, almost fat. The head was not in the drawing, nor were the lower limbs or the arms.

What was extraordinary was the fact that the

woman's body appeared to have been sliced open straight up the midline and the flesh and rib cage completely removed. The neck had been opened as well, revealing both the light tube of the jugular vein and the thicker and much more prominent carotid artery running up to and behind the ear. The lungs were bared as were the kidney and heart.

The liver was prominent and neatly drawn but the stomach appeared to have been removed to give a better view of the uterus and the opened vaginal barrel leading down from it. The cervix was carefully drawn in as were the labia at the other end. Ligaments and muscles supporting the uterus and the other organs were carefully included as were all the major veins and arteries of the circulatory system.

It was a beautifully rendered anatomical autopsy drawing of what appeared to be a middle-aged woman. There was only one thing wrong. Autopsies were not done in the Renaissance; it was called vivisection and the penalty for doing it was death. Leonardo da Vinci had been accused and tried for it although the charges had been dropped. Michelangelo, da Vinci's contemporary, had been accused but never brought to trial.

Over the years the memoirs of other artists and intellectuals stated that Michelangelo had, with the collusion of the church's prior, used the dead room at the Santo Spirito infirmary in Florence to do his drawings of bodies, but since Michelangelo's mythical notebook had never come to light there was no proof.

Finn continued to stare at the drawing. She had spent a year in Florence and most of that time was spent studying the work and times of Michelangelo. Even the writing running down the left and right sides of the drawing looked like examples she'd seen of his small, angular script. Without even pausing to think about it she went to her pack and took out her little Minolta digital. She knew she'd catch hell if she was caught but she also knew she had to have an image of this to study at her leisure. It would be a perfect illustration for her thesis. Alex Crawley, the director of the Parker-Hale, was a stickler for policy, and there would be an endless stream of documentation, permissions and just plain paperwork before he allowed her to even so much as think of taking pictures. She took a dozen quick shots then put the camera back in her pack, relieved that no one had seen her.

She carefully picked up the drawing, carried it to the light table and examined it more carefully, using a jeweler's loupe from the desk drawer. The handwriting was too faded to make out the words but she presumed it was notations made on the dissection of the woman's body.

According to existing documentation, when someone died at the Santo Spirito infirmary they would be placed in the dead room, wrapped in a sheet overnight then sewn into a shroud and placed in a coffin the following day. Given a copy of the iron key to the dead room, Michelangelo would sneak in at night, dissect the corpse to examine whatever section of the body he was interested in at the time and sneak out again before morning.

He was supposed to have used some strange metal device to hold a candle at his forehead to light his way but Finn wasn't sure she believed it. She'd been given a tour of Santo Spirito, including the dead room. From what she'd read of the economics of the time she was reasonably sure money had changed hands between the artist and the prior. She was also fairly sure that the rumors and stories were true.

Now she was positive—the drawing she was looking at had not been drawn from memory but from life, or rather death. It slowly dawned on her what she had discovered: this was an actual page from the near mythical Michelangelo's notebook. Finn even knew who had done the binding: Salvatore del Sarto, the binder friend of Michelangelo's who regularly bound together the sheets of cartoons he used to apply his frescoes. But why was it shoved in the back of a drawer in the Parker-Hale and how did it get here?

She checked the inventory number on the acetate covering and jotted it down in the stenographer's notebook. Taking the notebook down to the next niche with a computer in it she logged on, typed in the number and requested the scanned slide representation. Oddly there was none, just a blank white screen and the notation "Not Filed." She went back to the main menu and asked for any documentation relating to the inventory number and was given the name of a minor Venetian artist she vaguely remembered reading about named Santiago Urbino and a second number that took her back to the main menu and the provenance documentation files. The cross-index of image, artist and provenance all matched.

According to the computer file the drawing was by Urbino, had been purchased from a private collection by the Swiss branch of the Hoffman Gallery in 1924, sold again to Etienne Bignou Gallerie in Paris in 1930, to the Rosenberg Gallery in 1937 and finally from the Hoffman Gallery again, sold to William Whitehead Hale on his last trip to Europe before the war in 1939. It had been part of the permanent collection of the museum ever since.

Finn went back to the main menu yet again and accessed the museum's biographical file on Santiago Urbino. A contemporary of both Michelangelo and da Vinci, Urbino was arrested for vivisection of animals for immoral purposes, excommunicated and eventually executed. Finn stared at the screen, pulling her hair back and holding it thoughtfully. It made sense historically, but she knew that a minor painter like Urbino simply could not have executed that drawing.

"May I ask what it is you think you're doing, Miss Ryan?"

Finn jumped and turned in her seat. Alexander Crawley, the director, was standing directly behind her, the Michelangelo drawing in his hand and a furious expression on his face.

3

Crawley was a handsome man in his early sixties, his hair thick and gray, his face square, the eyes intelligent. He was no more than five eight or nine, and Finn was fairly sure he wore lifts in his expensive shoes. As always, he was dressed in a three-piece suit, but this afternoon he seemed even more dapper than usual, probably because of the fund-raiser tonight—the one she hadn't been invited to. She also noticed there were no white gloves on his hands even though he was handling a piece of the museum's inventory. Maybe when you got to be director your hands no longer had oils or potential pollutants on them. She commented on it to Crawley. His complexion went from red to purple.

"Whether I'm wearing gloves or not is none of your concern," he said. "What I am concerned with is your removing this drawing when you had no business to."

"It was in the drawer I was working on, Dr. Crawley. At first I thought it was just part of the regular inventory."

"At first?"

"I think it's been mislabeled."

"How is that?"

"According to the inventory number it's a drawing by Santiago Urbino, one of the minor Venetian painters."

Crawley looked professionally pained. "I know who Santiago Urbino was."

"I think it's a mistake. I think it's by Michelangelo."

"Michelangelo Buonarroti?" said Crawley, astounded. "You're insane."

"I don't think so, sir," said Finn. "I've examined it closely. It has all the earmarks of a Michelangelo piece."

"So we've been hoarding a page from Michelangelo's lost notebook for the past sixty-five years without knowing about it, and suddenly a young intern who is still cramming for her master's degree pops up with it out of the blue." He let out a little hollow laugh. "I don't think so, Miss Ryan."

"I looked on the inventory listings," said Finn, refusing to give up. "The museum doesn't have any other pieces by Urbino. Why this one?"

"Presumably, my dear, because Mr. Parker or Mr. Hale decided that he liked it."

"You're not even willing to consider that it could be Michelangelo's work?"

"And let you write a paper on it that would eventually lead to a great deal of embarrassment to the museum, and to myself as well? I prize neither your work here as an intern nor your ego that much, my dear."

" 'My dear'? It's Finn, or Miss Ryan," she said angrily, "and my ego has nothing to do with it. The drawing is not by Urbino, it is by Michelangelo. Whoever inventoried it was mistaken."

"Whom is the inventory of the piece credited to, and when?" asked Crawley. Finn tapped a few keys on the keyboard and tapped the space bar to move across to the end of the inventory line.

"AC, June 11, 2003." Whoops. A little political incorrectness could take you a long way.

"Alexander Crawley. Me. Not too long ago."

"Then perhaps it's *your* ego that's in question," said Finn.

"No, Miss Ryan, not my ego, but your competence—and, I might add, your arrogance."

"I studied Michelangelo's work in Florence for an entire year."

"And I have studied the masters all my working life. You're wrong and your refusal to admit that you're wrong and defer to a more educated judgment on the matter shows me that you're not the kind of person we need here. When your own ego gets in the way of the work, any professional sense goes out the window. I'm afraid I'll have to terminate your internship at Parker-Hale."

"You can't do that!"

"Of course I can." Crawley smiled blandly. "I just did." He smiled again. "I suggest that you gather up whatever personal belongings you have and leave now to avoid any further embarrassment." He shook his head. "A shame, too. You were a very pretty addition to our little department."

Finn stared at him for a long moment, not quite believing what the man had said, then walked out of the niche, grabbed her knapsack and ran off. She knew she was going to start crying and the last thing she wanted to do was show any weakness in front of that arrogant little son of a bitch. Five minutes later she was on her bike again and headed south to Alphabet City.

4

Once upon a time Alphabet City was the address heard crackling out of police radios on TV crime shows; now it's more likely to be the latest rapper's address or the place to find the newest edgy restaurant. The fact that the city built a brand-new precinct house on the other side of Tompkins Square Park might have had something to do with it. But it probably had more to do with New York's never-ending quest to renew itself as neighborhoods got hot for no particular reason, were gentrified, and then settled down to a comfortable, if boring respectability.

Finn's place was a small five-story brick apartment building on the corner of Fourth and A that only rated as a walk-up because the single elevator was so cranky. To the left of the building were the shops, bars and restaurants that made Alphabet City fun, and to the right lay Houston Street, the southern border of the Lower East Side, which was the hot new neighborhood du jour. Directly behind her was Village View, one of the old slab-sided, high-rise, 1960s-era urban renewal "projects" that used to stain the neighborhood like giant crime-infested cancers.

Still furious, she pulled up in front of her building, keyed herself in and locked up the old bicycle in the dark alcove behind the stairwell. She punched the Up button and was surprised when the elevator lurched into view, its round mesh-glass window making it look like some Stephen King one-eyed monster rising out of the building's depths. She climbed in and endured the slow jerking ride up to the top of the building.

The apartment was tiny by anything but New York standards. The extra-wide hallway leading from the front door was a living room at one end and a kitchen at the other. The kitchen looked out toward the Lower East Side, and had a table by the window big enough to accommodate a maximum of two guests for dinner. To the left was a small bedroom that looked out onto Fourth Street, complete with a chain lock on the window even though it was the fifth floor.

To the right of the kitchen was an alcove the super referred to as a "study" when he'd rented it to her. At the time it had looked like a walk-in closet or a nursery for an especially small baby, but she got a friend at school to build in some simple pine bookcases, then installed a drawing table that fit snugly and she had a place to work.

Beyond that was a bathroom with the smallest sink, tub and toilet in the world. When she was sitting on the toilet, her knees were under the sink. If she wanted to she could put the lid down on the toilet and soak her feet in the tub. An actual bath meant tucking her knees up under her chin.

When Finn had taken the apartment, everything had been painted a sullen nicotine yellow, but now she'd brightened things up with pink in the bathroom, forest green in the bedroom and a fawn color in the living room/kitchen. The study alcove was a workmanlike flat white. In her spare time she'd torn up the swamp green linoleum tiles and had a sanding party for the old hardwood floors.

Her computer was a used Sony laptop she'd picked up for peanuts from a sale at her mother's faculty office and was stored under the ratty red velvet couch in the "living hall" just in case a junkie had the energy to make it up five flights of stairs to steal it. To Finn, the cramped apartment was a palace and a magic doorway into her future. From here she could go anywhere—even though she couldn't really imagine herself being anywhere else at the moment.

Unlocking her door, fury unabated, she stormed into the apartment, threw her backpack on the couch and then began to undress, leaving a trail of clothes from the couch to the bathroom. She soaked herself in the minuscule tub for the better part of an hour, shaved her legs even though they didn't really need it and washed her hair as well, which didn't need it either.

Still furious after all that, she let the tub drain, ran a freezing cold shower and stood under it for as long as she could, counting her blessings and imagining Crawley wandering around Central Park waving a white cane in front of him, screaming, "I'm blind! I'm blind!" Serve the creep right. She pulled her worn terry-cloth bathrobe off the hook on the bathroom door, grabbed a towel and padded into her bedroom, looking for something to wear while drying her hair. She flopped down on the bed and stared blankly into her cupboard.

She groaned. This was her night of reckoning with Peter, her boyfriend of almost two months now. She was supposed to meet him and a few other friends at Max's Garden on Avenue B for dinner. There was an unspoken agreement that "tonight would be the night" at last, with most of the agreement coming from him and her getting tired of putting him off. Peter was handsome enough and smart enough and nice enough but Finn had always been very careful about who she went to bed with.

In Columbus, at sixteen, Finn had already been wonderfully beautiful and dreadfully shy. It was a deadly combination. Boys her own age were terrified of the beautiful dream and bolstered their own feelings of inadequacy by calling her the Red-hot Iceberg and the Red Snapper. The result was she never went out on dates and by the end of her sixteenth year she hadn't been so much as kissed on the cheek by a boy.

Eventually she'd thrown caution to the winds and told her problem to a young junior professor she babysat for, a widower in the English department at OSU who had a little two-year-old boy. She'd had a secret crush on him from the time they first met over a diaper change, so in the end she didn't have trouble believing that in one night she'd gone from never-been-kissed to not-a-virgin-anymore, and she'd never regretted it for a minute. It might be the kind of thing Oprah would have called sexual abuse, but she hadn't felt that way about it then, or now. To her it had been a miracle. On the other hand it wasn't the kind of thing you talked about very often.

The man had been kind, gentle and by later comparison, an astoundingly good lover. He'd also been smart enough to limit the relationship to a few months, not long enough to make her feel obligated to something beyond strong friendship. But he gave Finn enough time to gain the experience and the confidence she desperately needed, and taught her a few things about teenage boys.

He'd also given her a firm, practical grounding in condoms and how to use them and told her every excuse a guy was likely to come up with for *not* using one. By now she'd heard them all and more besides. She had a few condoms in her bedside table just in case, and there was always one tucked into one of the secret pockets in her wallet. Neither AIDS nor pregnancy was in the cards for her future, and somehow she didn't think Peter was either. Of the five men she'd been to bed with since the professor, only two had been worth all the complications and the emotional ups and downs; the others had been clinging, needy or jealously possessive—and in one case, all three.

She'd long ago come to the conclusion that sex and love got confused far too often and this time she was pretty sure she was confusing it with Peter. Right now he was looking for both sex and love, and she wasn't really looking for either. If she was looking for a relationship now it would be with a man to give her strong friendship as well. What she wanted was give-and-take; Peter was looking for all take and no give.

She reached out, grabbed the telephone on the bedside table and sat there with it in her hand, doodling on a little notepad. She could always beg off the date by telling him she was feeling under the weather, but he'd probably want to come over with chicken soup or something. She saw that she'd drawn a rough sketch of the Michelangelo drawing on her pad and grimaced. Who'd have thought finding an old master could get her into trouble? She still couldn't figure out why Crawley had gotten so angry. She started drawing in as many of the veins, organs and ligaments as she could remember and then gave up. She hung up the phone without dialing. The least she could do was tell him in person. She sighed, got up and started to dress. Tonight, she feared, was not going to be Peter's night after all. So how does one dress to tell a guy he isn't going to get lucky?

5

They walked back to her apartment, strolling slowly down Avenue A, listening to the music coming up out of the little basement clubs, smelling the aromas from a dozen different cuisines from around the world. Finn was in no hurry to get home from Max's but she could feel the tension coming off Peter in waves.

He had his arm around her waist, his hand slipped into the tight pocket of her Levi's and about every third step his hip would bump into hers. In high school she would have cut off her left boob to walk down a street with a boy like that but now it just seemed . . . high school. Like a guy going out and finding a street sign with your name on it and stealing it for you. She sighed. Maybe that was the point; Peter was just too damn high school.

"You okay?"

"Sure. Why?"

"You sighed."

"Sometimes people sigh, Peter."

"You're not getting your period or something?" He sounded nervous, as though menstruating was some kind of disease.

"Or something? Something like what? The clap? A yeast infection? Vaginal warts. Herpes maybe?"

He flushed, hurt at the hardness of her tone. "No, no, I didn't mean anything like that. It's just you've been down all evening and I thought maybe . . ."

"Thought maybe it would screw up your evening or something? Make things a little too messy for you? Blood and gore on the sheets?"

"No," Peter answered a little distantly. "I didn't mean that either." He took his hand out of her pocket and moved away from her side a little. He smiled tightly. "Where I come from girls don't talk like that."

"Yes, they do, Peter. You just never listened."

She sighed again. She was treating him horribly and it wasn't really fair of her. She was being a bitch and that wasn't her at all. It was one thing to let a person down easily, it was something else to shoot him down in flames.

"Look," she explained, "I just got fired from my job for no reason. I was pretty sure I'd done something good and it turned out to be bad and I got into a fight with someone and wound up looking like an idiot. On top of that, Alexander

Crawley is the biggest inflated-ego chauvinistic prick I've ever met in my life!"

"Gee," said Peter. "And I was worrying that it might be me." He gave her a boyish grin and her resolve wavered briefly. They reached the door to her building and she got out her keys.

Somehow a few seconds later she was kissing Peter. After the day she'd had at the museum she could feel her decision beginning to weaken even more. His lips felt soft and warm and his tongue poked coolly and insistently between her teeth. She could feel that little space right underneath her stomach begin to melt.

Then she tasted cinnamon Tic Tacs and realized he'd somehow popped one into his mouth a little while back, already planning his attack. His hand went up to her breast and she gently removed it. She broke the kiss.

"Not tonight, Pete. Really. I'm too tired."

"At least let me see you to the door of your apartment." He turned on the grin again. The grin and the Tic Tac seemed to go together.

"You don't need to do that."

"But I want to." He shrugged. "God knows what might be waiting for you in the elevator."

"The elevator monster," said Finn. "And you're it."

"Then I'll protect you from myself," he said. She laughed and turned the key and the two of them went inside.

Peter started kissing her again on the way up in the elevator and by the time the long jerky ride to the fifth floor was over she knew she was probably going to make a mistake and invite him in after all.

She also knew that she was just looking for comfort and distraction from the events of the day and Peter would try to turn it into much more than that, but right now she really didn't care. She wanted his taste and his smell and the feel of him. Maybe it was time she allowed herself to be the selfish one. After all, it wasn't her job to protect him from the realities of life. She wasn't his mother, for God's sake! She giggled at the Freudian implications of that thought and turned her door key in the lock.

"What's so funny?" asked Peter.

"Nothing, just a stupid thought. You might as well come in if you want." She stepped into the darkened apartment and Peter followed her.

"Gee, sound a little less enthusiastic, why don't you?" Peter muttered.

A man appeared out of nowhere like a soundless black shadow. A light flashed briefly in Finn's face and she lifted one arm to cover her eyes, her heart pounding in her chest as fear clutched at her throat.

"What the hell?" was all Peter had time to say.

There was a brief rustling sound from directly in front of them and Finn caught a quick scent of cheap aftershave before something hit her on the side of the head hard enough to take her to her knees. The flashlight? Maybe, because everything was dark now.

She heard Peter rush forward to help her, and in the last split second before the blackness swallowed her, she heard a distant terrible cry cut short by a drawn-out gurgling sigh and she wondered who it was making that awful noise.

6

The man looked as though he was in his middle sixties. He was on the short side, five eight or nine, maybe, and reasonably fit. He had gray crinkly-curly hair fading back to midskull from a widow's peak that made his forehead look abnormally large. The eyes behind his round, steelframed glasses were a very dark brown, almost black. He was wearing a nicely tailored navy pinstripe three-piece suit that was probably something safe, like Brooks Brothers, a simple, no-name, crisply starched white shirt and a Turnbull & Asser tie with thin, dark blue stripes. The shoes were Bally wing tips. The watch on his right wrist was a gold Bulgari that was a little garish but it matched the Yale ring on the index finger of his left hand. There was no wedding ring. He smelled faintly of Lagerfeld.

Someone had taken a nine-inch-long, curved-blade, Moroccan koummya dagger and jammed it into the man's mouth, slicing up through the soft palette and into the man's brain, the exposed end of the weapon sticking out between his lips like some sort of nasty silver-and-black tongue, the long, tooled-metal escutcheon keeping the head lifted slightly off the green leather-and-felt blotter that covered the antique desk. There was very little blood; that was the kind of detail Lieutenant Vincent Delaney of the chief's Special Action Squad was paid to look out for.

According to the title on the office door, the dead man with a dagger in his mouth was Alexander Crawley, director of the Parker-Hale Museum at Sixty-fifth Street and Fifth Avenue, directly across from the Central Park Zoo. Delaney glanced out the tall windows at the opposite end of the office. The old-fashioned green velvet drapes were pulled back and tied off with matching velvet ropes. Maybe a baboon in the zoo had seen something but Delaney doubted it. He never had that kind of luck. Actually, he'd never been to the Central Park Zoo and he wasn't even sure if they had baboons there.

There were four other people in the room: Singh from the M.E.'s office, Don Putkin, the crime scene specialist, Yance the photographer and Sergeant William Boyd, his overweight and badly dressed partner. Billy was watching the dead man's mouth while Singh turned the neck slightly to check for rigor. There wasn't any.

Downstairs at the cocktail party in the main reception hall there were nine hundred elegantly dressed suspects drinking martinis and wondering what the hell was holding up the hors d'oeuvres. Bigwigs, one and all, from the governor and the mayor on down. Delaney sighed. It was going to be a stinker.

"What's the word, Singh?"

The man from the medical examiner's office looked up and shrugged. "Dead maybe an hour, a bit more. No rigor yet. Strangled, probably with a piece of nylon rope. I've picked up a few fibers so far. Basically someone got in behind him and garroted him."

"Any ideas about the dagger?"

"It's not Pakistani or Indian. I can tell you that much. Too long. Probably Berber. Arabic of some kind, by the look of the design work."

"You said he was garroted," said Billy, still staring at the dagger. "He wasn't stabbed?"

"Maybe some kind of ritual thing. The victim was already dead when the dagger was inserted."

"Some kind of freak," said Delaney.

"Not for me to say." Singh shrugged again. "Who knows, maybe he just didn't like art."

Delaney's cell phone twinkled at him, playing the *Simpsons* theme. His teenage daughter had programmed it in as a joke, and he kept seeing Bart skateboarding through Springfield every time it rang. He popped open the phone, listened for a moment, grunted once or twice and then clapped the phone shut.

Delaney looked across at Billy. "Go find out if they've got an intern here named Ryan, would you? First name Finn."

7

The man sat in full uniform in the empty room. It was nothing more than a cell, really, with bare white concrete walls, a gray-painted wooden chair and a single small opening for ventilation in the far wall, always closed, always covered, even in the heat of summer. The only furniture in the room was an army cot and blanket in one corner, a chair and a long table for his work, a combination draftsman's lamp and magnifying lens clamped to one corner. It was the only light in the room—the only one necessary. He did not read there, or eat there or do anything else there except sleep and sit in his chair, working. Sometimes he thought for long periods at a time, but any thinking he did could be done in the dark. There was no sound except the hollow thunder in the distance and the rustling noises of small animals and mad things that could just as easily be in his overburdened mind.

He stood and went to the heavy steel door in his room. First he made sure all the locking mechanisms were in place and then he undressed slowly, hanging each piece of his uniform on the brass hook on his door. His boots he took and placed neatly at the end of his army cot. When he was completely naked he returned to his chair and sat down again. He saw that he was hard but he ignored it. He'd had no one to share his passion with for many years, so it was better to simply disregard it.

He reached out, picked a fresh pair of surgical gloves out of the box on his table and ran his fingers over the thick, carved leather cover of the immense, heavy book that sat in the absolute perfect center of the table.

The motif of the cover was simple and explicit, one of the first such things he had attempted: a deeply carved cross, lines radiating out from it like beams from a star. Hanging upside down was the Virgin Mother, hands nailed to the upright, legs spread on the crosspiece, revealing her agony at both her crucifixion and the birth of the only child she would ever have—a child born ascending, not to earth, but to his place beside his Father. God's child, his power killing her even as she died willingly on the cross to bear him, never to know the immensity of what she was birthing. The wonder of him and the fury, his commitment to a just and true revenge for the world. The naked man prayed briefly to the Mother then

opened the book to the last page he had been
working on and began a new verse.

Since it was the first of the column it would
need to be illuminated as in any Bible. He opened
the small glue pot, and, using his finest brush, he
drew a faint line of the thin, sticky liquid along
the penciled outline of the letter. He blew on it
carefully then used a block of gold leaf, sliding a
single sheet off the block with a cotton swab to
cover the glue line.

He waited patiently, letting the tissue-thin leaf
set with the glue, then used a wider and softer
sable brush to remove the excess gold. He'd already chosen the color he would use for the interior of the letter: copper red, just like the girl's
hair, like the smell of fresh blood on a hot summer
day, the way it must have been so long ago.

8

Finn sat huddled on the end of the couch as the paramedic dabbed at her temple with an alcohol swab. The woman was black and fat and very gentle.

"Must have used some kind of sap or something. Skin's barely broken. There'll be a bump but not much else. You were lucky, girl."

Finn nodded slowly and tried not to look at the huge stain on the carpet runner closer to the door. She didn't think she was lucky at all, but at least she was alive. Not like Peter. She felt the hot tears welling up in her eyes again and swallowed hard. The sound she'd heard before dropping down the dark well into unconsciousness had been Peter dying, his throat opened up in a single slashing sweep that had murmured past her like the wing of a night bird and then turned into that final, horrible liquid gurgle.

The apartment was crowded. Two paramedics,

packing up now, at least three uniformed cops and two detectives. A crime scene technician was covering everything with fingerprint powder and whistling softly under his breath. The paramedic was speaking to her again.

"Sure you don't want to come to the hospital, let the docs take a look at you. You maybe got a concussion. I don't think so, but still, you never know." The paramedic frowned. "There's the other thing too, maybe you want to have that checked."

"I'd know if I'd been raped," said Finn. "I wasn't."

"Okay then, sweetie-pie," the woman said. She snapped her plastic equipment case shut. "We'll be on our way then. Sorry for your trouble and your loss."

"Thank you."

"You bet." The paramedics edged out the door, skirting the bloodstain. One of the detectives came out of her bedroom, and she wondered why he'd been there in the first place. He'd introduced himself as Detective Tracker, which she'd thought was hysterically funny when he'd first said it. And it had been just that—a matter of near hysteria. He couldn't seem to take his eyes off her boobs and he had bad breath. He was tall, broad-shouldered and had greasy hair.

"You and this Peter kid friends for long?"

"A couple of months."

"Sleeping with him?"

"I don't think that's any of your business."

"Sure it is. You were sleeping with him. Some other guy gets jealous, breaks in and waits, like that. You're not sleeping with him, you got to wonder why, see?"

"I wasn't sleeping with him."

"So you didn't know the guy who killed him."

"No."

"How can you be sure? You said it was dark."

"I don't know anyone who goes around killing people."

"Anything taken?"

"I haven't really looked."

"Could have been a robbery then."

"I guess."

"Not much to steal."

"No."

"Student, right?"

"Yes. NYU."

"Peter too?"

"Yes."

"How'd you get together—same classes, mutual friends, what?"

"He's . . . *was* in the fine arts program."

"So? What's that got to do with anything."

"He took a life drawing class. I model."

"Like, naked?" His eyes dropped to her breasts again. For the first time in years stares actually bothered her.

"Nude."

"Same difference, sweetheart. You don't have any clothes on."

"It's different, Detective Tracker, believe me."

"You think maybe it could have been someone else in the class?"

"No."

"Nuts everywhere in New York."

Her head was pounding. All she wanted to do was curl up on the couch and go to sleep.

"It wasn't anyone from the goddamn class, all right?"

"Slow down, honey, I'm not the bad guy here."

"Then stop acting like it."

One of the uniformed cops smiled. Tracker frowned. There was a knock at the door and it opened. A tall, very thin man stood there. He had dark hair that needed cutting and a pinched angular face with deep-set eyes that matched his hair color. He had a smear of five-o'clock shadow on his cheeks and chin. He looked Irish. The man stared down at the pool of blood congealing on the carpet runner and frowned.

"Who the fuck are you?" asked Tracker. "This is a fucking crime scene and you're in the way."

The thin man reached into the inside pocket of his jacket and brought out a small, worn leather folder. As he pulled it out Finn saw that he was wearing a shoulder holster. Tracker saw it too. The man flipped open the folder and pushed it into Tracker's face.

"Delaney. *Lieutenant* Vincent Delaney, Special Action Squad." He smiled. "You are?"

"Tracker, Twenty-third Precinct."

"That's nice. This is Miss Ryan?"

"That's it, Loo."

"I'd like to speak to her if you don't mind."

"I'm in the middle of an investigation here."

"No, you're not," said Delaney. "Not anymore."

9

Dawn was breaking over the Vatican, the secret city behind the high walls still deep in shadow, the trees along its winding paths and around its ancient buildings whispering between themselves in the faint morning breeze.

Lights were on here and there. The man in the long black soutane could hear the faint sound of chanting as he came out of the State Department offices in the papal palace and turned down the narrow gravel walkway that led between the Belvedere Palace and the old brick power plant.

He clutched the decoded message from New York in one hand and quickened his pace down the path, his plain black lace-up shoes making crunching sounds on the dew-damp gravel. Once, early in his career, he had been in awe of this place and saw it as the active seat of God's will on earth.

Over the years his hair had thinned and his vision began to blur, but if anything, he now saw the Vatican with much clearer eyes. Once, he'd seen himself as a privileged priest, brought here for his piety and his love of Christ. Now he knew better; he'd been brought here for his facility with cryptography and his language abilities. If he'd gone to Harvard instead of Notre Dame he'd probably be working for the CIA right now.

Ah well, he thought, even God had need of spies, it seemed.

He continued down the path, then found a small entrance and went up into the library. It was not really the Vatican's library, but rather a tourist showpiece with its dozens of frescoed arches and its display tables of manuscript artifacts that were more colorful than important. He found a second staircase and went up to the floor above.

A long hall led down to a heavy wooden door guarded even at this time of day by an ornately uniformed Swiss guard complete with pantaloons, helmet and halberd. The priest knew that underneath the puffy-looking jacket the guard had a Beretta S12 submachine gun on a quick release sling on one side and a Beretta M9 service automatic on the other. The secrets of the Prince of Peace were guarded with some very sophisticated ironmongery.

The priest dug his plastic laminated ID card out of the pocket of his soutane, held it up where the guard could see it and watched him snap to attention. The priest gave the young man a brief nod then opened the door marked ARCHIVO SE-CRETO, the secret archives of the Vatican.

The man he had come to see was in the first of a score of rooms in the archives, waiting patiently at a plain wooden table, seated on a plain wooden chair. Around him were deep wooden shelves piled with documents. There was a small window looking down into the Pigna Courtyard. The man in the chair was Carlos Cardinal Abruzzi, presently the secretary of state, the second-highest position in the Vatican next to the pope himself. The priest knew that Abruzzi was far more powerful than the slight old man who sat in Peter's Chair. All the threads of power came to Abruzzi's hands eventually, and he plucked them like a well-played harp. He was aware, as few Catholics, or even Catholic clergy were, that the Vatican was less a center of religion than it was a center of business and government. In point of fact it was the second-largest corporation in the world and had an international population of almost two billion to govern, at least spiritually.

"What have you got for us, Frank?" Abruzzi asked, using the diminutive of the priest's first name. The priest handed over the decoded cable.

"Dear me, Crawley murdered," murmured the cardinal. "How unfortunate." The tone of his voice held no compassion or regret. "A Moroccan dagger?"

"I'm afraid so."

"Then we know who the killer is."

"Yes."

"Well, at least he's come to light after all this time."

"Rather dramatically."

"He'll have to be found and dealt with before the police trace him."

"Yes."

"An intern photographed one of Michelangelo's drawings?"

"Yes."

"How do we know this?"

"She was seen on the security camera at the museum."

"Was any attempt made to recover the photographs?"

"Yes. It failed."

"She'll have to be stopped as well." The cardinal continued to stare at the note thoughtfully. "This could be a great opportunity for us, especially with Crawley dead." The cardinal paused. "Is there any connection between his death and the girl?"

"Doubtful."

"But it could be made to look that way."

"Presumably."

"Who will you need?"

"Sorvino."

"Is he available?"

"Yes. He is waiting for your order, Eminence."

"Your order, Francis. I can have no part of this. You must understand."

"Of course, Eminence." He would take the fall if things went wrong.

"It would be a great thing if this could be brought to a conclusion once and for all. There is a great deal at stake, not the least of which is the integrity of the Church."

"And the sainthood of one of her popes," said the priest.

"If you can end this you might be beatified yourself." The cardinal smiled. "We could always use another St. Francis."

The priest returned the smile but there was no humor in it. "There are no saints consigned to the fires of hell, Eminence," he said. "And I'm afraid that will be my fate after this is done."

"Conceivably," said the cardinal. "But perhaps I can see to it that you wear the bishop's miter while you are consigned to this particular hell on earth. Would you like that, Francis?"

"I look for no rewards, Eminence. This is my job. It is how I serve."

"This is no one's job, Francis, man or priest, to clean up the moral defecations of someone who should have known better."

"No priest is anything but a man, Eminence. First and last, he is a man. And the pope is only a priest."

"You would teach me religious ethics?" The cardinal smiled gently.

"It is simple doctrine."

"Which we all learned long ago in the *seminaria*,

but an ordinary man would be deemed a fiend for what this vicar of Christ did. There was a time when he would have burned. Now he is to be a saint."

"It is a cliché, Eminence, but God works in mysterious ways, His wonders to perform."

"I doubt that this has anything to do with God or His wonders, Francis," said the cardinal. "I doubt that very much."

10

Delaney and Finn were alone in the apartment. He sat beside her on the couch. When he spoke, his voice was soft and gentle with just the slightest hint of a lilt she knew couldn't be real because he'd obviously come from New York's Hell's Kitchen and not Dublin's Fade Street—not that she really knew much about either. On the other hand, she had what she thought was a pretty good mind and a straightforward Midwestern distrust of people who were too nice for too little reason. The best candy is from strangers, her mother used to tell her.

"It was probably no more than a junkie looking for something to sell," said the detective. "A terrible thing, surely, but the murder of Dr. Crawley seems an awful coincidence. I'm sure you see that. And you having an argument with him this afternoon and all."

"I don't see what the possible connection could be."

"Neither do I, Finn, which is why I'm here—to see if there is one or not."

"There isn't."

"What was the fight about?"

"A difference of opinion about art. I found a drawing stuck in the back of a storage drawer. I was positive it was by Michelangelo. Dr. Crawley thought otherwise. We had words. He fired me."

"A difference of opinion hardly seems to be the stuff of being fired."

"I agree."

"Then why did he do it?" Delaney said, smiling calmly. "There it is again. You see, Finn, another mystery."

"I don't think he liked someone so young disputing his expertise. The man had an ego the size of a house."

"Did he know young Peter?" Delaney asked gently.

"No. I don't think so, anyway."

"Do you have any idea who would have been angry enough at Crawley to kill him?"

"I didn't know him very well."

"What happened to the Michelangelo drawing?"

Finn frowned. It seemed like a strange question and she told him so.

"A drawing by Michelangelo would be valuable, I presume," he answered.

"Of course."

Delaney shrugged. "So there's motive for killing him."

"The last time I saw it he had it in his hands. I'd put it back in its acetate cover—"

"Why did you have it out in the first place?" Delaney asked sharply.

Finn hesitated. Why was he so interested in the drawing? To her it didn't seem to have anything to do with Peter's death or Crawley's. She'd taken the cover off to get a clearer image when she photographed it, but she decided not to tell him—not yet, anyway.

"I wanted to get a better look at it." Not a lie, really.

"But it was back in its cover when he had it?"

"Yes."

"And that's the last you saw of it?"

"Yes."

"He didn't put it back in the drawer?"

"He might have after I left."

"But you didn't see him do it?"

"No."

Delaney sat back on the couch and looked at Finn. A beautiful Irish girl with a face as innocent as a child's and he was damned if he could tell if she was lying or not. He'd know better tomorrow after he looked at the surveillance tapes and talked to a few people.

"You're a smart young lady, aren't you, Finn?"

"I'd like to think so."

"Who do you think killed your boyfriend, and why would anyone have wanted to do anything so terrible?"

"I don't know."

"And if you were me, what would you be thinking?"

"What you obviously have been thinking: that there's some connection between the two deaths."

"Not deaths, Finn. Murders. There's a world of difference."

"Does there have to be a reason?" Finn asked. "Couldn't it just be coincidence?" Her voice was almost pleading. She was so tired it was almost a physical pain dragging at her. She felt as though she were the criminal, somehow, and not the victim.

Delaney looked at her for a long, thoughtful moment. Finally he spoke. "What do you think would have happened if you'd come back half an hour later than you did? That's the real question, isn't it? Or what would have happened if you'd gone to Peter's place instead?"

"Why are you asking me a lot of stupid hypothetical questions? Peter's dead. You don't know why, I don't know why, and it's your job to find out." She shook her head. "You keep on asking about the drawing. Why are you so goddamn interested in a drawing? I was wrong! It wasn't Michelangelo, okay!"

"Dr. Crawley had a dagger stuck in his throat. We think it's Moroccan. Called a koummya. You know what that is?"

"No."

"Peter might have been killed by the same kind of knife. Sure you never saw one around the museum?"

"No!"

"You're sounding a little tired, Finn."

"Guess who made me that way."

Delaney looked down at the old Hamilton he wore. It was after one in the morning. "Do you have someone to stay with?"

"Myself."

"You can't stay here alone, child."

"Oh, for God's sake! I'm not a child. I can take care of myself, all right?" It was taking everything in her power to hold back a flood of tears. All she wanted right now was to curl up in her bed and go to sleep.

Delaney stood up. "Well then," he said quietly, "I'd best be on my way."

"Yes, you'd best."

Delaney took a couple of steps toward the door, edging around the bloodstain. He turned. "You're sure it was a Michelangelo, aren't you?"

"Yes," she said flatly. "It was a Michelangelo. I don't care what Crawley said or why he said it."

"Maybe saying it is what got him killed," said Delaney. "Did you ever think of that? And your knowing about it might have gotten your friend Peter killed instead of you."

"You're just trying to scare me."

"Now why would I want to do a thing like

that?" He turned back to the door and let himself out. A few moments later she heard the thump of the elevator arriving and then it was gone. She was alone. She stared at the dark stain and then looked away. Why would he want to scare her, and why was he so interested in a drawing that perhaps wasn't by Michelangelo at all?

Finn climbed wearily to her feet, double-locked the door, put the chain on, edged around the carpet stain and went to her bedroom, leaving the living room light on; there was no way she was going to be able to sleep in the dark tonight.

In the bedroom she stripped off her clothes, found a long "Ohio—Home of Elsie" T-shirt with a huge illustration of the daisy-necklaced cow on the front and slid into bed. She turned off the bedside lamp and lay there, light spilling over the end of the bed from the open doorway. She could hear the city around her like a huge storm of energy that never ended. The building creaked, there were strange echoing sounds from the elevator, a scream from the projects behind her, the rumble of somebody dragging open a window downstairs. Maybe she had been stupid to stay here tonight.

She could remember when her father had died. She'd been fourteen. When her mother had told her that Dad had died from a massive heart attack in some godforsaken place in Central America while on a dig she'd lain in bed just like this, staring up at the ceiling, listening to the night sounds, wondering how things could go on with-

out the slightest acknowledgment that her father
had died—that he was gone and would never be
back, that he'd been totally removed from the entire scheme of things, exiled from the universe.
Peter was dead; she'd never hear his voice again,
feel his lips on hers, never even get the chance to
choose whether she'd make love to him or not.

She listened hard, squeezing her eyes shut, trying as hard as she could to sense some remnant
of his being still lingering in the apartment. She
could feel the tears coming again; it hadn't
worked when her father had died and it didn't
work now. He would come to her in haunting
visions instead.

She knew that like her father, she'd see Peter
for weeks, just turning a corner, a passing glimpse
in a crowd on a busy street, a face in the window
of a cab, the sound of a whispering voice that
wasn't there, and then slowly, over time, it would
all fade away like the rustle of old dead leaves in
the wind, and then it would be gone for good.
Memories and old bones—in her father's case, lost
in a jungle cenote, lying in the cold stony depths
of some black, bottomless well.

Finn lay there for a long time and finally sat up
in bed. She knew her mother was off in the Yucatán
digging up the royal tombs at Copan but the crazy
old girl had been known to pick up her messages
from time to time and Ryan really did need to talk
to someone, even if it was by voice-mail proxy.

She switched on the bedside lamp, picked up

the phone and began to dial her mother's number in Columbus from memory. She waited, listening to the ring, and as the recording of her mother's smoke-splintered drawl started, her heart almost stopped in her chest. Bile rose like hot acid in the back of her throat as she sat up, gently putting down the phone, not wanting to scare her mother with a message in her panic-stricken voice, because right now she knew that's how it would sound.

The doodle she'd made of the Michelangelo drawing was gone from the pad beside the telephone. She reached out gingerly and picked up the pad, rubbing her fingers across the blank page. Whoever had taken it had torn off several pages under it because there wasn't the slightest impression. It was as though it never was.

Had never been. Like Dad. Like Peter. Like she might be too, if the killer hadn't panicked. She twisted herself around and dropped her bare feet onto the cold wood floor. Crawley dead, Peter dead, the drawing she'd made gone. Somebody was trying to make it seem like the page from the notebook had never existed, but why? A forgery? Something that the Parker-Hale was trying to off-load on some poor unsuspecting curator at another museum? It didn't seem likely, not for a single misfiled drawing, not to mention the fact that a museum with a reputation like the Parker-Hale's wouldn't put everything on the line for a single possible Michelangelo drawing.

She swore she could hear the creaking step of somebody on the fire escape outside her kitchen window. She knew it was locked, but she also knew that a shirt wrapped around the hand and a single punch could break the glass. She looked around the bedroom frantically, saw her softball bat and glove in the corner near the door and flew to them, grabbing the bat and charging out into the living room. She turned to the kitchen alcove, stepped up to the sink and took a roundhouse swing at the dark reflective glass. It shattered into a thousand pieces as the blow struck, but there was no sound from the fire escape except the pattering of broken glass as it rained down five floors and eventually crashed into the Dumpster in the alley at the bottom.

Finn didn't waste time thinking about what she'd done; there could have been someone out there, and if Delaney was right about the man who had killed Peter and possibly killed Crawley too, eventually there would be somebody coming after her. Hanging on to the baseball bat she hustled back into the bedroom, grabbing her knapsack from beside the couch as she went.

She emptied her books out of the pack, strewing them across the bed, leaving only her digital camera and the makeup bag she carried with her everywhere. She went into the bathroom, loaded herself down with everything from shampoo to tampons, jammed it into the knapsack and then threw in four or five pairs of cotton underwear, two bras, half a dozen T-shirts and some socks.

She pulled and pushed herself into a skintight pair of black Gap jeans, slid on her sneakers and jammed her baseball cap on her head. A minute later she was out the door and taking the stairs instead of waiting for the elevator. She reached the bottom a little out of breath, unlocked her bike from its place behind the stairs and pushed out into the night. She checked the glow on her Timex: quarter to two. Hardly the best time of night to be on the run, but she didn't have much choice. Between Peter's death and Crawley's murder in his office she was feeling more and more as though she had a target painted on her back.

She dropped the pack into the big front basket, climbed onto the bike and pedaled herself up Fourth Street to First Avenue, got off her bike and went into the pay phone. She pulled her little black book out of the back pocket of her jeans, threw a quarter into the slot and dialed. It was answered on the third ring.

"Coolidge."

"Is that you, Eugene?" His real name was Yevgeny but he'd Americanized it.

"Is me. Who is this, please?" He sounded a little concerned, as though the KGB or his mother were calling him.

"It's Finn Ryan, Eugene. I've got a problem."

"Feen!" the young man exclaimed. He was one

of Finn's ESL students and he had a fixation on her breasts—or her ass, whichever happened to be facing him at the time—even though he'd denied it several times. "What is this problem you are having? I fix for you, no swee-at." Yevgeny was the night manager at the Coolidge Hotel.

"That's *sweat*," corrected Finn. "I need a room for the night."

"Here?" said Eugene, horrified. Finn smiled. She'd seen the Coolidge Hotel. It was a four-story, brick pigeon roost lurking under the Manhattan Bridge approaches on the tail end of Division Street, as if trying to distance itself from the flophouses on the Bowery. It was ungentrifiable and it didn't look as though anyone had even thought of trying.

"Yes. There. Don't worry. I've got a credit card. I can pay."

There was bitter laughter from the other end of the phone. Outside her phone booth half a dozen black teenagers were chasing an old man on a bicycle who seemed to be throwing old phone books at them, pulling them out of a frayed mailbag he wore across his shoulders. New York. She had to get undercover, fast.

"We don't take no credit cards here, Feen—cash only."

"We don't take *any* credit cards here," she said, correcting him automatically.

"Yes, any. That's right."

"But I don't have any cash."

"I do," said Eugene. "You pay me back later, yes?"

"Yes," she answered, not sure if she wanted to be indebted to an eighteen-year-old Russian boy with zits on his chin and designs on her body.

"You come now," urged Eugene. "Not good for pretty girl like you to be out this late." He laughed again. "Not good for *ugly* girl to be out this late."

"I'm on my way. If I'm not there in twenty minutes, call the cops."

There was a snorting sound from the other end of the phone line. "Eugene Zubinov never call for cop in his entire life. Not about to start, even for pretty girl like you, Feen. You hurry up your ass and get here quick so Eugene no worry no more, capiche?"

Finn smiled into the phone. "Capiche," she answered. She hung up the phone and got back on the Schwinn Lightweight, pausing for a moment to figure out her route. First was one way the wrong way and there was no way she was going to try riding on the sidewalk at this time of night. She could go over to Second, then down into the Financial District, but she'd be heading into a dead zone this late at night; if anything happened to her down there she'd never get help. Instead she turned the bike around and went back down to Avenue A, pumping the pedals full tilt as she sped past her building, then hanging a right, the fat tires hissing on the pavement as she stood up in the seat, getting as much speed as she could.

She turned onto Houston and into heavier traffic, even at this time of night, keeping as close to the curb as she could, watching for parked cars opening their doors and keeping her eyes peeled for the dangerous yellow rush of taxis playing thread-the-needle on her left.

By the time she reached Eldridge Street and turned left, heading toward the bottom of the island, she sensed that someone was on her tail. Every time she zigged or zagged around a car she'd catch a brief glimpse of another bike a hundred yards behind. In the streetlights it gleamed, sleek and expensive-looking, its gold and black molybdenum frame with rams' horn handlebars and razor-thin racing tires ridden by someone in the full package: skintight black racing shirt with dark Spandex cycle shorts, jet-black riding shoes and a black Kevlar raptor-style helmet, pointed down the back with an opaque angled visor in front. The kind of getup you saw on top-end bicycle couriers during the day running packages and envelopes all over the city, driving like bats out of hell and not giving a damn for anyone else on the road, from buses and garbage trucks right down to other bicycle couriers and even pedestrians.

He stayed on her tail, never gaining and never falling back, and by the time she got as far as Grand Street she was starting to get frightened. At first she thought the rider's presence had been simple coincidence—two people going in the same direction—but what bicycle courier is still working at two in the morning? It might have been a cop, but she knew they rode mountain bikes and wore easily identifiable, bright-colored nylon shells. She remembered the awful sound Peter had made just before he died and pedaled faster, the sweat running down her sides and between her breasts. There had to be some way to lose him.

The best way to lose him was to lose herself. Without pause she swung the bicycle to the right, suddenly finding herself in a dangerous maze of delivery trucks around the big residential block of Confucius Square, known to the people who traveled through it as Confusion. She skidded around a man carrying the gutted corpse of two pigs, threw herself down a narrow alley piled high with boxes of rotting vegetables, then turned again down an even narrower alley packed with wooden crates that went flying as she passed. She heard screaming in Chinese as the clutch of a hand grabbed at her T-shirt and a bottle flipped by in front of her face, smashing loudly into the brick wall on the far side of the alley.

Sobbing, she swerved, tires almost slipping out from under her as she made the turn onto Pell Street and into the thick of the late-night Chinatown trade. Slaloming around cars, she bounced the old bicycle up onto the sidewalk, sideswiped a display of mysterious fruits and vegetables outside a tiny storefront then cut in front of an old man in a black cap and bedroom slippers, coming so close her shoulder actually brushed the butt end of the hand-rolled cigarette from the man's slack lips, sending up a trail of sparks.

She came out onto Doyers Street and pulled hard left, still seeing her pursuer's reptilian helmet out of the corner of her eye. He was closer, less than a hundred feet, and now he was making no pretense about following her. Directly ahead of her was the intersection of Doyers Street and Bowery, the lights at the corner just going from yellow to red. Heart pounding and lungs aching she put out her last bit of strength, pushing as hard as she could on the pedals. Reaching the intersection just as the light went to red, she squeezed her eyes tightly shut, said a quick prayer and sailed across the opening. Eyes still closed, she heard the screaming of brakes and blaring horns followed by the satisfying crush of metal against metal. Without the time or the inclination to look back and see what kind of havoc she had wreaked, she kept on going across Kimlau Square and onto Division Street, then turned onto Market, following it down toward the East River in the shadow of the bridge, finally turning directly under the giant structure and in front of the grimy front entrance of the Coolidge Hotel. Panting hard, she dropped down off the bike, pushing it through the creaking wooden double doors and finally came to a stop.

Eugene, skinny, dark and dressed in a poorly fitting shiny black suit and a white collarless shirt

stepped out from behind the birdcagelike enclosure at the bottom of the stairs.

"You are in trouble, Feen?"

"Get rid of the bike for me. If a guy comes in
here dressed in Spandex bicycle shorts and one of
those dinosaur helmets, you never saw me."

"Dinosaur helmets?"

"Stick with the Spandex." She yanked her bag
out of the carrier basket, still breathing hard. "Get
me a key and I'll love you forever, Yevgeny." She
held the fat-tired bike while the young man ran
back to his cage, grabbed a key from the half-
empty rack on the wall and trotted back to her,
holding it out like one of the Magi bearing a gift.
He was very definitely staring at the sweat stain
between her boobs.

"Fourth floor, in the back, very private."

"Thanks, Eugene." She leaned over the bike,
kissed him on the cheek, then left him holding
the bike as she ran for the stairs. The young man
followed her with his eyes, a small, happy smile
lingering on his lips. After a few moments he
sighed and wheeled the bicycle around in the tiny
lobby of the hotel and pushed it through a doorway leading to the office behind his perch in the
birdcage.

"Feen," he whispered quietly to himself, lost in
some dreamy, damp-eyed adolescent fantasy.
"Feen."

11

Room 409 at the Coolidge was slightly larger than a prison cell and only a little better decorated. The room was roughly twelve by twelve with a single, small grimy window looking out into the tangle of steel supports for the bridge and a minuscule, cluttered view of the East River beyond. There was a faded square of blue carpeting on a wood floor, a brown metal bed and a beige three-drawer dresser with a crazed mirror.

Through the wall she could hear somebody else's bed squeaking and a headboard rhythmically striking the adjoining wall between them as a male voice repeated the words "Oh Mama, oh Mama" over and over again. There was a small bathroom done in shades of orange, with a used condom and the fizzled butt of a cigarette floating in the toilet bowl and two cockroaches standing motionless in the bottom of the tub. There were two separate faucets on the old porcelain sink and both of them dripped.

Finn dropped her bag on the narrow bed, went back to the door and made sure it was firmly locked. Then she went into the bathroom, ignored the toilet and splashed her face with lukewarm water from the taps. She looked at herself briefly in the cracked and chipped mirror on the front of the medicine chest then looked away again.

Her boyfriend's getting his throat slit and then her being chased halfway down the city in the middle of the night didn't do much for her appearance. Tense and exhausted didn't begin to describe it. She could probably pack a lunch in the bags under her eyes and imitate a raccoon while she was doing it. She used her sleeve to dry off her face rather than one of the gray Coolidge towels on the plastic bar beside the sink. Finn went back into the bedroom, flicked off all forty watts of the overhead light and lay down on the old iron bed. Light from a neon sign washed in the window, which was partially open with a screen insert in the bottom. "Oh Mama" next door had changed to "Oh God," but at least Finn had to give him credit for stamina. Outside and over her head, trucks rumbled over the old steel bridge and cars made smaller, insectlike sounds as their wheels spun over the grated surface of the road. "Oh God" changed to "I'm gonna let it go!" And then he did, in a series of incoherent grunts and squeals, and finally he was silent. She fluffed up the tiny pillow behind her head and looked at her watch. It was three o'clock in the morning.

According to her mother, anthropology and archaeology were guesswork and personal interpretation backed up by a smidgen of logic to make it look more scientific. She tried to apply the same system to her present situation. At first there didn't seem to be any connection between Peter's and Crawley's murders, but the disappearance of the doodles beside the phone and being followed by Raptor Head had changed that. Following her meant that he'd been watching the apartment, waiting for her. He probably had been willing to wait for the entire night. Following her in the morning would have been easier with all the traffic, and there was a good chance he wouldn't have been detected. The real question was why he was following her at all. The only connection she could see was the Michelangelo drawing: someone was so hell-bent on covering up the fact that it existed they were willing to kill—and more than once—to see that the secret was kept.

Finn frowned and yawned. That sort of made sense, but the logic didn't really hold up. Why come after her once she'd talked to the cop? And anyway, all Crawley had to do was hide or even destroy the drawing and the secret would have been safe, because the computer and all the material about the drawing's provenance said it was by Santiago Urbino, a sixteenth-century second-rater. The only proof one way or the other lay in the digital chip in her camera. She stared into the gloom at her pack nestled at the end of the bed. Could that be it? Did Raptor Head or whomever he worked for know about the shots she'd taken? It was impossible; the file room at the gallery had been empty when she'd photographed the drawing and she hadn't told anyone what she'd done, not even Peter. Finn yawned again. She had one last card to play, but that would have to wait for tomorrow. Next door she heard the sound of laughter and the sound of bedsprings creaking as one of the couple got up. She grimaced. At least someone had enjoyed their evening.

12

Finn knew she must have fallen asleep because she was suddenly awake. The sounds outside had faded to an occasional truck muttering its way across the bridge over her head. Thankfully her sleep had been deep and dreamless. She glanced at her watch, simultaneously aware that she'd slept in her clothes. She looked at the dial of the Timex and it took a little while for it to sink in. It was six in the morning and there was light coming in through the grimy window. "Oh Mama, oh God, I'm going to let it go" was quiet in the next room.

So what had woken her up? She stiffened on the bed, all her nerves jangling at full alert as she concentrated. Squeaks and creaks normal for an old building, rumbling echoes from the bridge, a distant siren and a scratching sound. Mice, or worse, in the walls? Rats? She'd heard of New York rats, even seen a few. Great big filthy things with yellow teeth sometimes so long they'd pierced their own lower lip. It was the stuff of bad horror movies at the drive-in.

No. Not a Hollywood rat. She let her eyes go wide and stared at a point in the air halfway between the bed and the ceiling, the same kind of thing she did in a life drawing class, concentrating on nothing, waiting for the sound to come again. And it did. Not scratching, but an insistent rubbing sound, metal on wood. She sat up quietly and looked at the door. There it was—a square tongue of metal moving slowly up and down the crack of the door, looking for the hasp of the lock. A steel ruler. Somebody was trying to get in and she doubted that it was Eugene. Raptor Head? More likely. She swung her legs off the bed and reached out, grabbing her pack. Here was one of those situations you never see in movies: the woman is about to get raped or murdered by the guy with jackknives for fingers coming through the door and she has to pee so bad she knows she'll wet her pants in another second.

"Shit," she whispered. She cleared her throat loudly and then thumped her feet on the floor. The scratching stopped, the gleaming end of the ruler frozen. On tiptoes she slipped into the bathroom and pulled down her jeans and panties. Without letting her bum anywhere near the toilet seat she squatted over the bowl, peed and wiped faster than she'd ever done in her life.

She turned and flushed, pulling up her panties

and jeans, watching the condom and the cigarette butt swirl desultorily away along with the two cockroaches who seemed to have moved into the toilet and formed a suicide pact while she was sleeping. She buttoned up her jeans, slipped out of the bathroom and grabbed her pack. Finn stared at the door. The straightedge was still there, not moving. She leaned over the bed and pressed down, making the bedsprings squeak, then heaved a dramatic sigh as though she were settling herself for sleep again. She moved over to the window and waited, her eyes on the door.

A full minute passed and then the sawing motion of the ruler began again. Pushing the pack up onto one shoulder Finn quietly pulled up on the window. She was surprised when it slid easily. She grabbed at the screen insert, easing it to the floor. With the window wide open she stuck her head out to see if there was any way to escape; if not, she'd have to stand by the door and belt the guy with her pack when he finally slipped the lock.

Outside the window there was a fire escape landing and another section of stairs that led to the roof. It wasn't much but it was better than nothing. She threw one leg through the opening, ducked her head and stepped out onto the fire escape. It seemed to shiver as she put her weight on it—she could actually see the rusty bolts pulling away from the brick wall. She began to climb as quietly as she could.

There was a curved handle at the top. She

grabbed it and pulled herself up and onto the roof. She'd been expecting some kind of doorway leading down to a stairway, but there was nothing— just a rippling, wobbly-looking expanse of tarred roof with puddles here and there.

There were half a dozen toilet standpipes and a curved vent stack, but that was it. She'd gone from the room below into the frying pan up here. There was no fire; things couldn't get any worse. Then they did. She clearly heard a loud clang as somebody stepped out onto the fire escape. It had to be Raptor Head. Finn figured she had about thirty seconds before he'd be joining her on the roof.

To the left, glittering in the early morning sun she could see the windows of the curving Confucius Tower. To the right was the dirty streak of the East River and the mosaic of rooftops between the river and the Coolidge. She could scream for help, it wasn't likely to get her any. She was on her own.

Five feet over her head were the lowest girders of the Manhattan Bridge. She ran to the middle of the roof, scrambled up the curving air vent and then reached up with both hands. She grabbed the broad girder, flipped her legs up and gripped the flanges on either side of the girder with her sneakers. Gathering her strength, she pulled herself higher, arching her back and then flipping herself over so that she was lying belly-down on the beam.

Once on the girder, she got up into a crouch
and looked across to the fire escape. She could
just see the top of the black helmet. She stood and
ran, keeping to the center of the girder, drawing in
her breath sharply as the Coolidge roof suddenly
disappeared and she was four stories above the
sidewalk.

Every now and again she ran into a vertical
girder and had to stop and edge around it. The
farther out over thin air she got the harder her
heart beat and the more unsure of herself she became. The empty space under the bridge was
mostly a repository for abandoned cars, and if she
fell now that's what she'd hit first. She risked a
look back and to her horror saw Raptor Head
playing acrobat on the girders as well, except he
didn't seem even remotely nervous as he deftly
made his way around the verticals, barely slow-
ing down.

He was gaining, and Finn knew she didn't have
a hope of reaching the far abutment to the bridge
where she could finally climb down. It took him
five minutes but he was eventually only a dozen
yards behind her and moving fast. At the next
vertical she'd have to slow down again and she'd
lose even more time; they'd wind up being on the
same girder. She heard a faint clicking sound from
behind her, and terrified, she turned. She'd heard
the sound before—last night, just before Peter
had died.

Behind her the blank-faced man in the black

helmet and skintight bicycle shorts was moving, poised and perfectly balanced along the girder, a long thin knife in his right hand, held between thumb and forefinger like a portrait painter's sable brush. He moved easily toward the last vertical between them and started to swing around it, one-handed. She heard a giggling, shallow laugh echoing from inside the helmet and something in her snapped. Instead of running from the dark, sinister figure in his obscenely revealing outfit she did the exact opposite, rushing back along the girder, stripping off her pack with one hand, her fiery hair blowing wildly in the wind as she swung the pack as hard as she could, catching Raptor Head right between the legs as he swung around the vertical.

He screamed as the knapsack connected with his groin, losing his balance at the worst possible moment. He lost the knife, the blade twinkling in the sunlight as it twisted and turned its way toward the ground, bouncing off the broken windshield of an old car before flipping off into a thin stand of weeds beside a tire. Raptor Head held on for half a second more before he found himself too overbalanced to pull himself back to the safety of the girder.

He fell, doing a slow half gainer with a twist, screaming all the way down and hitting the same windshield as his knife, going through it instead of bouncing off. The impact cracked the visor on his helmet like a black egg and she saw his face, a young bloody horror, Asian—either Chinese or Vietnamese. He wasn't moving. Sobbing, half with fear and half with relief, Finn stared down at him, wondering how her life could have changed so quickly and so completely. She slipped the pack on her shoulders again then turned away and headed back along the girder and to the street.

13

Lieutenant Vincent Delaney stood on the sidewalk with his hands stuffed in his pockets, looking up at the building on the corner. The street in front of him was littered with fire trucks, paramedic units and squad cars. Lights were flashing everywhere. There was crime scene tape all over the place and a lot of people in bathrobes and slippers behind it. Most of them had been there for several hours and they weren't looking too pleased about it. Sergeant William Boyd, his partner, rolled around the corner, two Styrofoam cups of coffee in his hand and a greasy bag held between his teeth like a St. Bernard. He reached Delaney, handed him one of the coffees, then transferred the paper bag to his free hand. He popped the top off his coffee, shook the bag open and offered it to Delaney.

"Doughnut?"

"Sure." Delaney peered into the bag, found a

chocolate glazed and lifted it out. He took a bite, then washed it down with some coffee. Boyd chose a banana cream. Delaney stared up at the building again. The entire top floor was a charred ruin. "What did you find out?"

"Fire started around four thirty. Apparently you can smell gasoline on the fifth floor landing, so it's definitely arson." Boyd finished the cream doughnut and dug into the bag for something else. A maple walnut this time. He chewed and slurped.

"Anyone up there?"

"Old guy in 5B. He gets up early so he smelled it first. Called it in and then got out himself. He doesn't know about 5A. Says the whole back part of the building was where the fire was." Boyd washed away the last of the maple walnut with the last of his coffee.

"Firemen been in there yet?"

"Yup."

"Find anything?"

"Nope." A cinnamon this time. The bag was now empty so he dropped his coffee cup into it, scrunching the whole thing into a sticky wad.

"Your flair for description is amazing, Billy, as is your appetite."

"Well, they didn't find anything. You want me to lie?"

"What about the canvassing?"

"The old guy in 5B says he heard someone go down the stairs at a little after two."

"He see who it was?"

"No."

"Anything else."

"The pay phone at the corner."

"What about it."

"I had the LUDs checked just in case," he said, referring to the local use details. "There was a phone call made about two ten."

"Interesting."

"Yeah, well, what's more interesting is where it was made to."

"Don't be coy, Billy. It doesn't suit you."

"The Coolidge."

"That flophouse by the bridge?"

"That's the one. I got a uniform to drive over and talk to the night manager about the call. Turns out the night manager's behind the counter with his throat slit. About ten minutes later some old wino comes in and says a black devil came through the window of his house and got blood over everything."

"What the hell's that supposed to mean?"

"Some Vietnamese punk in black bike gear got tossed off the bridge or something and came through the window of an old Chevy the wino was sleeping in. Messy. Funny thing is, a switchblade was found just outside the car in some weeds." Billy looked up at the building. "Think there could be a connection?"

"Yeah, Billy, I think there just might be. Maybe we should get over there and take a look."

They climbed into Delaney's unmarked Crown Victoria, Boyd behind the wheel, and drove against traffic up Sixth past the looming Village View project to the corner. Delaney glanced out at the phone booth and Boyd gave a whoop on the siren behind the grill, clearing the way across First Avenue. They continued along Sixth Street, Boyd's big red nose actually twitching as they went by the half dozen restaurants that made up Little India. Doughnuts or tandoori chicken, Boyd welcomed it all with a totally unprejudiced gullet.

The big unmarked G-car swung south down Second Avenue. They reached the corner of Second and Houston and Boyd was about to turn west when Delaney screamed at him.

"Stop the car! It's her!"

"Who?"

"Just stop the goddamn car, will ya!?"

Just as they'd gone into their turn Delaney had seen a flash of bright red hair coming up out of the Second Avenue subway station on the south side of Houston Street, the figure resolving itself into Finn Ryan. The tires on the Crown Vic screeched in protest as Boyd jammed on the brakes, and for some reason his hand jabbed out and pushed the siren button. The horn whooped and moaned as Delaney wove through the traffic.

Finn turned at the sound and saw Delaney pounding across the six lanes of Houston Street traffic toward her, dodging taxis and delivery vans like a running back trying to avoid being tackled. She stood for one frozen instant at the top of the subway stairs, then turned and ducked down into the darkness again. By the time Delaney reached the south side of Houston Street she was gone. He stood panting at the subway entrance. She was lost and he didn't have the slightest idea where she was going.

14

Finn rode the F train one stop to Broadway-Lafayette, changed for a downtown G train and then changed again for a Brooklyn-bound 4 train, which she rode all the way down to Bowling Green. She stood rigidly, her hand wrapped around the pole, staring at the doors and not really seeing anything at all or anyone around her. Seeing Delaney had been the last straw. The look of the man as he came hurtling across the street wasn't that of someone willing to offer a helping hand. He already thought she was somehow implicated in Peter's death and probably had something to do with Crawley's murder as well. Adding Raptor Head to the body count wasn't going to make him any less suspicious even if it had obviously been self-defense. She didn't even know who the Asian kid was, for crying out loud! Suddenly she was a suspect in multiple murders with cops chasing after her up and down New York streets and into the subway.

The train rolled into the Bowling Green station at the southern tip of Manhattan and Finn snapped out of her fugue. According to the map the next stop was Borough Hall in Brooklyn. She'd had a hard enough time learning how to navigate around Manhattan; this was definitely not the time to start on a new borough. When the doors slid open she stepped out along with a couple of dozen bright young things, male and female, out to make their mark on Wall Street, no doubt.

Finn climbed up to the surface, glanced briefly in the direction of where the Twin Towers had stood, then turned away and crossed over into Battery Park. She found a bench down by the jogging path that ran right around Manhattan's big toe and stared downriver at the Statue of Liberty, a distant ghost in the morning haze. She stripped off her knapsack, put it on the bench then sat down beside it, curling one long leg underneath herself, thinking out her options.

Her name was Fiona Katherine Ryan from Columbus, Ohio, and she was an art history student at NYU. She'd slept with fewer than half a dozen guys, she liked Häagen-Dazs better than Ben and Jerry's and she didn't really believe anything she heard on Howard Stern or saw on *Sex and the City* reruns. She'd traveled to Italy, spent a little bit of time in Amsterdam and Paris and she'd been well

and truly drunk about three times in her life. She
didn't smoke dope or take drugs except for Extra
Strength Tylenol when she had especially bad period cramps. She worried about zits in the winter.
The biggest secret she had was the knowledge that
she would have sex with Johnny Depp in the middle of Times Square if he asked her to, which
wasn't likely. She knew she was fairly intelligent,
maybe a little smarter than average. She knew she
was pretty, but not beautiful, which was fine with
her. She liked small animals, especially cats. She
didn't much care for spiders or anchovies.

In other words, she was completely normal. So
what was she doing being homeless, chased by
cops and guys with great big knives? She was
caught in the middle of something but she didn't
have the slightest idea what. All she knew right
now is that she wished she smoked. She sighed
and stared at the ripply patch in front of her
where the waters of the East River and the Hudson met. That was kind of how she felt right
now—swept along.

She had a twentieth-century English lit prof
they called the Bald Bear because he had hair all
over his body and none on his head. He was in
his forties, wore argyle socks and shorts to school
in the middle of February and talked on endlessly
about the Ambler theorem. Eric Ambler was an
early thriller writer and all of his books followed
the same pattern: an ordinary person suddenly
finds him- or herself in an extraordinary, and usu-

ally dangerous, set of circumstances. The Bald Bear had all sorts of his own theories about why Ambler wrote this way, but Finn was pretty sure he did it because he knew that spies and murderers weren't going to be reading his books— ordinary people were, so why not deal them into the game?

Well, that was her, and for the moment she couldn't see any way out. And in this case it was no game. If she went and handed herself over to Delaney she'd have to start everything by explaining why she ran. She had visions of *Law & Order* interrogation rooms, being interviewed by Lenny Briscoe and being thrown into some women's jail. The only other option she could see was simply getting out of town and going back to Columbus. She had a key to the house, a bank account and friends. She could camp out there forever, or at least until her mother got back from the Yucatán or wherever. At least she'd be safe there. Or would she?

Someone had been waiting in her apartment and had slashed Peter's throat. Probably the same person who had killed Crawley and had tried for her again this morning. She didn't kid herself that the Asian kid on the bicycle was anything else but hired help. Crazy as it sounded, someone wanted her dead because she'd seen, or simply knew about the drawing from Michelangelo's notebook, and they weren't going to stop chasing her now. How difficult would it be to find out who the nude model with the red hair was at the New York Studio School, or Cooper Union? Not to mention NYU. She wouldn't be difficult to trace back to Columbus at all.

A tug slid by, sending up a muscular-looking bow wave. So what did you do when you were drowning and going down for the third time? You screamed for help, that's what you did. Finn didn't have a bullhorn or a whistle but she did have a phone number.

"If it's really life or death and you can't get in touch with me for some reason phone this number." Her mother had given her the longest, dirtiest look ever and then scowled even harder. "And I mean real life or death, sister, or you can come back and finish college here and marry David Weiner."

The ultimate threat. David Weiner, aka the Weenie, had loved her since he was six years old and still carried a torch for her she could see from Manhattan on clear nights. He had been the only boy in Columbus to throw up during his own bar mitzvah, splashing the rabbi and narrowly missing the Torah he was supposed to be reading from. The Weenie was now a space architect, which wasn't half as exotic as it sounded. It meant he never actually designed anything; you told him how many people you had to fit into a building and he told you how many toilets you needed and how many cubic feet of air you were going to need so people wouldn't suffocate. David was, of course, now getting extremely wealthy, but was still dull as plaster drying. He had hair like a scouring pad and feet so big he could walk across Lake Erie and not get his ankles wet.

According to her mother the man at the other end of the phone number had worked with her father. Her mother had said it strangely at the time, as though her father had been something other than a professor of anthropology from Ohio State. Finn had quizzed her, but her mom had clammed right up. The look on her face said it wouldn't be wise to dig any deeper.

Her mother had used an indelible laundry marker to ink the number onto the inside flap of her knapsack, reversing the number and adding three extra digits to the left and two to the right. When she was finished doing that she made Finn memorize the number until she had it cold. Not the normal mother-henning you expect from a mom sending her daughter off to university, but then Amelia McKenzie Ryan was no normal mother hen. Whatever the case, this was the life and death situation she'd talked about. Finn lifted up her pack and walked back across the park to the pay phone at the edge of the sidewalk. She dug a quarter out of her jeans, dropped it in the slot and punched in the numbers. It rang three times and then anticlimactically it clicked over to an answering machine.

"This is Michael Valentine at Ex Libris, 32 Lispenard Street, New York. We are open by appointment

only. Please leave your name, telephone number and any other particulars you want and hopefully I'll get back to you sometime in the near future. Bye." There was a beep and then nothing.

"Well, screw you too!" said Finn, racking down the receiver. Appointment only? Hopefully? Sometime? The near future? One thing this Michael Valentine was *not*, was a businessman. This was the guy who was supposed to help her out of a jam? On the other hand he did have a nice voice; midbaritone, a little rough around the edges and with a sense of humor lurking in the background somewhere. The kind of person you hoped wound up looking like Al Pacino, except younger and taller. But they never did.

Since she didn't have the faintest idea where Lispenard Street was she hailed a cab and gave the driver the address. He had no idea where it was either, but at least he had a Hagstrom Five Borough Atlas to consult. After figuring out that it was close by, he did a circle around Beaver Street, went back up Broadway and let her out fifteen blocks later. It turned out Lispenard was a narrow street of old loft buildings that ran for two blocks between Broadway and Sixth Avenue. Halfway down the first block she saw an awning with Michel Angelo's Pizza on it and wasn't quite sure what kind of omen that was. The main floors of most of the buildings had been opened as shops, mostly galleries and cafés. Not 32 Lispenard; the windows had been boarded up and then covered with steel shutters all the way up to the roof. The only entrance was a plain gray door with a complicated lock and a faded business card thumbtacked at eye level.

Ex Libris
Antiquaria. Research information.
By appointment only.
Please look at the camera and smile.

The camera turned out to be a small black box the size of a walnut in the upper left-hand corner of the doorframe. She looked up at it, stuck her tongue out and frowned. "How's that, Mr. Arrogant Prick?" she muttered.

"That's fine, sweetheart, but I really would appreciate a smile." The answer came back almost immediately and Finn jumped back, blushing furiously.

"Step closer. You've gone out of range of the camera," said the voice.

Finn stepped forward again. "I phoned you but there was only a message."

"That's all there ever is. The number's unlisted. How did you get it?"

"Uh, my mother gave it to me."

"Your mother's name is 'Uh'?"

"My mother's name is Amelia McKenzie Ryan."

There was a brief silence. "Your dad was Lyman Andrew Ryan?"

"That's right."

"He had a nickname."

"That's right. He did."

"Tell it to me."

"Why should I?"

"Because if you don't, I won't open the door so you can tell me your problem."

"Why do you think I have a problem?"

"Don't be irritating. Your mother didn't give you this number because she thought you and I might sit around and have tea together. She gave it to you for extreme emergencies."

"Buck."

"Good girl. That makes you Fiona."

"Finn. And I'm not a girl."

"You're not a boy—that's for sure." There was a buzzing sound and the door popped open. "You'll see a freight elevator at the end of the hall. Take it. Press five. Close the door firmly behind you, please."

Finn did as she was told, making sure the door was shut tight. She walked down a narrow hall, brick on the left side, unpainted sheetrock on the other. She reached the oversized freight elevator, stepped in and pulled the knotted rope that brought the gate down. She pressed five on the old black control panel and the elevator began to creak its way upward.

What she saw through the slats of the gate as the elevator rose was nothing short of amazing. Each floor looked like a library envisioned by Ray

Bradbury as channeled by the Collyer brothers: metal grate floors with endless rows of tall gray bookcases and filing cabinets stuffed to overflowing, turns and corners indicating that there were secret depths to the maze you couldn't see from the elevator, all of this lit by dim bulbs in green pan-shaped fixtures hanging down out of the darkness. Once or twice she thought she saw movement among the seemingly endless stacks, like a giant shadowy rat, but she was pretty sure the image was caused by the state of her nerves and the gloom. The fifth floor was no different from the others. The elevator came to a smooth stop and she pulled on the rope, raising the gate. She stepped out of the elevator and brought the door down behind her. The elevator automatically moved down again, leaving a deep empty shaft behind. Finn took a step or two forward and looked down between her feet. The holes in the grated floor were large enough to let her see all the way down to the bottom floor. Once upon a time the building had been completely gutted of its interior walls and floors and replaced with a gigantic cage of mesh and struts that now made up the inside of the building.

She turned to the left and looked at the bookcase beside her. *Konstructive theoritsche und experimentelle Beitrag zu dem Probleme der Flussigkeitsrakete: W. Von Braun—1934.* The title had been hand-typed and then glued onto the spine. A university dissertation maybe? She reached out to pull it from the bookcase for a closer look. A voice stopped her.

"Don't touch the material, please. We don't want to disturb Enkel. He's very possessive about the material."

"Enkel?" she said into the gloom.

"Enkel Shmolkin. My archivist. I'm not sure where he is right now—somewhere in the stacks. Maybe you'll run into him."

Finn looked for a camera lens but this time she couldn't find it. "Where are you?"

"Straight ahead until you reach the end of the row. Then turn left. You'll come to a door eventually."

Feeling a little bit like Dorothy in *The Wizard of Oz*, Finn went forward, her feet ringing dully on the metal floor. The cases left and right seemed evenly divided between library-width bookcases eight or nine feet high and equally high file-drawer stacks. The file drawers each appeared to be fitted with a sturdy-looking steel Yale lock. The whole place was like the Fort Knox of libraries.

She reached the far end of the passage, turned left and kept walking. Eventually she reached a plain white door with no knob or lock. She put up one fist, preparing to knock, and there was a small clicking noise. The door slid open. It was metal, about three inches thick and had a piano hinge running all the way down one side, like the door to a bank vault.

The room beyond looked like something out of Dickens. It was a sitting room fitted out with several comfortable-looking club chairs, a table cluttered with several newspapers and a narrow, coal-burning fireplace. On the mantel of the fireplace there was a coal scuttle with a leather pouch in it, a violin standing on end and an old-fashioned-looking meerschaum pipe. Over the mantel, drilled into the pale striped wallpaper were the initials V.R. Finn smiled. It wasn't out of Dickens, it was out of Arthur Conan Doyle. The only thing out of place was a coffeemaker, cups and cream and sugar on a side table along with a plate piled high with what appeared to be freshly made Toll House cookies. "Enkel makes them," he said, noticing her glance. "Oatmeal and peanut butter too. We've both got a bit of a sweet tooth."

The man seated at the table smiled. He looked like a cross between John Malkovich and Willem Dafoe: high forehead, chiseled cheekbones, broad chin and big sexy mouth. His eyes were black, deep-set and intense. He looked to be in his mid-forties with just enough gray in his hair to make him look a little less dangerous than a younger version of the same man would have been.

"Finn Ryan," he said. "You don't look anything like your old man except for the hair."

Finn didn't know how to answer that so she looked around the room instead. "Sherlock Holmes's study," she said finally.

"Very good," said Valentine.

"Was it a test?"

"Not at all," he said. "I just like it when people are literate enough to know what they're seeing. I just did it for fun. Next time I do something with it, I thought I might try Nero Wolfe."

"You're not fat."

"I'd be Archie Goodwin."

"That might work."

"So what's your problem?"

"Murder, funnily enough."

"Did you do it?" said Valentine, waving her toward one of the club chairs.

"No," said Finn.

"Then there's no problem," said Valentine. "There's just a situation that has to be resolved."

"I think it's a bit more than that," said Finn.

"Explain."

So she did.

15

Half an hour later, while munching on cookies and drinking coffee, her legs drawn up under her in one of the big club chairs, she had brought Valentine up to speed.

"So what do you think?" he asked.

"I think Peter got in the way and died because of it. I think Crawley died because I saw the Michelangelo and I think I'm next."

"Interesting."

"It's more than interesting. It's my life, Mr. Valentine."

"Michael, please. I didn't mean that part of it was interesting. I meant the part about someone dying just because they saw a particular work of art. It doesn't have any logical basis . . . yet."

"I don't think it has a logical basis *period*. It doesn't make any sense at all."

"It makes sense to whoever killed your friend and the director of the Parker-Hale."

"Why do I get the feeling we're going around in circles?"

"Because we are," said Valentine. "The circles get smaller and smaller, and finally you come to the little point of truth right in the center."

"Way too Zen for me," answered Finn. "My mother gave me your number if I ever got into real trouble, which is what I think I'm in right now. Aren't you supposed to do something? We've been sitting around drinking coffee and eating cookies and we're not getting anywhere."

"Depends on your point of view," said Valentine. "I know a lot of things I didn't before. I know what you look like, I know where you live, I know that among other things you're a nude model, a teacher of English as a second language, a recently fired intern at a prestigious art museum and you've been involved in two violent deaths. Any one of those facts could be vitally important to the situation at hand."

"Why does everyone harp on the nude model part?"

"Because it forces people to imagine you with no clothes on. For some people that's probably very uncomfortable, for other people it's probably a delight. It's a lot different than saying you work as a waitress at IHOP, you've got to admit." Valentine sighed. "My dear Finn, it's my job to look at details, very small details. When I'm doing a valuation of a rare book for someone, the shape of a letter can mean the difference between the work being authentic or a forgery. If I'm advising somebody on a piece of crucial information, that information has to be exactly right. If you look closely at things you see the details, you see the flaws and sometimes you see the absolute perfection. They can be equally important."

"You mean the Michelangelo?"

"As an example, sure. That may be the problem right there—it might not be a Michelangelo at all. It wouldn't be the first time someone was killed over a forgery."

"It was the real thing. I'm sure of it."

Valentine smiled. "No offense, kiddo, but you hardly qualify as an expert."

"And you do?"

"You told me you had a digital image of the drawing."

Finn nodded. She dug around in her pack, which was leaning by the chair, found her camera and handed it over to Valentine. He opened the flap at the camera's bottom, withdrew the firewire connector and plugged it into the black, flat-screened IBM on his desk. Finn got up and came around to stand behind him as he worked the keyboard. She looked around but she couldn't actually see the computer itself.

"It's a server down in the basement," said Valentine without looking up from what he was doing, as though reading her mind. "It's cooler down there."

"What do you have?" Finn asked. "A super-computer or something?"

"Not quite," he answered. "But close. I do a lot of work for some people in California. They pay me in computer technology." He sat back in his chair. "There we go." On the screen was the Michelangelo drawing, full size. The detail on the screen was flawless.

"Well?" Finn asked.

"I've got to admit it looks pretty good. Authentic at first glance, anyway." He tapped some more keys and the drawing vanished.

"What are you doing?"

"Comparison test. I've got some material on file. If we need more, I can get it out of the stacks."

"Comparing what?"

"The words in the corner there. See if the handwriting's the same."

The screen stayed blank for a moment, then resolved itself into a windowpanelike alignment of four sections. Each one appeared to hold a small piece of handwriting. He then hit another key and a fifth pane in the window appeared with the Michelangelo drawing. After another keystroke, the drawing dropped away, leaving only the writing.

"Now we'll see," said Valentine. He tapped keys with his long fluid fingers and for a moment Finn found herself thinking that they'd be very sensitive touching her. She wiped the thought out of her mind as quickly as the images on the screen disappeared. Now there were only two sections to the window—one on the left with a scrap of obviously very old handwriting in cursive Italian, the other a blown-up version of the writing on the drawing.

Finn leaned over Valentine's shoulder, her hair cascading down over his cheek. She read the lines easily:

"What joy hath you glad wreath of flowers that is
Around each hair so deftly twined,
Each blossom pressing forward from behind,
As though to be the first her brows to kiss."

Valentine picked it up at the beginning of the next line:

"The livelong day her dress hath perfect bliss,
That now reveals her breast, now seems to bind,
And that fair woven net of gold refined
Rests on her cheek and throat in happiness."

Finn stepped back, blushing, realizing that she'd been standing much too close to Valentine while they read. "It's one of his sonnets to his mistress, Clarissa Saffi. She was a courtesan, actually."

"The first one he wrote about her, if I remember correctly," agreed Valentine. "You're very good."

"You're not bad yourself," she said, taking another step away, grabbing her hair nervously and holding it against her neck. "Most people don't even known he wrote poetry."

"Everyone wrote poetry back then," said Valentine, smiling and showing off his large square teeth.

He turned back to the screen. "I think poetry took the place of game shows." He played with the keyboard again. "Now let's see if we can get them to match up." Slowly he used the mouse to drag the writing from the drawing across and atop the other one. He fiddled with the mouse, clicking it from time to time, then entered a series of instructions. The screen cleared again, split down the middle with five individual letters on each side:

```
        A                   A
        E                   E
        I                   I
        O                   O
        U                   U
```

Valentine then used the mouse to drag one set of letters so that they covered the first:

```
        A
        E
        I
        O
        U
```

"Looks like a match to me," said Finn.

"Me too," said Valentine. "I'd say your drawing was definitely a Michelangelo." He stared at the screen. "Certainly the handwriting is the same." He paused. "Did Delaney tell you how Crawley was killed?"

"He said he was strangled but somebody stuck

some kind of ritual dagger in his mouth." Finn made a face. "I didn't like Mr. Crawley, but it still sounds gross."

"This ritual dagger, what kind was it—do you remember?"

"He called it a koummya or something."

"Spanish. Andalusian. Sometimes from southern Morocco."

"You know everything?"

"A little bit about a lot," he said. "That's what makes me dangerous."

"You're dangerous?"

"I can be."

Finn went back to her chair and sat down again. "So now what do we do?"

"I'm not sure, exactly," he murmured, still staring at the screen. "This is interesting but . . ."

"It's not the kind of evidence we can take to the police."

"It's all electronic, for one thing. There's no actual drawing. Did Delaney mention anything about finding it in Crawley's office?"

"No. He kept on asking me where I saw it last, I kept on telling him Crawley had it in his hand." She frowned. "I think he figures I stole it."

"There must be surveillance cameras."

"There are. I don't know if I'm on them. If I am then that'll prove I didn't take it."

"But it would also prove you photographed them," said Valentine, "which might be enough reason to come after you at your apartment."

"I thought of that, but it still doesn't make any sense. It's as though the very existence of the drawing, phony or not, is evidence of something . . . something worth killing for."

"It's like I said about going around in circles." Valentine smiled. "Eventually you get to the little dot of truth at the middle of the vortex. Which I think perhaps you just did."

"What truth?"

"The existence of the drawing is worth killing for."

"What kind of truth is that?"

"A dangerous one."

16

The man in the priest's collar got off the Delta flight from Rome at three fifteen, ran his small black fiber suitcase through the machines and then showed his Vatican passport to a hard-eyed uniformed INS man. The passport identified him as Father Ricardo Gentile and his occupation as priest, which seemed fairly self-evident. In fact none of the information on the passport was true, and the passport itself, although genuine, did not exist on any records at the Vatican passport office in Rome. The INS man handed him back the passport after a brief glance then gave him an "I am the first line of defense in the war against terrorism" nod and allowed him into the United States.

Father Gentile followed the crowds out into the afternoon sunlight, picked up a cab and told the Nigerian driver to take him to the JFK Holiday Inn. He avoided speaking to the driver in his native Anaang although he spoke it fluently; the last thing he wanted to do was make an impression on anyone at this point. As usual the dog collar was bad enough.

The drive took only a few minutes and by three forty-five Father Gentile was checked into the office building slab of the hotel at the junction of the Van Wyck Expressway and the Belt Parkway. The room was narrow, simply furnished and small. The color scheme was predominantly a grape-tinted purple. His window looked out over some sort of Japanese garden. He couldn't have cared less. He swished the blinds closed and switched on the desk light. There was no overhead; it was something he'd been noticing recently on his travels, the lack of overhead lighting. He went to the closet, found the hard-shell suitcase that had been left for him earlier that afternoon and unlocked it with the key that had been Fed-Exed to him the day before in Rome. He removed the contents, which included two suits, several Arrow shirts in different colors, still in their wrapping, a pair of black James Taylor and Son elevator shoes that added two inches to his height and a Glock 21 10mm automatic pistol with a fifteen-round law enforcement magazine and a Patrick Johnakin muzzle-up spring-loaded shoulder rig to go with it. He stripped off his priest's clothes, redressed—complete with the Glock and holster—then neatly placed everything into the hard-shell suitcase and locked it again.

He reached inside the pocket of the suit jacket

and withdrew two wallets, one large and European, the other an ordinary American-style billfold. The large wallet identified him as Peter Ruffino, an Italian agent of the Art Recovery Tactical Squad (ARTS), which was itself a division of Allied International Intelligence, or Alintel, a worldwide concern representing everybody from Lloyds to the British Museum, including several royal families, dozens of major corporations and even a few governments.

The other wallet was filled with the Homeland Security credentials of one Laurence Gaynor MacLean. Both sets of documents were authentic and subjectible to deep background checks. As Father Gentile was well aware, despite endless denials of its existence, the Vatican secretary of state had the single-longest-running intelligence department in the world, an organization that in one form or another had existed since St. Peter came to Rome and underground Christians had chalked the sign of the fish on catacomb walls. Documents and the "legends" to go with them were never a problem. Gentile decided on the Homeland Security persona of good old Larry MacLean, working for a minute in front of the bathroom mirror to spin away his Italian accent and replace it with something vaguely Midwestern, then left the room.

He went down to the lobby, asked for a taxi to take him into the city and half an hour later he was in Manhattan, checking into the Gramercy Park Hotel and telling the desk clerk that Delta had lost his luggage once again. He registered as Laurence G. MacLean and paid with a Bank of America Visa check card that was hooked into what was effectively a bottomless well. He spent ten more minutes in front of the bathroom mirror of his suite practicing a flat Kansas drawl, then left the hotel and began to work.

17

The store was called simply "Maroc" and occupied a tiny space on Lafayette Street about three blocks away, at the corner of Grand. A tinkling bell announced Finn and Valentine as they entered. It was like some kind of doorway that took them halfway across the world—the air was suddenly full of the scent of cumin, caraway and cinnamon, the walls hung with rugs of every size and color, tables piled on tables, stacks of everything from baskets to ancient muskets—all of it overseen by a fat man at the back smoking an oval cigarette and wearing a fez, dressed in a pure white linen suit that made him look as though he'd just stepped out of *Casablanca*. Finn expected Humphrey Bogart to appear at any minute with Ingrid Bergman right behind him. Valentine gave the man a small Islamic salutation and the man replied in kind. He looked at Finn curiously and Valentine introduced them.

"Finn Ryan, this is my friend Hassan Lasri."

"*Salaam*," said Finn, doing her best. Lasri smiled.

"Actually it is *Shalom*, since I am a *Juif Maroc* as they say in that other language of my nation, but it was a good effort." He smiled again. "I am like a well-trained dog—I answer to any number of calls, especially from such a pretty *checroun* as yourself."

"*Checroun?*"

"Redhead. They are said to be particularly lucky, among other things, and since my own name brings me nothing but bad luck . . ." He shrugged.

"*Lasri* means left-handed in Arabic," Valentine explained.

"The worst kind of luck for an African like myself I'm afraid, but maybe you'll bring me better." He gestured toward a pair of ornately carved chairs and they sat down. He snapped his fingers incredibly loudly and a young man appeared in a long white robe and a small white embroidered cap. He gave Finn one wide-eyed appreciative look, then turned to Lasri, who spoke in rapid-fire Arabic for a few moments. The young man nodded, gave Finn another look and then disappeared.

"That is my nephew, Majoub. Clearly he is madly in love with you."

Finn could feel herself blushing.

"Have no cause for embarrassment. You are very beautiful, it is true, and a wonderful example of a *checroun*, with sprinklings of freckles like stars and skin like milk, but I'm afraid Majoub would fall in love with a female chimpanzee if one came in the door. He is at that age. Harmless, believe me." A few minutes later the young man was back with an enameled tray loaded down with three small cups, a Moroccan coffeepot and a plate of something brown, sticky and very fattening. Majoub cast a final glance at Finn, sighed and then disappeared for good. Hassan poured the coffee, spooning a tooth-aching amount of sugar into each cup and then passed around the plate of sticky brown things. "I have no idea what Majoub calls these but they are made from toffee and pecans and cashew nuts and are supposedly good for one's prostate. You do not have to worry about such things, Finn, but we men must look to our health." He grinned, popped two of them into his mouth one after the other and then washed them down with a swallow of coffee. Finn took a small bite out of the corner of one of the little bars and felt twenty years of careful dentistry in serious jeopardy. They were delicious.

"Now then," said Hassan, "what is it that I can help you with today?"

"A man was killed yesterday. A ritual dagger was used. A koummya."

"Oh yes," said Hassan, nodding. "The director of the museum."

"You've heard about this already?" asked Finn, startled.

"Americans are Americans, Arabs are Arabs— even Jewish Arabs like me. You think the world runs one way. We know it runs another. When a koummya is used to still someone's tongue that is Moroccan business, Moroccan news, therefore we hear about it quickly." He smiled with a twinge of sadness. "These days it is better for people with large noses and dark skin to have their story straight before the men from Homeland Security show up at your door with your ticket to the Guantanamo Hilton."

"Tell us about the koummya," said Valentine.

"The koummya, or sometimes called the khanjar, comes from the northern part of the country. It is usually thought of as a right of passage, a sign of a boy's admission into manhood, you know?"

Valentine nodded. Finn waited. She thought about having another one of the little gooey pecan-cashew-toffee things and then decided against it. Just as Hassan Lasri produced a little silver box and lit another one of his oval cigarettes Finn found herself wishing she smoked. No smoking, no drinking, no pecan-cashew-toffee things and no sex—she might as well be a nun.

Lasri took a long drag on his cigarette, blew the smoke out of his wide hairy nostrils and popped another square into his mouth. He chewed and looked thoughtfully at Finn. "Of course," he continued, his mouth still half full, "the koummya had another purpose."

"What was that?" asked Finn.

"Other than being used for circumcisions— Arabs and Jews alike circumcise their children, you know—it is only the Christian and Asian infidels who do not—other than that, the dagger was used to cut out the tongues of traitors. Traditionally, that is; I haven't heard of it being done recently. 'To still the tongues of traitors' is the official terminology."

"Could that have applied to Crawley?" asked Finn.

"How should I know, my dear? I never met the man. I do, however, know where that particular koummya came from."

"How?"

"A policeman showed me a picture of it this morning. A man named Delaney. He was apparently aware that I was head of the local Moroccan Friendship Alliance. At any rate, I told him what the dagger was, its background and uses."

"And whom it belonged to?" asked Valentine.

"He didn't ask me."

"But you know."

"Of course. Except for the cheap tourist-quality knives they sell in the souks in Marrakech and Fez and Casablanca and the like, a properly made koummya—especially a Moorish one of great antiquity—is as personal as a fingerprint." He grinned broadly and popped yet another square into his mouth. Finn drank more coffee. "Not to mention the fact that the owner's name is usually

embossed in silver on the hilt or the scabbard."
He smiled. "Mr. Delaney, of course, does not
read Arabic."

Finn's brain was beginning to cloud over from
the wreaths of smoke wafting around the store
from the man's cigarettes. He swallowed, drank
the last of his coffee, tonguing up a mouthful of
the fine-grained grounds at the bottom of the cup
and smiled again. "The grounds are very good for
the colon, you know," he said. "Moroccan men
have a very low incidence of colon cancer." He
opened his silver box, took out another cigarette
and lit up. Here was a classic example of what
they called an oral-compulsive back in psych 101.
"On the other hand," he continued, "they have
a horribly high incidence of lung cancer." Lasri
coughed harshly as though making his point.

"The dagger," murmured Valentine.

"It came from the collection of a young men's
private school in Connecticut," said the man.

"The name of the school?" asked Valentine.

"Greyfriars," said Lasri, eyeing the last gooey
square on the plate. "The Greyfriars Academy."

18

He entered the room and went through his ritual with the uniform. Naked, he crossed the room to his chair and sat down. He examined the leather cover of the book as he always did when he came here and then opened it carefully, turning the pages filled with minute but perfectly clear script, pausing every now and again to whisper the words like hateful prayers: *"Genus humanum quod constat stirpibus tantopere inter se diferentibus non est origine unum descendus a protoparentibus numero iisdem."*

For it was true: all men were different, their origins different, some base, some blessed, some damned from birth. Some were born as demons, others as saints. Since the words were immutable and divine they could not be argued with and so, by their very nature, following those words would be the act of a divine. It was all so simple when the order of it all could be seen.

He turned the page and the farm stood before him as it had been, the photographs fading now, the faces gray, but full of life in memory. He knew each one like a brother. Patterson in his glasses like that Beatle who was shot wore, Dorm, the guy they called Dormouse, Winetka, Bosnic, Teitelbaum and Reid. Pixie Mortimer, Hayes, Terhune, Dickie Biearsto. He could see them all, cold in the late winter chill, slipping up through the forest, ten guys from the forty-four playing babysitter to a bunch of art freaks from back home. But in the end they all smartened up, didn't they? They were spies first and art types second and they'd all been in the fucking war long enough to know that war was for what you could get out of it once you got by the survival part. War was a game of bullies and bastards, not heroes.

There it was, right in front of him, the Altenburg farm and beyond it the little tumbledown Benedictine abbey called the Althof, long abandoned for want of monks or nuns in a part of the world that had forgotten that God had ever existed. Rain was coming down, cold and thin, the way his blood felt and he dropped his neck a little farther down into the collar of his jacket, not that it did much good. He was soaked through, his nose was running and he couldn't keep a cigarette lit for more than a few seconds before it fizzled out on him.

They'd come down out of the mountains at last, moving through the trees down whatever goat paths they could find. There had been no way to stick together, and eventually the squad had come apart like a crumbling piece of old stone. There were ten noncoms, all with Garands and .45s; Pixie, the skinny fruit from Jersey City carrying a thirty-cal. across his back like he was Christ, and Dick Hayes, the wild-hair bald guy carrying the mortar and talking about what he'd really like to do—and I mean *really* like to do would be to *slllide* it into that Greer Garson babe—and he'd felt that way ever since he saw her in *Mrs. Miniver*. When Pixie told him she'd married the guy who played her son in the movie he almost shit and told Pixie that before the war was over he'd find an excuse to cut his fuckin' good-for-nothing nuts off. Ten right guys and the three spooks from the ALIU, the Art Looting Investigation Unit, which everybody knew was part of the OSS and all they really wanted to do was catch Nazis with their hands in the cookie jar. McPhail, Taggart and Cornwall. McPhail thought he was some kind of big shit with his Boston accent and that funny Skull and Bones signet ring he wore; Taggart talked to himself, and Cornwall didn't talk to anyone, he just had that notebook of his out all the time, writing. Altogether a weird crew.

Dick Hayes, the bald guy with the mortar took the first hit. It was one of those Russian SVT-40s the Germans liked so much; it had that flat, slap-in-the-face sound that hardly left an echo, even in that kind of countryside. Hayes was just ahead of him and to the right and the sergeant saw his whole right arm blown off at the shoulder leaving nothing but some blood and bone and some white twisted things he figured were tendons. Then that sound like someone dropping the lid on a child's desk in grade school and then Hayes just dropped and the way he was lying you could look into his rib cage and see his lung and his heart swimming around in a lot of blood and purple stuff. One shot and he was gone and that was it for him and any chance with Greer Garson.

Everybody hit the dirt, and it seemed like everyone but Hayes made it to the ditch that ran at an angle across the meadow, more like it had been some kind of earthworks defense a few hundred years ago when they were fighting some other stupid war. Anyway they all got down behind it. The three guys from the ALIU were all lieutenants except for Cornwall, who was a captain, but none of the three of them knew shit about how to fight a fucking war, so they left it up to him because he was a sergeant and he'd also managed to keep from getting killed over here for the last few years and he didn't think any of them had been here longer than since Christmas.

The sergeant looked up for a second to get his bearings and the Kraut with the SVT took another shot, knocking out a groove in the dirt about three inches to the left of his head. He got what he wanted, though—the lay of the land.

The farm looked more French than German: half a dozen buildings including a barrackslike barn probably used for cows, a big house—low, two stories, the thatched roof like a hat pulled low, heavy linteled window with the glass shot out long ago leaving black holes like dead eyes. All of this surrounded by a stone wall about five feet high and three feet wide and covered with half a dozen generations of blackberry and bramble—more effective than barbed wire. The wall ran off to the left and connected with the old abbey, two stories high like the farmhouse, the roof slate looking very dark in the light rain. The windows on the second floor of the abbey were very narrow and most of them were covered by wooden shutters. Some of them hung on one hinge, letting you look into the blackness beyond. Almost certainly where the firing had come from.

The sergeant got out the little pair of caramel-colored binoculars he'd traded a Canadian for and took a closer look at everything. They were on the upslope of the meadow that went down to the road so from where they were they could see over the wall and even over the roofs of the farm buildings. That's when he started figuring something was different about this whole thing because behind the barracks-type building, the big low barn, he could see half a dozen of those three-tonner Opel Blitzes the Krauts used for just about everything. These ones were closed with canvas backs. They didn't have any unit designations that the sergeant could see except for the bumper plate on the one closest to the edge of the building. The number plate had SS lightning bolts on it but the metal pennant plugged into the passenger side ferrule was orange, which meant they were *feldjager*—military police. Six three-ton trucks capable of carrying maybe a hundred men out in the middle of nowhere? It didn't make any sense at all.

"What we got, Sarge?" It was Dormouse. He had snot running down both sides of his fat lips like a little kid and his eyes blinked all the time.

"Wipe your fucking nose, Dormouse."

"Sure, Sarge." He did, but his nose continued to run. "That Hayes who got hit?"

"Yeah, sniper in the old church place there— the abbey, I guess you'd call it."

"What's the fucking point of defending an old ruin? And if this is a bunch of Krauts on the run what are they doing with a sniper?"

"You ask too many questions, Dormouse. One of these days it's going to get you in the shit. And wipe your nose again. You look fucking disgusting."

The sergeant stared through the binoculars, looking at the trucks, wondering what the hell was inside them. It was a funny war now. Time was you picked up a gun and got moving and shot Germans and they shot back at you. Now it seemed like they were all in some kind of secret maze, looking for secrets and things that properly didn't have a fuckin' thing to do with fighting any war he'd ever heard of. He picked up the binoculars again and looked down at the farm. Military police?

19

Greyfriars Academy was located on the Sark River in the hilly, wooded countryside a dozen miles north of Greenwich, Connecticut. The closest civilization was the small crossroads village of Friardale on the way to Riverview and Toll Gate Pond. Passing through the village, Michael Valentine followed the signs to Oaklane and drove along beside a low fieldstone wall capped with wrought iron spikes to the main gates of the school. Directly ahead, down a slightly curving gravel drive lined with mature oaks, was the main building. It looked like a cross between a medieval church and a weathered, ivy-covered English country house. It was huge and looked very old.

"Like something out of a Harry Potter story," Finn commented, staring through the windshield of Valentine's rental as they went down the sun-dappled drive toward the school.

"More like Frank Richards," murmured the older man.

"Who?"

"Never mind."

They continued up the tree-lined drive. To the left there were half a dozen outbuildings, including a porter's lodge, something big enough to be a swimming pool or a gymnasium and a small chapel complete with miniature bell tower. To the right was a baseball diamond, tennis courts and something that could have been a stable. Behind the main building and running back to the wall was an orchard, the stunted trees laid out in neat rows. In between everything there were winding paths, neatly trimmed lawns and a number of artfully placed flower beds. It was clearly a school for rich kids.

They parked in a small lot outside the main quadrangle. The lot was empty except for a burgundy-colored mid-nineties Taurus station wagon with one of its windshield wipers missing and an old, humpbacked Jaguar Mark II saloon in British racing green. The Taurus had a toddler-sized car seat in the back.

They left their rental car and stepped into the hot morning air. The sun was almost directly overhead and everything had a flat, baked, deserted look about it. A school in midsummer was like an abandoned husk until September. They entered the main quadrangle. Directly in front of them was a stone fountain topped by a large, classically draped figure of a woman with a tilted amphora on her shoulder, spilling water down into the granite pool below. It looked as though the figure had stood there spilling water for a hundred years, the pool never filling, the container on her shoulder never emptying. The burbling water was the only sound and movement in the place. They turned to the left and went up a set of wide stone stairs. Valentine pulled open one of the dark oak doors and they stepped into the cool interior of the school.

They found themselves in a large reception hall paneled in the same oak as the front doors. The floor was marble, laid out in alternating squares of light and dark. The ceiling was more coffered oak set in the center with a massive wrought iron chandelier. Finn expected to see suits of armor and crossed halberds ranged around the room but instead she saw dimly lit display cases filled with dusty trophies and old framed photographs. Just inside the doors there was a massive granite slab bolted to the wall, etched like a tombstone, which is what it was, in a sense. Picked out in gold, the inscription running along the top of the memorial said simply: 1916–1918—1941–1945. Below the dates were a dozen columns of names. Apparently for Greyfriars, history had stopped at the end of the second world war and paid no heed to the conflicts that had followed. Either that or they'd simply run out of space and the Greyfriars dead from Korea, Vietnam and Iraq were left to fend for themselves.

Finn and Valentine crossed the entry hall, following the seesaw sound of an old dot-matrix printer and the blurred clatter of fingers on a keyboard. Through the main hall they found a narrow corridor disappearing left and right, half paneled in oak, with ancient ochre-colored plaster above. A number of small rooms led off the corridor; only one had an open door. Valentine peeked in, tapping lightly on the doorframe. A small, plain woman was working away in front of a keyboard, her feet neatly tucked under her desk, her head erect and posture perfect. She wore glasses and had her hair drawn up into a loose untidy bun. She looked up at Valentine's knock, eyes going wide behind the glasses. Valentine smiled.

"I'm Dr. Michael Valentine from New York. This is my assistant, Miss Ryan."

"Dr. Valentine?" The woman looked even more startled now, a rabbit frozen in high beams. "No one here is sick that I know of. There's really nobody here. A few of the masters, the head."

"You are?" Valentine asked.

"Miss Mimble. Jessie Mimble. I'm the receptionist."

"We'd like to see Dr. Wharton, if you don't mind."

"Do you have an appointment?"

"No. It's about the stolen knife."

"Oh dear."

"Right. We're here about that." The young, rabbit-eyed Miss Mimble stared up at them as though expecting further orders. She seemed transfixed by Valentine.

"Dr. Wharton?" Finn reminded.

"Oh, right," said the woman. She got up from behind her desk and scuttled off to an adjoining door, knocking mouselike before entering. Watching her go, Finn noticed that she had an enormous rear end and jutting hips, as though the body of a much slimmer woman had been grafted onto the waist of a Bradley tank camouflaged in a flowered skirt. She was back a few moments later, pulling open the door and standing aside.

"Dr. Wharton will see you now." She gestured them into the room and closed the door behind them.

Dr. Harry Wharton was in his mid-fifties, bald, clean-shaven and wearing bright red reading glasses which he took off and dropped on the pile of papers in front of him on the desk as Valentine and Finn Ryan entered the room. The room itself was pleasant and bright. The curtains on the tall window behind Wharton were bright red and drawn back to let in the sun. The desk was dark oak, large and modern. The carpet matched the curtains and the tack-upholstered red leather chairs that sat in front of the desk. On the wall behind the headmaster was a framed aerial photograph of the school. The rest of the walls were taken up with floor-to-ceiling bookcases. Very professorial, like the *Architectural Digest* version of a private school headmaster's office. Finn smiled; just the kind of thing to set rich parents at ease. The room smelled faintly of apple-flavored pipe tobacco. There was no ashtray.

Wharton stood up, most of his attention on Finn. She noticed the tie he was wearing was bright red with small blue heraldic shields on it. His suit was a dark pinstripe and the toe caps of his brogues shone like the top of his head. He reached out a hand across the desk and smiled. The smile seemed perfectly pleasant and genuine. Finn took his hand first. The grip was dry and firm and he wasn't one of those people who kept pressing the flesh for too long. He sat down again.

"Dr. Valentine, Miss Ryan, what can I do for you?"

"We're here about the koummya."

"The knife." Wharton nodded. "It was stolen several weeks ago."

"Yes," said Valentine.

"I'd like to know why you're interested?" Wharton asked. His voice was still pleasant enough but there was a faint edge to the question.

"I'm generally interested in antiquities but I'm more interested in how this one was put to use."

"The murder."

"Yes."

"You're with the police then?"

"I sometimes do consulting work for them."

A nice bit of evasion, thought Finn. Not the

truth but not necessarily a lie either. Said without a twitch or hesitation—an expected question, the answer ready. As her mother might say, Michael Valentine certainly was a caution.

"Unfortunate," said Wharton. "There's no connection to Greyfriars, of course. It was simply the weapon used. Nevertheless, it reflects poorly on the school. We can only be glad that it took place during the summer holidays." Not the kind of thing that attracted the rich and famous, certainly, Finn thought.

"Alexander Crawley wasn't an alumnus of Greyfriars?"

"No."

"You're sure."

Wharton's otherwise pleasant and neutral expression suddenly hardened. "Absolutely. In the first place, I checked the records of the New York Police. Given Mr. Crawley's age he would have attended Greyfriars at the same time I did. I was here from 1955 to 1967. If he'd been a student here, boarder or day boy, I would have known him."

"I see."

"There was a robbery. The knife caught the thief's eye. Unfortunately Mr. Crawley became his victim."

"Seems a little far-fetched, don't you think?"

"It seems like an odd conjunction of events, and a tragic one, but I can assure you that's all it was."

"Why did Greyfriars have the knife in the first place?" Finn asked.

"We have a small museum here. What they used to call a cabinet of curiosities. The knife was a gift from one of the alumni."

Valentine glanced across at Finn. She took her cue instantly.

"May we see it?" she said brightly, giving Wharton her best smile. "The museum, I mean."

"I don't really see the point," the headmaster responded. "The knife is no longer there, after all."

"Please," said Finn. She stood up, putting the brass button on the front of her jeans roughly at Wharton's eye level. He barely paused.

"I suppose," the headmaster answered gruffly. He stood up, the fingers of his right hand automatically going to the button of his jacket and doing it up. He smoothed his tie. "We can get to it through the school but it's easier if we simply go across the quad."

The headmaster led them out into the hallway, informed the goggle-eyed Miss Mimble of their destination and went into the main entrance hall and then outside. He made no effort to talk to either Finn or Valentine, striding quickly down the narrow gravel pathway that cut through the well-tended grass, almost as though he was daring them to keep up with him.

They reached a small set of stone steps on the far side of the quadrangle, climbed them and went through a small glass-paned door that led into a small cloakroom space fitted out with rows of brass coat hooks on either side. They were at a right angle between two wings of the large building and two narrow hallways led off left and right. Without a word Wharton turned to the right. Immediately on their left an open door led into what was obviously a science lab. Beside it was a door with a neat wooden sign that said DARKROOM. Wharton turned and stopped in front of a door on the left. He reached into his trouser pocket, took out a large ring of keys and fitted one into the lock.

"You lock the door to the museum?" Valentine asked.

"We do now," Wharton answered sourly. He turned the key and the door swung open. He flicked a switch on the wall and several overhead fluorescents crackled to life.

The museum was small, no larger than the average living room. There were maps and paintings on the wall and glass-topped display cases ranged around the walls. The room had an old-fashioned look about it, like photographs Finn had seen of early displays at the Smithsonian. The display cases held everything from a collection of bird eggs resting on small beds of yellowing cotton balls to an old stereopticon with several slides to an Olympic gold medal for track and field from 1924 and somebody's Congressional Medal of Honor from WWII.

High on the wall above one case were a pair of Brown Bess caplock muskets from the War of

1812, and in the case itself, a collection of Civil War memorabilia including an old navy Colt revolver. Beside the revolver in gruesome juxtaposition was a pair of brass-bound binoculars with the right lens smashed and the eyepiece a twisted, exploded mess. Finn grimaced. It gave a whole new meaning to "Don't shoot till you see the whites of their eyes."

Far to the right, almost invisible, was a small, rather amateurish-looking oil painting of a monkey. The painting looked as though it hadn't been dusted in years. Below it was a wood-and-glass case. A roughly triangular section of glass had been removed from the case, clearly cut with a diamond glass cutter and pulled off with a lump of putty. The scored piece of glass was still sitting to one side of the hole and the whole display case was cloudy with fingerprint dust. Finn looked through the opening, and could see where the curved knife had lain against the green baize cloth that covered the bottom of the case, leaving a darker, unfaded ghost impression of itself. A small printed card said: MOORISH RITUAL DAGGER. GIFT OF COL. GEORGE GATTY.

"Who was George Gatty?" Finn asked.

"He was here in the thirties, according to the records. Went on to West Point."

"One wonders where he came across a Spanish dagger," murmured Valentine.

"Presumably during the war. Spanish Morocco, Casablanca, somewhere like that."

"You know your twentieth-century history," Valentine commented.

"In addition to being headmaster I'm also head of the history department. I teach sixth form."

"Sixth form?" asked Finn.

"He means grade twelve," said Valentine. "Do you know anything more about Gatty?"

"No. Only that he went here in the thirties and went on to West Point. That's all the information on him I was able to give the police too."

"You don't know where we could find him?"

"Tracing down old students isn't my job, Mr. Valentine. That's what the alumni association is for."

"Dr. Valentine."

"Whatever you call yourself." Wharton turned on his heel and left the museum.

"Short-tempered fellow," Valentine observed.

"I'll say," commented Finn. "You think we'll be able to track down Colonel Gatty?"

"With a name like that I don't think it'll be too difficult."

Valentine took a last look at the small painting over the display case and then followed Wharton out of the little museum. The man was waiting beside the door. As Finn and Valentine stepped out of the room he closed the door and locked it.

"Is there anything else I can help you with?" asked the headmaster.

"No," said Valentine, shaking his head. "I think I've seen enough."

Wharton gave him a sharp look. "In that case, perhaps I'll say good-bye then."

"Thank you for your help." Valentine nodded.

"No problem," answered Wharton. He turned away and went back toward the cloakroom entrance. By the time Finn and Valentine followed he was nowhere to be seen, his footsteps echoing away as he headed back to his office through the school corridors. They exited through the smaller door out into the quadrangle and the hot sunlight.

"Well, what did you make of all that?" said Valentine as they headed back across the quad.

"Is this a quiz?" said Finn.

"If you want it to be."

"Where do I start?"

"The beginning, of course."

"His office smelled of pipe tobacco but I didn't see any pipe."

"Yes, I caught that too."

"Uh, he wanted to make sure we didn't go through the school on the way to the little museum place, so maybe there was somebody he didn't want us to see . . . the pipe smoker maybe."

"Anything else?"

"I think he was lying about Crawley. I bet if we checked we'd find out that Crawley went to Greyfriars."

"Go on."

"I think he was lying about this Colonel Gatty as well. I'll bet he knows more than he's telling."

"Why do you think he'd be doing something like that?"

"I'm not sure. Protecting him for some reason, I suppose."

"Anything else?"

"Not really, except that you seemed awfully interested in that painting in the museum. Looked like a dingy Picasso knockoff."

"It's by Juan Gris."

"The cubist?" Gris, a Spaniard like Picasso as well as his neighbor in Paris, had been one of the early exponents of the style along with George Braque. She'd studied him briefly in her second year. If Valentine was right, the painting was worth a lot of money.

"If the painting is genuine it's an untitled canvas from 1927. It shouldn't be there."

"Why not?" said Finn. "Another generous ex-student?"

"Doubtful," answered Valentine. "It was looted by the Nazis in 1941 from the Wildenstein Gallery in Paris and hasn't been seen or heard of since."

"How would it turn up here?"

"Now that's a mystery, isn't it?"

They reached the rental car. The Taurus was still there. The Jaguar was gone. "We can presume the Taurus is Miss Mimble's."

"I thought the Jag belonged to Wharton."

"So did I until I saw the aerial photograph behind his desk. It shows quite a large house tucked in behind the main building. The headmaster's residence."

"So who owns the Jag?"

"The person who was smoking the pipe in Wharton's office just before we came in."

"Shit," muttered Finn. "We should have got the plate number."

"It was a New York World War Two veterans plate. 1LGS2699."

Somehow she wasn't surprised that he remembered the number. "Colonel Gatty?"

"Probably. Easy enough to find out." He tossed Finn the keys. "You drive." She unlocked the car and got behind the wheel. Valentine climbed in the other side. He reached down, picked his laptop case up from under the seat and plugged it into the empty lighter socket. He booted up the computer, turned on the GPRS wireless modem and tapped his way effortlessly into the New York Department of Motor Vehicles database. Finn ran the car up the long drive and then turned onto the road that led back to the highway. Within a few minutes Valentine had what he wanted.

"It's Gatty. He lives near the Museum of Natural History."

"That didn't take long."

"Anything Afghani terrorists can do, I can do better." He grinned. He punched a key on the laptop and closed it. They drove back to New York.

20

Night was falling and the nighthawks were making their swooping, booming mating calls in the purple sky overhead. Instead of being dark, the farmhouse and the outbuildings were bathed in light from half a dozen security lamps on tall poles, lit by the chugging of a small portable generator somewhere. Who had the gasoline to light up a stupid farmhouse these days, making it an easy target for Allied planes overhead, or passing patrols? But Allied flights never got this close to the Swiss border, and there weren't any patrols wandering around in this area except for them. This was a dead zone, where whatever war that existed was a private one.

They had made a cold camp just inside the tree line using the remains of an old dry stone fence covered with bramble for cover. One of the spooks, Taggart, was whispering to Cornwall, who was making notes using a small pad and his pocket flash. Everyone else was having M-3 meat and vegetable stew or M-1 meat and beans, which tasted as bad as it looked cold and not much better heated. Not that the sergeant much cared; after eating that shit for three years all over Europe his taste buds were cardboard anyway. Shit filled you up just like good stuff and it all came out the same—C-3 accessory-pack toilet paper. Like everyone said, it was a shitty war.

Wonder of wonders, Cornwall was actually talking to him.

"Sergeant."

"Sir."

"We're going to need to get a little closer to the farm."

"We, sir?"

"You and a patrol. As many men as you think you need." Stupid fucking question. I need the whole fucking U.S. Army if you've got it to spare. The light from the German lamps twinkled off the man's glasses like he had no eyes at all. He had a voice like a history teacher, like he knew everything in the fucking world. A drone. "What do you want to know, sir?"

"Reconnoiter the situation, Sergeant. How many men, weapons—that kind of thing."

"Fine." They were going to do the hard part and Cornwall and McPhail and Taggart were going to sit back here and talk about art. Jesus!

He chose Teitelbaum and Reid because they could keep their mouths shut. They slipped over the hedge and through the last of the trees just after the moon had set. It took them almost an hour to make their way down to the narrow dirt road that ran in front of the farm. It was just on the edge of the pools of light thrown by the pole lamps and offered enough shadow and cover in the roadside ditch to keep the sentries from seeing them.

The sergeant got out his binoculars and swung them slowly from left to right. Everything was the same as it had been before, only closer. He could see the break in the bramble-covered stone wall and the post and a few splintered pieces of wood that had once been the gate into the place. There was a guard just visible on the left side, looking miserable in a canvas rain cape even though it had stopped raining hours ago. The sergeant could see the glow of a cigarette moving in an arc from the man's hand to his mouth. It would have been an easy shot, payback for Hayes, but who the fuck cared about Hayes anyway? If the sniper was still in the tower of the abbey he'd pick up the muzzle flash and take him out easy as one two three. No, this was a look-see, no more.

The sergeant could also see that getting over the stone wall was going to be a bitch. Too high and covered with brambles. They'd get hung up like birds in a fucking net. As far as he could see they'd have to go through the front gate if they were going to go in at all. On the other hand, if he told that to Cornwall or either of the other two phony officers, they'd probably do it and wind up getting them all killed. Like somebody told him back before France, to know more was to have more. He told Teitelbaum and Reid to park it, gave them the evening password and told them he'd be back in a while. If they smoked and got themselves picked off by the sniper in the abbey ruins, that was their lookout.

He slipped back into the trees and moved north. He'd seen the big topo map that Cornwall carried and he knew there was the vague possibility of one of those monster King Tigers coming down the road and blowing them all to hell with its 88mm, but he hadn't seen one yet and he didn't think he was likely to. The worst he'd seen was a burned-out old Panzer I that looked like it dated back to the Spanish civil war lying half in the ditch at the top of the hill. He'd been sidetracked with the OSS dudes and as long as they didn't do anything stupid that was fine with him. He was no hero—that was for sure. At this point all he wanted was to do his time and then go back to Canarsie.

He moved through the trees, his eyes automatically scanning the ground for deadfalls or trip wires, his ears cocked by long practice to the sounds around him, his mind in some kind of automatic autonomic state that was more animal than human, ready to react at any moment to any sight or sound that was out of the natural order of things. Eventually he reached another drainage ditch, this one leading to a culvert that ran under the road to the field on the other side. If there was going to be any kind of warning mechanism, mines or trips he knew it would be here, but there was nothing. The plates on the trucks said SS but this was no crack unit. Those pricks, hell, even the straight army types would know better than to leave their flank open like this. He checked the ground carefully; no cigarette butts, no matches or food waste, no stink of piss that would give away a perimeter guard. Nothing. He smiled to himself, glad he'd left the others behind. Something was going on here, something as squirrely as Cornwall and his two so-called lieutenants.

The sergeant squatted by the culvert, staring at the ground. He'd been with the little band for more than six months now, him and the others taken out of Antwerp just after Holland was liberated and attached to G2 by orders of God knows who. Since then they'd been working their way across Europe, mostly talking to people without the slightest sign of combat. Two weeks ago they'd been sitting around fifty miles from Koblenz waiting for the Brits to make up their minds and Cornwall had found out something that had them pushing south and east like a coon dog with a bitch's scent up his schnoz. Maybe what he was sniffing was this: a phony SS unit out in the middle of the fucking Bavarian nowhere and six Opel Blitzes.

At this stage of the war a gas guzzler like the

Blitz—capable of at least thirty miles an hour, or even more with a good enough road—was worth its weight in gold, and that had the sergeant thinking quick. The trucks had to have some kind of special designation and documents to get this far south, and from here they could head for Switzerland, Italy or Austria. The Russkies were to the east, the Allies were to the west and they were being squeezed like a pimple. Odds were they were heading for Switzerland, since Italy had already surrendered and Austria wasn't far behind. That meant Lake Constance, no more than sixty miles away.

The sergeant looked through the culvert, wondering how much trouble his curiosity could get him into. Say the shipment in those six Opels really was valuable, and say that Cornwall meant to take it. But the real question was, what did he intend doing with it after that. His job was to recover the stuff then get it through proper channels back to its owners, but he was beginning to wonder. Maybe now they were past war, and playing finders keepers. Maybe it was every man for himself. Maybe it was time for the boy from Canarsie to cut himself a big slab of that pie. Maybe.

The sergeant let his hand drop to the butt of the firearm holstered on his hip. Three phony officers who weren't really army at all, who all had soft jobs stateside, who were probably true-blue as all get-out. It would be easy enough, but then what would *he* do with the six trucks? It was all in the paperwork.

He stood up. The dawn was coming on pretty quick and the ground fog was running through the trees like so many torn rags. Six trucks and close enough to the Swiss border to make it in a day, maybe two. It was worth thinking about. He peered through the patchy fog at the distant entrance to the farm. For a moment he was almost sure he saw a figure moving across the gated opening. He lifted his binoculars. Not a guard. A man in uniform. A general, right down to the red stripe on his fucking jodhpurs. But he was way too young—hawk-faced, pointy chin, young side of forty. Some kind of disguise, maybe. He stopped at the edge of the gate and a second figure appeared. A woman in a sweater and a headscarf. The guy in uniform lit her cigarette. They were laughing about something. A young woman; now that was interesting. The farmer's wife or daughter, someone along for the ride? Six Opel trucks, a phony general and a woman. What was that all about?

21

Gatty's residence was a six-story house on West Seventy-second that looked as though it had been transported away from beside a canal in Amsterdam a few hundred years ago. To the left was a brownstone, to the right there was a fair-sized apartment building. The front door was in the basement and they had to walk down into a little well surrounded by a wrought iron fence. The door knocker was huge: a black hand on a hinge holding something that looked like a small cannonball. In the middle of the cannonball was an unblinking eye. Valentine tapped the knocker twice against the heavy oak door. They could hear it echoing inside and then they heard the sound of footsteps on stone.

"Spooky," said Finn.

Valentine smiled. "The kind of money that can afford a house like this on the West Side usually is," he answered. A light went on over their heads. There was a short pause and then a man in a plain black suit answered the door. He was in his seventies and the little hair he had on his head was silver-white. He had dark eyes that had seen too much and a thin mouth. A scar pulled his upper lip upward, revealing a piece of yellow tooth. He'd been born before operations for split lips and cleft pallets were commonplace.

"We'd like to speak to the colonel, if you don't mind," said Valentine. "It's to do with Greyfriars Academy. He was just visiting there, I believe."

"Wait," said the man. There was a slight snuffle to his voice but it was clear enough. He closed the door on them and the light went off, leaving the two standing in the darkness.

"The butler did it," said Finn. "He's *really* spooky."

"Not just a butler," Valentine commented. "Bodyguard. He's wearing a shoulder rig. I saw it when he turned away."

The butler-bodyguard returned a few moments later and let them in. They followed him into a gloomy, slate-floored foyer set with old-fashioned wall sconces, then up a wide flight of worn oak steps to an enormous room on the main floor. It was two stories high, a blend of church nave and baronial hall. The ceiling was plaster, worked in ornate clusters of ivy and grapes, the walls paneled three quarters of the way up in dark oak, the floor done in wide planks. At one end of the room three arched windows, heavily leaded, looked out

onto Seventy-second Street while at the other end
more than a dozen smaller windows rising from
floor to ceiling looked out onto a small walled
garden, dark except for two or three small lights
set into the corners of the wall.

There were dozens of paintings on the walls,
almost all of them Dutch: meticulous DeWitte architectural renderings, DeHooch domestic interiors, seascapes by Cuyp and Hobbema's gloomy
castles. The only exception was a large Renoir, the
head of a young girl, placed in a position of honor
above the large tiled fireplace.

Heraldic banners hung around the room from
a second-floor gallery running around three sides
of the room, and there were four blue-black suits
of armor, one in each corner. A bright red rug
covered most of the floor and on it, facing each
other were two large, tufted leather sofas in cara-
mel brown. Between the sofas, resting on a large,
splayed zebra skin was a square coffee table
framed in teak and surfaced in squares of heavy
beaten brass. There were end tables and side tables here and there loaded with photographs in
silver frames and assorted small treasures from
ornate gold cigarette boxes to at least three silver
koummyas that Finn could see.

"I see you are enjoying my things," said a voice
from somewhere above them. "Please, enjoy yourself." Finn looked up and saw the face of a heavily
jowled man looking down at them from the gallery. The man disappeared and there was a low

humming sound. A moment later the man appeared at the far end of the room. He was dressed in a very formal-looking Saville Row suit at least thirty years out of date. He had a full head of flat black hair that might have come out of a tin of shoe polish, Ronald Reagan–style, and his large blue eyes were washed out and pale. He had large liver spots on his gnarled hands and when he walked, he leaned heavily on a three-point cane. His right leg appeared to hitch a little as he moved and his left shoulder was fractionally higher than his right. Despite the black hair he appeared to be well into his eighties. Using his left hand, he gestured with the cane.

"Sit," he said pleasantly, pointing at the brown leather couches. Finn and Valentine did as he asked. The old man chose a heavy-looking straight-backed wooden chair at right angles to them. The butler-bodyguard appeared carrying an antique silver coffee service. The man put it down and disappeared. "Edward Winslow," said the old man. "People often mistake it for Paul Revere." He took a gnarled briar pipe out of his jacket pocket and lit it with a World War Two–vintage, black, crackle-finish lighter. He snapped it shut with a practiced motion and blew out a cloud of apple-scented smoke. *One mystery solved*, Finn thought.

"Winslow was much earlier than Revere, though," commented Valentine. "And better, in my opinion, especially his smaller pieces. Revere was like his politics, a little bit melodramatic."

"You know something of silver?"

"And politics." Valentine smiled. "Especially the melodramatic kind."

"Who is your young and singularly pretty companion?"

"My name is Finn Ryan, Colonel. We're here about the koummya you donated to Greyfriars."

"The one that wound up being shoved down poor Alex Crawley's throat, you mean?" The old man laughed. "Much as I would have enjoyed doing it, I seriously doubt that my arthritis would have allowed it, not to mention the stroke I had a year or so ago. I don't get around the way I used to."

"You knew Crawley?" asked Valentine.

"I knew him well enough to dislike him. He was what they refer to as a bean counter. Had no feel for the art he represented."

"How did you know him?" Finn asked. "Through the museum or through Greyfriars?" The old man gave her a long, almost predatory look that made her skin crawl.

"Neither. Not that it's any of your business. Look around you, Miss Ryan. Do I have your name right? I live for art. I purchase a great deal of it. When you buy art at the scale I do you often find yourself making purchases from deaccessioned works from places like the Parker-Hale.

They had a number of Dutch works—Dutch is what I collect."

"Except for the Renoir," Valentine commented, nodding toward the painting over the fireplace.

"Yes, I purchased that just toward the end of the war."

"Oh." Valentine let it hang. Gatty was a collector—a vulgar one, if the décor of his living room was anything to go by—and collectors loved to boast.

"In Switzerland, as a matter of fact."

"Odd posting."

"Not really. I was army liaison to Allen Dulles in Berne."

"Really?"

"Yes. Cloak-and-dagger stuff. Still can't talk about most of it."

"Dulles ran an OSS listening post. How does Renoir come into it?"

The colonel seemed surprised that Valentine knew as much as he did. He raised an eyebrow, then smiled. "There was a great deal of art for sale in Europe. Before, during and after the war. I merely took advantage of what one might call a downturn in the market. The provenance is perfectly legitimate."

"I didn't say it wasn't," Valentine answered mildly.

"I still buy from them now and again."

"Who might that be?"

"The Hoffman Gallery," replied Gatty. Finn made a small startled movement. Valentine casually dropped his hand onto her knee and left it there. Finn wasn't sure which was more shocking—the touch of Valentine's hand or the name of the gallery. Hoffman was the same name as the one on the computer file for the provenance of the Michelangelo drawing. It was no answer to the mystery, but at least it was another piece of the puzzle put into play. The dagger, Greyfriars, Gatty's connection to Crawley and now the Swiss art gallery linking everything together. Connections, but no real meaning.

"Doesn't it seem a little strange that a murderer would go to all the trouble to break into a school in Connecticut for a murder weapon he used in New York?"

"As far as I know it was a coincidence. A robbery in one place, the dagger turning up in another. The killer could just as easily have purchased the knife from a pawnshop here; there's nothing to say they were one and the same person."

"I suppose if you were defending yourself in court that would be true."

"But I'm not, am I?" Gatty answered. "And not likely to be."

"No, I suppose not," answered Valentine. One finger tapped lightly on Finn's knee. Valentine stood up and she followed suit. The old man remained in his seat. The white-haired bodyguard appeared as though Gatty had pressed some kind of hidden button.

"Bert, show these two people out." The old man gave them a cold smile and the bodyguard led them to the front door.

"What was that all about?" asked Finn as they walked down the block to the rental car. "You never really asked him about anything except the Renoir. And how did you know there was a connection to the drawing?"

"I didn't," said Valentine. "I knew I'd seen the Renoir before, though."

"Where?"

"The same place as the Juan Gris back at the school—on an International Fine Arts Register Bulletin. The Renoir disappeared along with a Pissaro landscape in 1938. It was being shipped from Amsterdam to Switzerland. Supposedly it never arrived. That's two pieces of stolen art in one day." He paused. "And that's two too many."

22

The top floor loft of Ex Libris was as stark as the lower floors were overflowing. Returning from Gatty's, Valentine keyed the big freight elevator and they rode up in silence. Finn stepped out into a five thousand square foot expanse that looked like something out of a Fellini film. One huge, high-ceilinged room led into the next. The first had faux brick walls in pressed tin painted Chinese red with a centerpiece table surfaced with a huge slab of black Georgia marble. From there they went into a wide hallway set out with John Kulik neon sculptures on deep green walls and round Chinese carpets on the gleaming black tile floor. The third area, obviously a living room, had more Chinese carpets on the floor and a huge Sidney Goldman surrealist canvas of nudes and nuns on the far wall. Finn sat down on one of three couches in the room and looked around. Valentine disappeared around the corner and came back a few minutes later with a tray holding two immense, stacked bagels and a couple of long-necked beers.

"Blatz?"

"From Wisconsin." Valentine smiled. "I went to school in Madison and got a taste for it."

"My dad taught at UW," said Finn, taking a swallow of beer. She bit a chunk out of the bagel and chewed, staring across at Valentine as he sat down across from her.

"That's right." Valentine nodded. He drank from his bottle and ignored the sandwich on the tray in front of him. "That's where I met him."

"How did you meet him?"

"He was my anthropology prof."

"When was this?"

"Late sixties, early seventies."

"He must have been young."

"He was. So was I—even younger." He laughed.

Finn took another bite of her sandwich and another swallow of beer. She looked around the room at the furniture and the art, thought about the piece of New York real estate she was sitting on top of, thought about Valentine. It was all so tiring. Her head began to whirl. Overkill.

"You didn't buy this place selling old books, Mr. Valentine."

"It's Michael, and that sounds like a passive-aggressive statement, Ms. Ryan."

"I'm really not a fan of dime-store shrinkology. You do more than sell books and do research."

"Yes."

"You're some kind of spook, aren't you?"

"Spook?"

"Spy."

"No, not really."

"And my dad, what was he?"

"An anthropology professor."

"When he died they shipped his body back to Columbus for the funeral."

"Yes?"

"It was a closed-coffin funeral. I didn't really think about it much back then. I was just mad that I'd never get to see his face again."

Valentine said nothing.

"But later, a lot later, I started thinking about all the places he'd been—always politically unstable, always dangerous—and then I wondered why he had a closed coffin when he supposedly had a perfectly innocent heart attack."

Valentine shrugged. "He died in the jungle. Maybe it took time to get his remains back to civilization."

"Or maybe he was missing his fingernails, or maybe he was tortured, or maybe it really wasn't my father's body in that coffin at all."

"You're saying you think your father was a spy?"

"I'm from Columbus, Ohio. I'm what my teachers used to call a linear thinker. Straight lines, you know—line up the facts like dominoes and see where they take you. In this case my mother gives me your phone number, you're definitely no stodgy old bookseller and you used to be a student of my dad's . . . probably more than a student. Is my analysis wrong? My boyfriend gets murdered, I get attacked, my ex-boss winds up with a dagger stuck into him and you don't turn a hair . . . Michael."

"You sound just like him."

"Who?"

"Your dad. He used to count facts off on his fingers like that too." He smiled. Finn looked down and realized what she'd been doing with her hands. She flushed, remembering her father at the dinner table, explaining something, his hands playing over each other, one finger on another. When he ran out of fingers the lecture was usually over.

Finn closed her eyes, suddenly exhausted. What she really wanted to do was find a bed and fall into it for the next month or so. How long had it been, twenty-four, thirty-six hours? Something like that. Like a bolt of lightning. Like driving in a car one second and finding yourself wrapped around a telephone pole the next. Life didn't happen this way, or it wasn't supposed to. She'd done all the right things, got good grades, brushed her teeth from side to side as well as up and down, played well with others, colored inside the lines, all of that, so this just should . . . not . . . be . . . happening.

She opened her eyes.

"I don't want any more bullshit, Michael. I'm not playing games, and I'm not playing Holmes and Watson. This is my life—or maybe my death we're talking about. Murder. I want the truth. And I want to know just who the hell you are."

"You may not like it."

"Try me."

"Do you know anything about your grandfather—your paternal grandfather?"

"What's that got to do with anything?"

"A great deal."

"He was some kind of businessman. My father never talked about him. He was Irish, obviously." She sighed. "This is all ancient history."

"Ancient history is what we are and where we came from. You know the old saying 'Those who forget history—' "

" 'Are doomed to repeat it.' "

"Lots of people know the quote, but do you know who said it?"

"No."

"A Spanish philosopher named George Santayana. He was born in the middle of the nineteenth century and died in 1952. Your grandfather actually met him once."

"You always go the long way to get home?"

"Your grandfather was born in Ireland but his name wasn't Ryan. It was Flynn, Padraic Flynn—

which figures, because Flynn in Gaelic is O'Flionn, which means red-haired."

"Jesus wept," Finn groaned. "You mean my name is really Finn Flynn?"

"He changed it legally when he left Cork in a bit of a rush. He was part of the Easter Uprising in 1916 and had to get out of town. He came to Canada and he wasn't in business. He was a bootlegger. He got rich by taking rowboats full of booze across the Detroit River from Windsor."

"This is all very interesting, but where's it leading?"

"When he got to the American side of the river he met up with my grandfather, Michelangelo Valentini. He changed his name too. He called himself Mickey Valentine but everyone called him Mickey Hearts. He was famous for a while, like your grandfather. Patrick Ryan retired after Prohibition and moved to Ohio. Mickey Hearts was gunned down in the seventies gang wars in New York. After that, Gotti and his freaks took over."

"Okay, so we both come from criminal backgrounds—if it's true, which I'm beginning to wonder about any of this. Just what is your point?"

"The point is neither my grandfather nor yours wanted their children growing up criminals. For them it was rooted in the necessities of poverty. For their children there was the freedom of education. They both went to Yale, you know. During the war my father worked for the judge advocate general and your father worked for the OSS."

"I didn't know that," said Finn, "but I still don't see what it has to do with Crawley's murder or my boyfriend, Pete's."

"I'm beginning to think it has a lot to do with it, at least peripherally."

"So finish your story."

"After the war my father went to work for the CIA and your old man taught anthropology—which meant, in the early days, the fifties and early sixties, he did a lot of traveling, mostly to Southeast Asia and Central America. He even looked the part—horn-rimmed glasses, bald, red beard, big smile, tweed jacket with elbow patches . . . he even smoked a pipe. Nobody paid any attention to him. He wrote papers on the Hmong and the Montagnards in Vietnam and Cambodia before most people could find the places on the map. He also correctly predicted the revolution in Cuba and pointed out Fidel Castro as a potential problem several years before he came to power."

"You're saying he was a spy."

"No. Not officially, but my father enlisted him as a freelancer—one of the best in the business—and your dad, in turn, recruited me. He was an information specialist on a human scale. I broadened out into history and . . . other specialties."

"Like crime?"

"I was connected. My grandfather was still alive then. My father had broken off any relationship years ago, just the way your father was estranged from his father, but I was always curious about my roots, and like it or not, Mickey Hearts was blood."

"Which equals murder and stolen art."

"Art theft has been a major source of income for me for the past twenty years: finding it, recovering it, authenticating it. I work for private individuals, insurance companies, museums. Anyone who needs me."

"Including brokering it for the thieves."

"Sometimes it has to be that way, or the art suffers."

"Ars Gratia Artis," Finn scoffed. "Art for art's sake. And a big fee." She shook her head again. "We're a long way from my dad."

"Not very far—or your mom either."

"Mom? She's a little old lady."

"She might surprise you. She was as deep into it as your father."

"Into what, exactly?"

"Your father wasn't killed because he was trying to destabilize some rickety tin-pot dictator in some banana republic. He was killed because he discovered that the tin-pot dictator—a man named Jose Montt—was murdering villagers by the truckload and raping archaeological sites all over central Guatemala. The man who actually did the killing was the head of one of Montt's death squads, Le Mano Blanco, the White Hand. His name was Julio Roberto Alpirez. They were doing a hundred million dollars' worth of business a year in looted artifacts. Your father got in their way. He also made a stink about it, which was even worse."

"What happened to Alpirez?" Finn asked, her voice taut, her face even paler than usual.

"He died," said Valentine.

"How?"

"I killed him," said Valentine, his voice flat. "He had an apartment in Guatemala City, Zone Four behind the old Church of St. Agustin on Avenida Quattro Sur." Valentine took a sip from the bottle on the table in front of him. He stared at Finn but she could tell that he wasn't looking at her at all. "I went to his apartment and I found him asleep, alone, stoned out of his mind on cocaine and drunk on twelve-year-old single malt. I taped his hands and feet and then I woke him up with a lit cigarette and I talked to him for a few minutes and then I wrapped a very thin piece of piano wire around his throat and pulled it tight and cut his head off. The artifact thefts stopped after that.

"Your father was my teacher, my mentor and my friend and I come from a long line of people who are great believers in the power of revenge." Valentine finished off his beer and stood up. "It's late. I'm going to bed. You should try to get some sleep too. Your room's at the end of the hall." He gave her a brief smile, turned and left the room.

23

The residence of the cardinal archbishop of New
York is a handsome one-hundred-year-old mansion at 452 Madison Avenue, directly behind St.
Patrick's Cathedral and connected to it by an underground passageway. The first floor of the mansion, generally referred to as the museum, is filled
with formal antique furniture and is usually used
for photo opportunities, cocktail parties and various high-level fund-raising events. The second
floor contains offices and the private rooms for the
archbishop's staff, which includes a cook, three
housekeepers, the two priests who serve as the
archbishop's secretaries and a monsignor who acts
as chancellor of the archdiocese. The two "secretaries" are both trained marksmen, have completed a number of special weapons and tactics
courses at the FBI Academy in Quantico and are
usually armed when accompanying the cardinal

archbishop off the premises of the mansion or the cathedral itself.

The archbishop's private apartment on the third floor of the mansion includes a bedroom, bathroom, small kitchen, sitting room and a study. The sitting room is sparsely furnished with a couch, a few chairs, a small but well-stocked bar and a very large color television set. The study has several large stained-glass windows, a cathedral ceiling and a long, old, refectory table the archbishop uses as a desk. The apartment's bedroom lies between the study and the sitting room and is small, a mere twelve by fourteen feet. There is a king-sized bed, and a single window, covered with brown-and-white draperies that match the bedspread. The glass in the drapery-covered window is bullet-proof and plastic laminated to prevent splintering in case of a bomb attack. Over the head of the bed there is a rather tasteless painting of Christ entering Jerusalem on a donkey, and on the wall opposite there is a large fourteenth-century gold crucifix that once was part of the altar of the Cathedral of Wroclaw. At the far end of the room is a tall ironwood vestry containing the archbishop's ecclesiastical garb including copes, chasubles, surplices, several scarlet-and-black mantelettas, or cloaks, edged in gold thread and ermine and an emerald-studded gold pectoral cross he favored for the evening masses on Friday, the only day he personally offered the sacrament.

The man known variously as Father Ricardo
Gentile, a priest of Rome, Peter Ruffino of the Art
Recovery Tactical Squad and Laurence G. Mac-
Lean of Homeland Security moved silently
through the rooms of the archbishop's third-floor
apartment, his footsteps hushed by a pair of cheap
black Nike knockoffs. He had hidden in a small
storeroom behind the sacristy until the cathedral
closed at eleven, then followed the directions he'd
been given to the basement crypt and the passageway leading to the mansion.

For a city and a country so recently and vio-
lently attacked, the ease with which he'd reached
the private apartment of His Eminence David
Cardinal Bannerman had been truly alarming. The
Americans were still amateurs at this sort of thing,
and remarkably innocent, still refusing to accept
that they could be so deeply hated by people seriously intent on doing them harm for no other reason than their being American. The Vatican had
been dispatching assassins to do the Devil's work
in the name of God for the better part of a millen-
nium or more and other nations had been doing
it for much longer.

There had been more political assassinations in
Switzerland by the twelfth century than had ever
taken place in the United States and the only
country with fewer was its next-door neighbor,
Canada. Even that bland and desolate country of
ice and snow had suffered more distinct "terrorist
attacks" in its time. It was, Father Gentile knew,

mostly a matter of not learning from history—which the Americans were very good at, preferring to believe that, on a world level, all other nations revolved around them like planets around the sun. Perhaps a few more wealthy, certifiable zealots and madmen like Osama bin Laden and airliners thrown like so many sticks and stones would eventually teach them.

He reached the open doorway of the bedroom and paused to screw the suppressor onto the tapped muzzle of the ugly little Beretta Cougar he carried in his right hand. He looked into the room. Bannerman was asleep, snoring lightly, his thick gray hair on the single pillow. He slept on his back in the exact center of the large bed, hands folded across the coverlet like a corpse, sheet drawn up to his chin. Gentile could see the collar of his silk pajamas. Probably from Gammarelli's, around the corner from the Pantheon. He crossed the room and sat down on the edge of the bed. He gently tapped the cold end of the suppressor against the bridge of the cardinal archbishop's patrician Irish nose.

"Wake up," he said quietly.

Bannerman's snoring broke and he muttered something. Father Gentile rapped him on the nose a little harder. The cardinal's eyes shot open, the pupils widening, pain creasing the man's forehead.

"What the hell?"

"Wake up," Gentile said again. "We must talk.

Keep your voice down; believe me, you don't want us to be interrupted."

Bannerman's eyes crossed in a silly expression as he focused on the muzzle of the suppressor. It was now four inches away from his nose. A shot that close would blow his brains all over Jesus and his donkey.

"Who are you?" said Bannerman. He was an old man, well into his seventies, but his voice was still firm and strong.

"Vincit qui si vincit," the priest with the gun responded. *He conquers who conquers himself.*

Bannerman's eyes widened at the quotation. It was something every man in his position knew and also dreaded. In those few words and their response lay the seeds of a scandal of unimaginable proportions. Bannerman knew in an instant who the man was, what his authority allowed him and whom that authority came from. He also knew that he would be a dead man if he didn't give the correct answer within the next few seconds. They were words he had never expected to say.

"Verbum pat sapient," he whispered. *A word is enough for a wise man.*

"Are you a wise man, Eminence?" asked Father Gentile.

"I know what you are here for. I can read the e-mails from ASV as well as any other man."

"What am I here for, Eminence, the *Archivo Secreto Vaticano* aside?"

"You're here because of the murder of Alexander Crawley. To investigate his death." The cardinal eased himself up on the pillow, eying Gentile in the half-light coming through the bedroom window.

"Only partly, Eminence. I have been charged with a much more complex assignment than that. Crawley is no more than the tip of the iceberg. There will be more killings, as you well know. The more killing, the more danger to the Church and her situation. This cannot be allowed to happen."

"What do I have to do with any of this?" asked Bannerman. "This is none of my doing. It all happened more than half a century ago. This is all Spellman's doing—him and his damn chorus boys! He was Pacelli's friend, not me."

"You are Archbishop Spellman's inheritor, I'm afraid. It comes with the proud-looking manteletta you keep in your closet over there. It is as much a part of your congregation as the people of New York."

Bannerman sat up fully, aware that the gun barrel followed his movements, its aim never far from a spot roughly between his eyes. He watched the man sitting beside him on the bed carefully. Early middle age, fit, ordinary face, the obscenity of his holy collar. He wondered if the man really was a priest at all, or whether the guardians of the ASV simply chose their operatives wherever they could. Not that it mattered. What mattered was that the man was here, now, in his bedroom and with a gun.

"What do you want?"

"I want as much information on the boy as possible."

"There is very little. All the files concerning the child were destroyed when he entered the country. It was part of the agreement to take him in the first place."

"It was an agreement made with criminals. It was an agreement made under duress. You know as well as I do that such agreements have no weight. It is my understanding that files were secretly maintained, that you have kept track of him through the years."

"This is all too dangerous."

"Of course it's dangerous. If it was a walk in the park, as you Americans call it, I would not be here."

"If the child's existence were to be discovered the repercussions would be enormous. The Church has gone through a great deal in recent years. Things have been difficult."

"Of course. If all those whining victims had kept their mouths shut none of this would have happened, right?" The priest with the gun shook his head. "Any evangelist television preacher could quote you Ecclesiastes 11:1, Eminence: 'Cast your bread upon the waters and it shall be returned to you tenfold.' What most of them would forget to tell you is that it works both ways, good as well as bad. That's what this is all about. I need the files on the boy. In addition, I will need as much information as you can give me about the Grange Foundation."

"One has nothing to do with the other!"

"Crawley's murder would indicate otherwise." The only thing he had been told by his employers was that an organization by that name would bear closer scrutiny and that Crawley's unfortunate demise was somehow involved. The cardinal's violent reaction was instructive.

"You are trifling with information that can only come to no good. This is insanity. One false move and I will be pilloried in the media."

"Then perhaps in your next mass you should pray that I make no false moves, for all our sakes. Now where can I find the files on the boy?"

The cardinal looked at the gun and then into the face of the man holding it. Lying was not an option. "They are kept in the records of the Community of Sant'Egidio at St. Joseph's Church in Greenwich Village."

Gentile nodded. Sant'Egidio was a large lay movement that did a lot of work with orphans and displaced children. "Under what name?"

"Frederico Botte."

"How do I get the files?"

"If I ask for them the office would become suspicious at my interest. Not to mention the fact that the file is very old. It will not have been computerized."

"I can deal with that. The Grange Foundation?"

"I will find out what I can."

"No intermediaries, no secretaries. I deal with you only."

"All right. How do I get in touch with you?"

"I will get in touch with you." He reached into the other pocket of his dark jacket and took out a tiny Globalstar satellite pager. He dropped it onto the cardinal's scarlet chest. "Keep this on you at all times. It vibrates. Call the number you see in the little screen. The number will change. Call from this phone." He dropped another small device beside the pager—an extremely small cell phone.

"One thing more," said Gentile, standing.

"Yes."

"Don't try to have me followed. Don't try to trace me through the machinery. Under no circumstances call the police. The one thing you must know is that I am not your enemy. You must also know that I would not hesitate to sacrifice you for the common good. Don't be foolish, Eminence. Please."

With that, Gentile slipped away, leaving the archbishop of New York shaking nervously in his own bed. Outside, over the sharp neo-Gothic spires of the cathedral, the moon began to rise.

24

She went to his bed and found him still awake in the darkened room, hands clasped behind his head, staring at the ceiling, perhaps reliving a distant violent past. He turned to her as she stood beside the bed, the moon at her back, unbuttoning her shirt, staring down at him.

"You don't have to do this, you know."

"I know." She pulled off the shirt, then reached behind her back to unclasp her bra, tossing it on the floor. She slipped the buttons on her jeans one by one, knowing that he was watching her, trying not to think about what he was thinking, trying not to think of anything at all except the moment. He said nothing more.

She slid off her jeans and the plain white cotton panties with them and stood there finally, naked in front of him, the light from behind her turning her hair into a glowing tangled halo, catching the curve of her hips and the long, strong muscles of her thighs with a soft plain glow. She waited like that for a moment, letting him see her, wanting him to see everything that she was, simple in the moonlight, and then she got into the bed with him, slipping under the covers, remembering the touch of his hand on her thigh at the colonel's house, knowing this was going to happen even then, the touch like a fist in an iron glove and also as tender as a lover.

For the second time she wondered about the abstract moments and twists of fate that could turn a person's life upside down within the space of time from one sunrise to another. For a split second she thought about Peter and that final, terrible cry, and bizarrely she suddenly had an image of her mother's dressing table in the house on Doderidge Street back in Columbus and the wedding photograph in its silver frame.

Her mother and father standing together, somberfaced, her father in tweeds and tortoiseshell-rim glasses towering over her mother—so much younger, bright-eyed in a perfect wedding dress and holding a spray of white flowers in her hand, the tall trees and the rose gardens of Whetstone Park in the background, all in that pale yellow of old black-and-white photographs. For a moment she felt very young as she brushed against the hot dry skin of Valentine's hip and then it was too late for good and all and he reached out and put his hand on her flat, taut belly and she turned to him and he slipped into her immensely as though he had belonged there from the beginning.

He began to move and she moved with him and none of the other things mattered even though she had no idea if she was doing it for him and his pain, for her father or for herself. Nothing mattered at all except right now and that was enough for both of them.

25

Lieutenant James Cornwall of the Monuments, Fine Arts and Archives unit attached to the ALIU—the art-looting division of the OSS—in western Germany sat on a rock with his sergeant trying to find a way into the farmhouse hidden behind the screen of trees. He wasn't having very much success. His group was running out of food, there were dozens of retreating German patrols in the area, and according to the sergeant, they were sitting ducks if even one German tank decided to move in their direction. He lit a Lucky, pushed his metal-rimmed glasses up on his forehead and wondered how a man who'd completed two years of study at the Sorbonne in Paris and graduated summa cum laude from Yale could wind up sitting on a rock in Bavaria beside a man who stank of sweat and cigarettes and who carried a Garand rifle strapped to his back. He was assistant curator of prints and drawings at the Parker-Hale Museum. Right now he should have been having breakfast at the Hotel Brevoort and palling around with Rorimer and Henry Taylor from the Met, not getting shot at in Bavaria.

"So what do you think, Sergeant?"

"I don't get paid to think, sir."

"Don't be an ass."

"Yes, sir." The sergeant paused and lit a smoke from the crumpled pack he kept in the well of his combat boot and looked out over the early-morning mist that lay on the hillside and filtered in through the trees. "Well, sir, except for the sniper, I don't think we're dealing with combat troops. It's something else, sir."

"Like what?"

"Some kind of special mission. Six trucks—Opels, not Mercedes. That means they're gas, not diesel, and that means they're meant to move fast. Six trucks like that wouldn't be used to guard troops, and they wouldn't waste more gas on them lights like they were doing last night. It's maybe bigwig Krauts taking a powder, but you'd think they'd be in staff cars. The officer I saw was wearing a general's uniform but he was too young, no more than thirty-five. He's gotta be a phony."

"Your conclusion?"

"Like I said, some kind of secret thing, hot-footing it, you know. They're carrying something—loot, papers, something valuable." He paused and cleared his throat. "And then there's the broad."

"The woman you mentioned."

"Yes, sir."

"A phantom perhaps, wishful thinking?" Cornwall said with a faint smile.

"No, sir. She was real enough."

"You mentioned before that it might have been some relation to the occupant of the farm. What about the hypothesis?"

I don't know about any hypo thing, but I know she was real and if she was some farmer's wife or something she wouldn't have been walking around free like that in the middle of the night."

"Do you think it might be important? Tactically."

"Tactics aren't my business any more than hypo-watsits. I saw a broad. I thought you should know, that's all."

"All right," said Cornwall. "Now I know."

"So what do you want to do?" the sergeant asked. "The sniper saw us coming. They'll make a move before we do, try to break out, maybe."

"What would you do?"

The sergeant smiled. He knew that Cornwall was looking for more than just advice. He was asking for some kind of plan because he didn't have any fucking idea of what he was doing.

"Depends on whether or not you want to keep those trucks from getting blown to shit or not."

"That would be preferable."

"Then we hit them first, before they can do anything. Hold them down with the fifty-caliber, blowing the fucking sniper out of his fucking tower with Terhune's M9 and go in hard."

"Day or night?"

The sergeant resisted the urge to tell Cornwall not to be an asshole. "Night."

"All right," the lieutenant said again. "Let me think about it."

Just so long as you don't think about it for too fucking long, thought the sergeant, but he kept his mouth shut and thought about the broad and the bogus general instead.

He reached out and let his long, bony index finger play over the faded photograph pasted neatly into the Great Book beside the careful drawing of the farm: Stabsfuhrer Gerhard Utikal of Einsatzstab Rosenberg, last seen in the early spring of 1945 near Fussen and Schloss Neuschwanstein in the Bavarian Alps. In the picture he was in his early thirties, wearing, illegally as it turned out, the uniform of a Wehrmacht Hauptman, squinting into the sunlight in three-quarter profile, trees and a large ornamental pool behind him, the snapshot probably taken at Versailles or the Tuileries Gardens in Paris sometime between 1941 and 1943, his years of duty there.

The naked, gray-haired man smiled vaguely, remembering. Gerhard Utikal had been the first, so long ago now. According to all the files Utikal had vanished like smoke, but in time he'd found him, living in Uruguay, dividing his time between an apartment on the Playa Ramirez in Montevideo and a huge ranch in Argentina on the far side of the River Platte. By then Eichmann had been taken and the Butcher of Riga, Herberts Cukurs, had been liquidated by an Israeli death squad after boasting to journalist Jack Anderson that he was "invincible."

Utikal wasn't invincible, just smarter. Instead of keeping a set of neatly pressed Nazi uniforms in his closet like the Latvian had, he had chosen instead to hide in plain sight, adopting the identity of one of the interned sailors from the scuttled battleship *Graf Spee*. It worked for the better part of twenty-five years, but not quite long enough or well enough.

The naked man put the tip of his finger over the face in the photograph. The first of many, and more to come. Utikal had screamed as the first tenpenny nail was pushed slowly into his left eye, then died, twisting horribly in the chair as the second three-inch sliver was pushed into the right. The naked man closed the Great Book.

"*Mirabile Dictu*," he whispered softly. *Miraculous to say.* "*Kyrie eleison.*" *Lord, have mercy on our souls.*

26

Valentine's kitchen on the top floor of Ex Libris was a paean of praise to a fifties that Finn had never known. The floors were covered in blue and white linoleum tile, the cupboards were yellow with chrome handles and white interiors, and the two small country-style windows that looked out onto the roof garden planted with staked tomatoes were trimmed in blue chintz.

The stove was a forty-inch Gaffers & Sattler factory-yellow four-burner gas range with a thermal eye, heat-timer griddle, and a fifth burner. The refrigerator was a 1956 turquoise Kelvinator. There was a Rival waffle maker on the yellow-flecked Formica countertop along with a bullet-shaped chrome toaster and a huge chrome breadbox that actually hid a very up-to-date microwave.

There was a four-seat yellow vinyl and chrome dinette set in the middle of the room, and off in one corner there was a sky blue vinyl breakfast nook under one of the windows. Finn, wearing her panties and one of Valentine's crisp Sea Island cotton white shirts, was lounging in the breakfast nook, drinking coffee brewed in the big silver GE percolator. Valentine, nude except for an idiotic barbecue apron that said "A little sugar for the chef makes sure the cookin' is sweet," was making scrambled eggs at the stove. Finn reached out onto the breakfast nook table and toyed with the green-skirted, hula-dancing, ukulele-playing ceramic boy and girl salt-and-pepper shakers. According to the tail-swinging, eye-rolling cat clock over the sink it was just after eight in the morning. Apparently everything in the fifties had been in pastel shades of "cute." Tellingly, there was no visible dishwasher—or at least one that she could see at first glance.

The whole thing was ridiculous to the point of fetish, but she knew it was almost certainly accurate down to the plastic laminated cowgirl placemats and the bright yellow "Mornin' Ma'am" cowboy coffee mugs. She felt herself remembering their time in his bed the night before. She stretched in her seat, a shiver running through her from the back of her neck to the pit of her stomach. There was no doubt that Valentine was a perfectionist in everything he did.

"You always show your women a good time like this?" She grinned.

He turned and smiled, looking at her, the expression on his face taking ten hard years off his face.

"There aren't that many to show a good time to," he answered. Finn almost said something but stopped herself. She had a pretty good idea that Valentine was a lot like the guys she'd yearned after in high school. They didn't have the slightest idea they were attractive, which in itself made them even more so. On the other hand, his love-making had been smooth, practiced and knowledgeable. Could you know a lot about women without knowing a lot of women? She stopped herself from thinking about it at all. They'd made love for hours and it had been wonderful. That was all she needed—or wanted—to know right now, certainly not his reasons for doing it, or hers. Maybe she'd been in school for too long; this was the real world. And she didn't want to think about *that* too much either.

Valentine took two plates out of the warming oven, slid a mound of scrambled eggs onto each then went back for the toast and bacon. He picked up both plates and fitted them into his right hand, then snagged the ketchup off the counter with his left. He brought the meal expertly across the room, put everything down on the breakfast nook table and slid onto the blue vinyl seat. He slid the plates onto the placemats, and they began to eat, talking easily between bites with no obvious discomfort at their situation. To Finn it felt as though they'd been lovers forever, which was a little scary.

"What's with the retro stuff?" she asked.

"It's the easiest way to decorate a room," he said. "Pick an era and then pick up things from the period. It's fun. You get to look for things without it being serious. I can get as excited about a 1954 first edition of the *Betty Crocker's Good and Easy Cook Book* as I can about finding a Vermeer stolen from an Irish country house."

"I heard about that when we were doing a Dutch masters class," said Finn, her eyes widening a little. *"Lady Writing a Letter with Her Maid.* They even wrote a book about it. That was you?"

"It was the second time the painting had been stolen. There was a drug connection. I helped track it down from this end." He shook his head and took a sip of coffee from his cowboy mug. "Once upon a time art theft was something you saw in the movies starring David Niven or Cary Grant. Now it's usually got some kind of other link—usually with drugs, sometimes with guns."

"I don't get it," said Finn. "They don't have anything to do with each other."

"Sure they do," responded Valentine.

"Explain."

"Most criminal activity deals in large volumes of cash. Cash is hard to keep and hard to spend. Stealing art helps both problems."

"How?"

"It's currency. Most works of art, valuable ones,

have a well-established value. A painting or draw-ing can be sold for X amount. Instead of doing deals for money, big drug dealers and weapons dealers—especially the ones in the terrorist market—trade in art. It's portable, it's easy to move across borders and it's usually insured in one way or another. I can name you half a dozen galleries in Europe that knowingly traffic in stolen art and twice that many just in New York. It's a very big business."

Finn shifted on the seat across from Valentine, tucking one leg up underneath herself, thinking. "Is that what we're dealing with here?"

"I'm not sure. If it's drugs it's very sophisti-cated, beyond anything I've ever seen. On first glance I'd say no. It's something else, and it's been going on for some time."

"Why do you say that?"

"Crawley was pretty high up the ladder. You said the provenance for the Michelangelo had his initials on it?"

"No, the inventory line."

"What about the Hoffman Gallery receipt. Who was it sent to? Crawley or somebody else?"

"It's all on computer. One of the founders of the Parker-Hale bought it from the Hoffman Gal-lery in 1939, I think. Before Crawley's time."

"But he inventoried it?"

"Yes. As an Urbino, a few years back."

"Too many coincidences and not enough an-swers," murmured Valentine. He finished his eggs and chewed on a piece of bacon. Finn refilled his coffee cup and her own. A silence fell across the pleasantly anachronistic kitchen. Somewhere far away she could hear the morning traffic sounds on Broadway, and closer, the whine and thunder of the garbage trucks behind Lispenard.

"Okay, let's put together what we have," said Valentine. "This all starts when you accidentally trip over a Michelangelo drawing and Alex Crawley catches you."

"You make it sound as though I was stealing something."

"That's the point," said Valentine. "You weren't doing anything wrong, so why was Crawley so upset? All he really had to do was say that you were mistaken, and it was only after you insisted it was a Michelangelo that he fired you."

"What are you saying?"

"Either he didn't want you or anyone else knowing the gallery was in possession of that particular drawing, or it's a fake. More likely the former rather than the latter because it's obvious there was already a cover-up in motion since it was identified in the inventory as the work of another artist. The question, of course, is Why?" He tapped his fingers rapidly on the Formica surface of the table. "I'd love to see the original paperwork. It's got to be somewhere and it would be easier to trace than computer files, harder to fake."

"It's a company called U.S. Docugraphics Service. I've seen their trucks in the parking area behind the museum.''

"All right. That makes things easier,'' he said. He thought for a moment, picking up a toast crust and dabbing it with a knifeful of E. Waldo Ward Rhubarb Conserve. Even that simple act made the muscles in his arms and shoulders stand out and she remembered being in his arms last night; he'd been enormously strong and had a tough, hard body that came from more than three times a week at the gym. Definitely not the abs of a librarian. They were lovers now but he still hadn't told her everything.

"Penny for your thoughts.'' He grinned in that slightly savage, predatory way, his perfect teeth gleaming, the intelligent eyes focused on hers.

"Not a chance,'' she said, laughing. "So what do we do now? Run away to a desert island and wait until things die down?''

"I know just the place.'' He smiled. "But I don't think it's a possibility yet.''

"Then where do we go from here? Crawley's murder is being investigated by the cops and so is Peter's. We've established some kind of relationship between Gatty, Crawley and Greyfriars Academy through the missing knife and the Juan Gris, and that creep—the headmaster, Wharton—is probably involved. We know Gatty's involved in stolen art, at least as a buyer, because he's got that Renoir. None of it fits together.''

"Sure it does. We just don't know how yet."

"So how do we find out?"

"I want to talk to a dealer I know. Then maybe go to the Parker-Hale and ask a few questions."

"Under what pretext?"

"I'll tell them I'm your godfather and that you're missing. Your boyfriend was murdered and obviously I'm concerned."

"I don't know if I like you referring to yourself as my godfather. It makes me feel as though I was in a cradle that was just robbed." She grinned.

"Think of it in the Marlon Brando sense, then." He grinned back. He stuck out his foot under the table and let his big toe slide down her calf. She shivered. He gave her a strange look.

"What's that?"

"My best Christopher Walken leer."

"Can you back it up?"

"That remains to be seen."

"What am I supposed to do . . . afterward?"

"Get on the computer and find out how all the pieces are connected."

"Okay."

"You finished?" He glanced down at her plate.

"Yup." She slid out of the breakfast nook and started undoing the buttons of her shirt. "Gentlemen, prepare to defend your aprons."

27

Without being asked or ordered, the sergeant went out an hour or so after dawn broke, leaving everybody else behind this time except Reid. He was part fucking Cherokee or something and he looked like the front of an old nickel. Quiet enough to stand in front of a cigar store and yet he could pick off most anything with his M1 from a couple hundred yards.

"Where we going, Sarge?" Reid asked.

"Same as before. Maybe somebody's up and around. Maybe do a head count or something."

"Sure, Sarge," and that was it. Reid unslung the M1 and followed him into the woods.

This time the sergeant kept his eyes on the forest floor. There seemed to be three well-worn paths, one going straight through, one moving to the left and one to the right. They all came together in roughly the center of the woodlot at a small clearing. Rabbits maybe, more likely deer.

There were chewed-off branches about five feet up, which would be right for a deer, or maybe a young moose. He wondered if there were moose in Europe. He put the thought out of his mind; waste of time to think about anything except the here and now. The sergeant gestured to the left and Reid nodded. The sergeant headed along the left-hand path with the other man a few yards behind him. Reid didn't make a sound, which was more than you could say for most of the others.

When they reached the edge of the woods, the sergeant made a "get low" gesture. Sitting on his haunches, he had a brief conference with Reid.

"There's a ditch and then the road. There's an old Panzer, burned out, catercorner. The hatch is open. We should be able to get a pretty good look down into the farm. The tank's at the top of the hill."

"The sniper?" Reid asked.

"If we come up low the tank will be between us and that tower. Unless he's looking for us it should be okay."

"What do you want me to do?"

"Watch my back."

"Okay."

They waited just inside the screening woods, trading puffs from one of the sergeant's Luckies. The sniper might not be looking for them, but a sharp eye might see cigarette smoke wafting up in the still, early-morning air. The overcast sky wouldn't help either. No smoking, drinking or screwing while you were fighting a war. He field-stripped the smoke, grinding the hot ash under his combat boot. Didn't quite seem right; you should be able to have one last bit of pleasure before you were snuffed with a bullet from some invisible Kraut's Steyr 95.

The sergeant slid out through an opening between the trees and dropped down into the ditch that ran beside the road. He crawled forward until he was in the shadow of the old tank. Coming at it low, from the rear, he saw that it wasn't as badly damaged as he'd first thought. He could see the exposed rear differential blown to shit and one of the treads had been blown off the right rear assembly but that was about it. From the way the road was chewed up behind it the tank looked as though it might have been strafed by a fighter. American, Brit, Russkie, who knew? The Panzer 1 had been designed originally as a practice tank. It had thin 8mm armor and only a couple of machine guns with no cannon. Good against infantry but no better than a tin can if it ran into another tank, even a crappy old M1 or a guy with a bazooka. On the pro side—if you were a Kraut—was the fact that there were thousands of them and they used only a two-man crew: The driver and a combination commander, observer and machine gunner.

The sergeant left Reid down on the ground behind the left-hand tread. He climbed up the side of the tank, avoiding the sharp, sheet-metal mud flaps and the cheese grater–pierced metal of the muffler cover. He pulled himself up to the turret, using the big eyebolts used to hold a spare length of winch cable, then slithered through the hatchway and into the gunner's chair. There were foot pedals to swing the turret and each of the twin guns was on a swivel, able to move up and down independently. Between the guns was a long metal telescopic sight. The sergeant peered through the eyepiece but the far magnifying lens had shattered during whatever firefight had stopped the tank.

The inside of the tank was the usual sandy beige color and there didn't seem to be any blood, so maybe the crew had gotten away clean. The fact that the tank was still here meant the road wasn't used very often, which almost certainly meant that the trucks down on the farm had come from the east. That was something to chew on, since that's where Hitler's place was supposed to be— Berchtesgaden or whatever it was called.

He tried to imagine coming face-to-face with King Kraut and couldn't imagine it. For the past four years when he thought about Hitler it always came out like Charlie Chaplin. You couldn't really take the guy seriously with that mustache, could you? On the other hand, you could take a bunch of guys with those big fucking helmets seriously, that was for sure.

The sergeant eased himself out of the gunner's seat and slid down into the bottom of the tank. All the ports were open so he squeezed into the driver's seat. He eased the binoculars out of their case and looked down at the farm. He could immediately see a great deal of activity.

Several men in shirtsleeves were sponging off the trucks' windshields and more men were hanging out laundry on a makeshift line that ran from the side mirror of one of the trucks to a post beside a well opening on the other side of the cobbled courtyard. Two men in civilian clothes—lightweight crumpled suits, one brown, one blue—were smoking cigarettes beside one of the small outbuildings. Both men had eyeglasses on.

A woman in a blue dress and brown shoes with fat Cuban heels walked casually about, chatting and smoking. A second woman, dressed in the flat brown uniform of the Wehrmacht women's auxiliary was sitting on the edge of the well casing, her head tilted back into the sun. The only man in full uniform was a youngish-looking officer in a black SS uniform.

The shirtsleeved soldiers cleaning the windshields carried no weapons. Nobody except the SS officer had a sidearm. The sergeant turned his attention to the abbey tower. The small opening at the top of the tower looked dark and empty, but that didn't mean anything. Snipers were good at keeping in the shadows.

The sergeant turned and spoke quietly out through one of the rear observation ports. "You catching any of this, Reid?"

"Yeah" came the faint response from outside the tank.

"Whadya think?"

"Not army, not military. I dunno who they are," said the disembodied voice.

"Take a guess."

"Civvies."

"What do you think of the women?"

"They're women. What am I supposed to think?"

"Why would they have women along?"

"Why does anyone have women along."

"Gotta be more than that."

"Why?"

"Something pretty strange going on, you ask me."

"Is anyone asking you?"

"Don't be an asshole." The sergeant was silent again. He looked back through the front port. "What's east of here?"

"Mountains, bunch of castles."

"West?"

"Lake Constance. The Krauts call it something else. Switzerland's on the other end."

"South?"

"Austria."

"Who's there now, any idea?"

"Forty-fourth. The Russkies, I think."

"Germans don't like Russkies—am I right?"

"How the fuck do I know, Sarge? Why are you asking me all these questions? I'm just a redskin off the reservation, remember? 'Ugh, How, Kemosabe,' like that."

"Hey, Reid, how come your name isn't Running Bear, or Moon Blanket or something?"

"My father was a garage mechanic in Kansas who like fucking squaws when he got drunk, okay?" He almost laughed. "Where you come from it was 'Nigger in the woodpile.' Where I'm from it was 'Choctaw in the cornfield.' "

"You know what? You're okay, Reid." The sergeant shifted gears. "They had to come from the east, or else they would have had to get those trucks around the tank and there's no sign of that. They're not going north, 'cause that's where the war is, and the Russkies and us are in Austria, so they're not going there."

"So they're going to Lake Constance."

"Yeah. The Bodensee or something, that's what the Krauts call it. I wonder if they got some kind of ferry service or something that would handle six trucks like that."

"Probably." There was silence from Reid for a moment. The sergeant turned his glasses on the courtyard again. If the sniper was up in the tower he was their only line of defense. If the machine guns in the tank still had ammo he could probably do pretty much of a clean sweep. He reached down and opened the big ammo bin and saw

enough belts to keep the guns going steady for
ten or fifteen minutes. The only problem was
you'd have to have the engine going to power
the turret; with the sight gone it would be dead
reckoning. Still . . .

"You cooking up some kind of plan, Sarge? It
feels like you're cooking up some kind of plan."

"I'm working on it."

"What is it?"

"I'm not sure. Hey, Reid, how many real Krauts
you see down there? Soldiers."

"Maybe a dozen or so, the guys cleaning the
windows."

"They're not even armed. The tags say they're
Feldgendarmarie but army cops wear gray and
those guys have brown pants on. It's like they
picked up uniforms where they found them. I
wonder how many truck drivers they conscripted
who wear glasses."

"Maybe they had no choice."

"And maybe they're in a big hurry to get what's
in those trucks out of here."

"What do you think's in those trucks, Sarge?"

"Somethin' good, Reid. Somethin' to get you
doing your best war dance and sharpening your
tommy-hawk." He focused on the trucks again,
trying vainly to catch a glimpse of what was inside them. They were closed up tight, even the
back flaps. As he watched, some of the men
pushed a big open staff car out of one of the
smaller outbuildings and began to gas it up using

jerry cans pulled down from the sides of the trucks.

"They're getting ready to move," said Reid.

"Yeah. We gotta get Cornwall and his friends off their duffs or it's going to be too late."

"We going to get a piece of what's in the trucks, Sarge?"

"I think that's fair, don't you. To the victor go the spoils, right? And my middle name's Victor."

"Funny," said Reid. "So's mine."

"Maybe we're related."

"Anything you say, paleface."

"How many people you count down there?"

"Dozen at the trucks, four, no, five more outside, walking around."

"Plus the sniper."

"Yeah, there's him. But most of the others don't look like regular army."

"There's gotta be a few somewhere. I saw a guard with a 98k on his back and an MP40 in front last night by the gate."

"Could have been one of the motor pool guys."

"Maybe. Point is, he was armed."

"They aren't armed now."

"The way they're cleaning up that staff car or whatever it is, looks like they're maybe getting ready to bug."

"Maybe we should go back and report."

"Yeah. I'm coming down." He climbed up out of the tank and back down the side. On his way down he tapped a couple of the jerry cans strapped to the hull. At least half full. A machine like this was usually stripped pretty quickly, and he began to revise his thinking about how long it had been here. He also began revising his tactics about taking the farm. He and Reid slipped back into the woods.

"You know anything about tanks, Reid?"

"Not much."

"Think you could handle her machine guns?" He thumbed over his shoulder.

"I could figure it out. Is there ammo?"

"Yeah."

"Need gas to run the turret, wouldn't you?"

"They've got it but you might not need it. The guns are already facing down into the courtyard. There's a crank wheel to lower the elevation."

"So what do you figure?"

"Knock out the tower with Terhune's bazooka. Then go in through the front gate. You keep a cross fire going from up here as soon as we put up a flare."

"Sounds like it would work."

"So let's tell Cornwall and get on with it." They moved into the deeper shadows of the woods. "We're running out of time."

28

The Newman Gallery was located in Chelsea, on West Twenty-second Street between Tenth and Eleventh Avenues. The gallery had moved with the times, from Greenwich Village in the thirties to Soho in the seventies to Tribeca in the eighties and finally to its present Chelsea location in the early nineties. During all that time a series of Newmans had stuck to the credo laid down by the gallery's founder in 1889: "Don't buy what you can't sell." To the founder, Josef Neumann of Cologne, that meant buying quality, which meant sticking to the proven. In more than a hundred years the Newman Gallery had never succumbed to the vagaries of taste. Because of that, they had prospered, riding out waves of flash-in-the-pan art, quietly expanding over the years, stocking up on Dutch masters and French Impressionists when they were out of favor, trickling them back on the market when the tide turned, which it inevitably did.

The gallery occupied a narrow space on the ground floor of a renovated warehouse building and was bracketed by a nouveau Japanese restaurant and an upscale kitchen store. The walls of the gallery were painted flat white, the floors were heavily polyurethaned oak planks and the ceiling was a black steel grid capable of virtually any lighting arrangement.

There were only three paintings on display: a Franz Hals portrait a yard square, a Jacob van Ruisdael about the same size on the opposite wall and, at the rear of the gallery, a massive Petrus Christus religious scene as large as the other two put together. By Valentine's quick estimate there was at least twenty or thirty million dollars' worth of art in the long narrow room. Valentine also knew that the three pieces were only the very tip of the iceberg; the gallery's real inventory was in a climate-controlled storage vault in New Jersey.

As Valentine stepped through the door, Peter Newman came out of the office in the back. Newman, as usual, was dressed in funereal black. He was in his early seventies, bald and stooped. He looked more like a mortician than an art dealer, although it occurred to Valentine that both professions were similar: a mortician cared for dead bodies, an art dealer of Peter Newman's stature cared for dead art. Both jobs were remarkably profitable.

"Michael," said Newman, smiling as Valentine came down the room. "It's been ages. How have you been?"

"Well enough," said Valentine. "Taking care of business."

"Business," huffed the old man irritably "Feh! Art is supposed to be art, not business. 'I got fifty million worth of Van Gogh,' says one of the little Japanese businessmen. 'That's nothing,' says the man beside him at the sushi bar. 'I got a hundred million in Picassos in the trunk of my car.' " Newman made a snorting sound. "And by sushi bar I don't mean the restaurant next door." He slipped his arm through Valentine's and led him into the rear office. The little room was cramped. An old and probably valuable escritoire stood against one wall, and the other wall was taken up by floor-to-ceiling bookcases crammed with ledgers that probably dated back to the gallery's origins. In them Valentine knew were the sales records and provenances for every painting the Newmans had ever sold, and in a sense it was those records that were the real value of the gallery—the family trees of ten thousand individual pieces of art and the record of a hundred thousand transactions that covered Europe and North America like an invisible network. What wasn't in the records was probably crammed into Peter Newman's head, information handed down from father to son for more than a hundred years.

Valentine sat down in an old wooden office chair and watched while Peter Newman shuffled around in front of the coffeemaker at the very rear of the cell-like office. He brought back two ancient Delftware cups and saucers and handed one to Valentine. Then he sat down at the escritoire and sighed as he settled into his seat.

"So?" he said, sipping his coffee, peering at Valentine over the milky edge of the cup.

"Juan Gris."

"He's dead," Newman cackled.

"The Nazi connection."

"He was Spanish. He stayed in Paris during the war. He was one of the so-called 'degenerates.' The Nazis looted some of his early work. He's part of the whole mudslinging match between European galleries about who did what during Hitler's reign. I never had much feeling for the man myself."

"Renoir, *Head of a Young Girl.*"

"More Nazi loot."

"If I told you I'd seen a looted Juan Gris and the Renoir portrait in one day what would you say?"

"I'd say you'd paid a visit to Colonel George Gatty."

"Why haven't I heard of him before?"

"He lives in a very rarified strata. He never buys at a public auction. Very discreet."

"Both the Gris and the Renoir are reasonably well known. Why doesn't somebody tell the police?"

"The colonel has some very important connections."

"Anyone in particular?"

"Is the president of the United States particular enough?"

"Impressive."

"Not in the art world. The man is a pig. No one reputable would buy or sell for him."

"Somebody is."

"Who said the art world was entirely reputable?" Newman cackled again, finishing his coffee.

"Come on, Peter, it's me you're talking to."

Newman sighed and put down his cup and saucer. "I would not like to be accused of being a bigot," he said. "Such things are not good when you are an old Jew like me. Bad for my reputation."

"Spit it out," Valentine said, smiling.

"Let me say only this," Newman murmured. "The archdiocese of New York has some very fine collections under the purvue of its archives division. They also have ready access to the Vatican collections in Rome. Colonel Gatty, by the way, is what they refer to as a 'Friend' of the Vatican museums."

"You're kidding."

"Not at all," countered Newman. "The Vatican museums were founded in the 1500s. Their collection is . . . how shall I put this . . . extensive. Like any other museum, they regularly deaccession. When they do, the colonel is first in line."

"The Vatican is dealing in looted art?"

"I never said that. Not really." Newman pursed his lips into a small smile.

"Christ," Valentine whispered.

"I seriously doubt that *he* was directly involved," said Newman, cracking himself up again.

Valentine tried to clear his thoughts. "All right," he said after a moment. "Forget about the Vatican. What about the Parker-Hale?"

"Private art museum with an endowment about as big as the Whitney but smaller than the Getty."

"A player?"

"Undoubtedly."

"Alexander Crawley?"

"Like Juan Gris, he too is dead. Nasty."

"His reputation?"

"Academically it was unblemished. Columbia, Harvard or Yale—I forget which. Studied conservation in London at the Courtauld Institute of Art, curator at the Fogg in Boston, that sort of thing. Went to the Parker-Hale under the wing of the director, James Cornwall, in the mid-nineties. Took over as acting director a year ago when Cornwall passed on."

"Passed on?"

"It is how *alter cockers* like myself refer to dropping dead. And by the way, in Cornwall's case it was peacefully—*Az a yor ahf mir*, May I be so lucky—in his sleep. He'd had several heart attacks. He was in his eighties, I believe."

"You said Crawley was academically clean; what about otherwise?"

"Socially very good with people, an excellent fund-raiser. He tended to cheat when it came to buying and selling."

"How so?"

"It was in the way of being a ring; you know what that is, of course."

Valentine nodded. In the business of art and antiquities a ring was a secret association of dealers who conspired to keep the prices down at auction. Not only were they frowned upon, they were illegal, constituting both fraud and price-fixing.

"He had his friends, then?"

"That's right, and it was a circle that is very difficult to break in to." Newman frowned. "An interesting connection, if that's what you're looking for."

"What's that?"

"He often sold works to the archdiocese of New York and vice versa."

"Any idea why someone would want to kill him?"

"He was not a very nice fellow, I'm afraid, unlike his predecessor. James Cornwall was a good and fair man. He showed no favorites."

"He must have thought well of Crawley, though."

"Perhaps at first. They had a falling-out toward the end. I hear rumors to that effect. He certainly wouldn't have been Cornwall's anointed heir."

"But he became acting director."

"James Cornwall's health had been failing for

some time. The man he'd chosen to take over
when he retired had resigned under something of
a cloud." The old man shrugged his shoulders.
"Although it should not be so, these things are
sometimes political. Crawley had his friends on
the board of directors. He stacked the deck in his
favor, so to speak."

"Who was the man who resigned and under
what sort of cloud?"

"His name was Taschen, Eric Taschen, and the
cloud had quite a purple tinge to it."

"Sex?"

"I'm afraid so, Michael." The old man in the
black suit let out a heartfelt sigh. "As ever it was
and ever shall be."

29

The priest, this time using his Larry MacLean persona, sat at an empty table in the enormous, high-ceilinged Main Reading Room of the New York Public Library. High over his head, the frescoed clouds were lost in the gloom above the dusty chandeliers. The only real light came from the old-fashioned shaded lamp on the table in front of him.

For the past few hours the library's dumbwaiters had delivered him every possible piece of information concerning the Grange Foundation from the miles of stacks below him. He'd been making notes on a pad of yellow paper but it didn't amount to much. In fact, most of the information was contradictory.

According to the public record the Grange Foundation was established in 1946 from the bequests of Frederick Henry Grange (1860–1945), and his wife, Abbie Norman Grange, nee Coleman

(1859–1939). His wife had been an heiress and Grange himself had been a self-made man, a shanty-Irish son of a Boston Back Bay cop. He rose to become an investment banker, entrepreneur and brokerage owner with Kennedys and Fitzgeralds as both partners and clients.

One of his most lucrative investments had been in the Chicago stockyards. By the early 1900s he was a millionaire and began investing in railroads. By the time of his death he had profited from two world wars and had assets of 172 million dollars, while his wife had left behind a second, earlier trust worth almost twice that much.

As a fully private trust the Grange Foundation was not required to file anything but the most basic disclosure documents. Since all of its activities were not for profit and dispensed from tax-paid funds they were not required to report to any government agency. The foundation was located on St. Luke's Place in Greenwich Village, looking into the park that had once been the churchyard where Edgar Allan Poe had meandered, composing his strange, unsettling poetry.

According to the foundation's brochure it was dedicated to supporting museums, all types of performance groups, visual arts organizations, art service organizations, community arts programs and organizations providing high-quality arts experiences for young people.

It also had a separate section, the McSkimming Foundation, that provided art law services, particularly focusing on Holocaust victims, forgery and stolen art. McSkimming had been a close friend of Frederick Grange, an avid collector of art and the senior partner in the law firm that managed Grange's interests and those of his wife. They were close in another way: McSkimming's son, James, had married Grange's daughter, Anna— James dying during the war, and his wife predeceasing him, dying in childbirth in 1940. The child was born with severe mental retardation and was institutionalized.

All very well, at least superficially. A closer look revealed that most of it was either misdirection or an outright lie. According to his Google search after logging on to one of the library's computers, he had discovered a great deal about both Frederick Grange and his foundation. Grange had indeed been shanty Irish and the son of a cop, but he had never been an entrepreneur, brokerage owner, investment banker or railroad tycoon. He had, in fact, been a clerk in the firm of Topping, Halliwell & Whiting, where McSkimming had been a junior partner.

Topping, Halliwell & Whiting basically dissolved at the close of the war with the blasting away of half its partners and even more of its younger associates, although the firm still existed in corporate fact. It was purchased in 1945 by several unnamed partners and hired its own lawyers—and it was this group of lawyers who created the Grange Foundation and the McSkimming Art Trust, purportedly given family trust tax status by the use of the institutionalized heir, Robert McSkimming.

In 1956, following the death of the boy at the age of sixteen, the foundation was quietly reincorporated as a tax-deductible charity while retaining its name. It was no longer a family trust or a foundation; it was the shell of one, run from behind the scenes by several directors, who, under the charter of the organization were not required to identify themselves. Nowhere did there seem to be any record of the names of those directors, since the directors of the public board were all the newly recruited lawyers now operating under the defunct Topping, Halliwell & Whiting banner. By 1956 all traces of the original participants in what had to be a completely fraudulent operation had vanished. But the foundation remained, on its way into the early part of the next century, still in existence after sixty years. It didn't make any sort of sense; an elaborate, complex and very expensive hoax, but to what purpose and what eventual end?

Since the regular audit statements filed of their grants to other institutions with the IRS had never been a cause for suspicion, that meant that the three or four hundred million dollars' worth of assets held by the Grange Foundation were real enough even though they obviously had not come from bequests made by Frederick Grange or his wife.

The Grange Foundation was a front to disperse funds that had no real source. It was money laundering on an enormous scale, and it had now been going on for more than half a century. It was quite extraordinary, and remarkably simple. But where was the money coming from that needed laundering, and how was a small boy spirited away from a convent in the north of Italy involved? The Grange Foundation was a small part of his quest here in America. According to his contact in the Vatican, the boy from the past and his present whereabouts were crucial. He scrawled his name on the pad:

Frederico Botte

He knew that once, the boy had been given another name—a dangerous name—and it was his job to make sure it would never be revealed. He wrote the second name below the first:

Eugenio

He glanced at his watch. It was well into the afternoon but there was probably time to get back to the hotel and change into his Father Gentile garb before going off to his meeting with the good friars at St. Joseph's Church in Greenwich Village.

While checking out the Grange Foundation on the Internet he'd run a quick check on the staff at the Community of Sant'Egidio and discovered that there was no one working there who went back as far as Frederico Botte's arrival in their care, but he knew he could probably find out something of use.

He switched off his lamp and left the football field–sized room, the clouds in the frescoes far above him frozen in a perpetually blue and sun-drenched sky. Unfortunately real life wasn't quite that simple. He went across the main lobby, his footsteps echoing on the shiny marble floor, then pushed out through the main doors and discovered that in real life it was raining hard. Ducking his head he ran down the steps, paused to buy an umbrella from one of the enterprising vendors who always seemed to forecast the weather better than the weathermen, then headed for his hotel.

30

Carl Kressman eased weary old bones out of bed at his normal early hour, then went up into the tower of his Florida-style beach house to take a look at the day. As usual, the weather was nearly perfect: cloudless sky, limitless azure Gulf, gentle breeze and a temperature that was somewhere in the eighties already.

Kressman went down to his bedroom again, slipped into his bathing suit and gave himself a quick once-over in the full-length mirror on the bathroom door. At seventy-five he still had most of what he'd had at twenty, except now some of it was chemically or mechanically enhanced. Viagra and a couple of other potions kept his pecker up when it was necessary—which wasn't all that often, if truth be told—and a pacemaker that looked like a pack of cigarettes stuck under the skin of his chest kept his ticker tocking. For some reason, unlike most of his friends, he still had all his hair—white, now, of course—and trifocal contact lenses kept his vision twenty-twenty. He was tanned, fit and in good spirits, completely in command of his senses and rich as Croesus. What else could a man want?

The tanned old man took the circular staircase down to the main floor, went to the all-white kitchen and poured himself a cup of coffee from the automatic machine. Standing by the sink and looking out at the big swimming pool at the back of his lot he shook his head, savoring the rich flavor of the brew. Life was certainly a strange thing; there was a time when he had counted his life in minutes. The thought of living out the last of his long life in a place like this, with beach houses, swimming pools and machines that made coffee for you before you woke was almost too much to comprehend. He had come through wars, hurricanes and untold other disasters and had more than just survived—he had prospered. He laughed out loud at that. At twenty years old he had barely heard of shrimp let alone tasted one, and in the end the wonderful little morsels had made him rich.

Kressman finished his coffee, rinsed out his mug at the sink, then put it in the rack to dry. He crossed the tile-floored living room, went out through the screen door onto the covered porch and then down the steps to the pool. More than one person had made fun of him for having a pool when his house was only fifty feet from the

Gulf of Mexico but he enjoyed the convenience. The pool was filled with saltwater pumped in from the Gulf, filtered and heated to eighty degrees, night or day. There was no surf to get in the way of his exercise and no currents or riptides to deal with.

He walked down the concrete apron around the pool, slipped out of his slippers at the foot of the diving board and picked up his goggles out of the little plastic basket he kept there. He went out to the end of the board, bounced twice, lightly, then arced into the air, slicing into the breeze-rippled water with the near professional ease of long practice.

Kressman began his regular laps, his mind clearing as he went through his routine of alternating crawl and breast stroke. As he swam he let his mind go free, memory skittering over his life, his happy years with his wife—dead now after a short, painful battle with cancer—his two children, boy and girl, one a doctor now, the other a professor in New York. He thought of his businesses, taking half a dozen old shrimpers from Fernandina Beach, refurbishing them and putting them to work, half a dozen becoming a hundred, a hundred becoming a freezing and packaging depot, the depot station becoming one of the biggest seafood companies in the south. Investing in Alabama coast real estate and getting even richer.

All so he could wind up swimming in his pool in the early morning, all by himself with his memories. He reached the end of his routine, did one more lap just for the hell of it, then floated on his back for a minute or two, staring up into the young morning sky, thinking about having a big breakfast down the road at the new and improved Nolan's, recovered from the hurricane now, and back in business better than ever. Steak, eggs and pan fries and to hell with his cholesterol for once. *"Liegt der Bauer unterm Tisch, war das Essen nimmer frisch!"* as his papa used to tell him.

He flipped over onto his front, treaded water for a moment and then paddled forward until his feet touched the slightly grainy gunite of the shallow end. He stepped forward, pushing through the water with a side-to-side sweeping motion of his arms, barely feeling the first spike of glass as it sliced through his foot. By the third step he was aware that something was wrong; like a lot of men his age, Kressman had type 2 diabetes and had lost a great deal of sensation in his feet, but by now the pain had gone farther up his legs. He looked down and saw that the water around him was turning pink.

Another step and one of the deadly, invisible weapons sliced through his right Achilles tendon. He staggered, then fell, his arms outstretched. One of his hands was punctured and another piece slashed into his left calf. Kressman, already going into shock, knew that he was in terrible trouble. As well as diabetes, Kressman also suffered from a number of minor heart ailments, all of them requiring the administration of blood thinners. One of them was Coumadin—also known as Warfarin, a powerful rat poison. Multiple cuts like he'd just received and in warm water could easily result in his exsanguinating—bleeding out in a matter of minutes.

He crawled forward, trying to reach the safety of the steps leading out of the pool. His other hand was cut, his index finger almost amputated. He gave a gurgling scream and fell to one side, and he was pierced twice more, once just below his ribs on the right, cutting through his thin flesh into his liver, the second piece of glass goring him in the thigh, opening up the femoral artery close to his groin.

He screamed again, his mouth half underwater and he began to choke. He tried to roll over and failed, his torn hands flailing, trying to find purchase on the bottom of the pool only to meet with more agony. As the ripped artery in his leg poured out his lifeblood the water around him turned from pink to red. His eyes rolled back in his head and he slowly rolled over, his face fully underwater. A moment later he died, the battery in the pacemaker still jolting his heart with electricity every few seconds and getting no response, the organ still jerking spasmodically in the dead man's chest.

31

Detective Sergeant Bobby Izzard—known inevitably as Izzy since his days playing box ball on the busy sidewalks outside his apartment building deep in the bowels of Queens—studied the long breakfast buffet on the lower level of Zeke's Down Under, then filled up his plate with scrambled eggs, bacon, home fries, a few fried oysters, a scoop and a half of marinated Royal Reds and some dirty rice to balance things out.

Like just about everyone else on the Gulf Shores Police Force his belly hung over his belt and it was probably killing him along with the beer, the cigarettes and watching football on Sundays instead of playing it, but frankly, he couldn't give a good goddamn. He'd escaped his nagging wife, New York winters, a homicide caseload that never seemed to get any smaller and a twisting pain in his gut that was threatening to turn into an ulcer, or maybe something worse. In Gulf Shores, Alabama, of all places, he'd found paradise, and one of its fundamental joys was eating breakfast at Zeke's Down Under.

Paradise for sure. In the first place, lots of people died in Gulf Shores, which was why there was one full-time funeral home in the town of five thousand and two more in the town of Foley, just up the road. Died, yes—murdered, no. Almost all of the deaths were from old age, almost all the dead bodies had been under a doctor's care, and none of them had any interest for Izzy.

As part of a three-man detective squad, Bobby Izzard spent most of his time looking into purse snatchings, the occasional bunco beef where some jerk tried to slick an old lady's life savings, and missing persons, most of which turned out to be people with Alzheimer's who'd wandered off. Once in a while during the snowbird season— when the town's population trebled and quadrupled as northerners poured into their high-rise beach condos—Izzy would hook himself up with the marine squad and go out in the big cruiser to look for floaters and annoy boaters who looked like they might be trying to smuggle in a bale or two, but in the three years he'd been on the job serving and protecting the people of Gulf Shores, Alabama, he'd never drawn his gun, only twice used his cuffs and had never had anyone lift a hand in his direction, let alone fire a shot.

And that was just the way he liked it. This wasn't *NYPD Blue* or *Law & Order* or *CSI* or even

Kojak. This was Gulf Shores, Alabama, home of petting zoos, miniature golf courses and shark fishing charters. Gulf Shores, where the living was high-fat and who cared? Where dying was just a simple question of your heart stopping after a nice round of mini golf with your friends at Pirate's Cove. If anyone got murdered it was in Mobile or Pensacola and that was none of his damn business.

He picked up a pot of coffee on his way back to his table, sat down with his favorite view of the marina and the wharf and started to methodically work his way around the oversized plate. It was too early for most people. With the exception of a few hungover-looking charter boat captains and a tottering group of old tourists in yellow T-shirts and Tilly hats to guard against the sun he had the place to himself. For a minute.

He'd just speared his first Royal Red and was swirling it around in the sugary marinade when he saw Kenny Frizell out of the corner of his eye. Kenny was a go-getter, a local, and, God help him, Kenny was his partner, the second man in the so-called investigative team that made up the Gulf Shores Detective Bureau. The third man was the K-9 end, a good old boy named Earl Ray Pasher whose only love was El Kabong, his enormous, drooling, grinning American bloodhound.

Kabong was at his happiest when sniffing around the bloated corpse of a drowning victim, a suitcase full of cocaine, a growhouse basement full of hydroponic weed, or picking out the trailer down the bayou back roads that was actually a crystal meth lab. Kabong was so good at his job that he and Pasher were constantly being borrowed by other forces in Alabama as well as out of state, and neither one of them was around much. Anything that smelled of anything in Gulf Shores had long since been given the once-over by the Kabonger.

Kenny looked like a cartoon character in a suit. He had carrot red hair in a marine corps buzz, a build like Popeye on steroids and a face like Howdy Doody, except he wasn't old enough to remember the famous puppet. The only reason he was a corporal and a detective was because he'd completed a two-year associate's degree in criminal justice at Faulkner State Community College, Gulf Shores campus. Kenny didn't pause in front of the buffet—wasn't even tempted. He didn't even hook himself a coffee. Kenny just came on in those big black shoes, the freckles on his round cheeks all aglow. Unlike Izzy, who after three years was tanned a nice tea-stained color, Kenny just burned. He always looked like he'd been gone over with a blowtorch or stepped out of a pizza oven. Watching him cross the floor, Izzy began to lose his appetite. Kenny looked serious. Worse than that, he looked worried.

The young detective sat down across from his partner.

"We got a problem, Iz."

"No, you've got a problem. You haven't told me what it is yet, so I'm still enjoying my breakfast." He picked up a piece of bacon, wrapped it around one of the marinated Royal Reds and popped the morsel into his mouth, chewing and doing his imitation of Homer Simpson, which almost always got a laugh out of Kenny. Not this time.

"We've got a body in a swimming pool."

Izzy sighed. Kenny liked to get full value for all that education, which meant it took him forever to get to the point.

"Presumably a dead body."

"Yeah."

"Old person?"

"Yeah."

"So old people drown in pools all the time."

"Except he didn't drown. I don't think anyway. It looks as though he bled to death in the pool. He's floating faceup and the water's red." Faceup was a little strange. Natural flotation usually made bodies flip onto their fronts.

"He in the deep end of the pool or the shallow?"

"Shallow."

That explained it. He was probably grounded on the bottom of the pool.

"Somebody call Maggie?"

"On her way."

Gulf Shores was lucky enough to have a county coroner who was not only a doctor but also a pathologist, working out of the morgue at the Baldwin County Medical Center up the road in Foley, a ten-minute drive away down Route 59. Maggie was in her early fifties, like Izzy, but she had an ass like an eighteen-year-old and she knew it, which was fine with Izzy.

"Hemorrhoids, maybe?" Izzy ventured.

Kenny's mouth twisted up into a cross between a scowl and a simple look of distaste. Somebody with an associate's degree didn't joke about possible murder victims. Izzy, on the other hand, even made jokes about the extraordinary number of pedestrians killed crossing Gulf Shores Boulevard— most of them half blind or carrying walkers or canes—referring to it as the annual roadkill count. Men were squirrels, women were beavers. For Izzy violent death was a job; for Kenny it was a calling.

"I think it was murder," said Kenny, his voice heavy with doom.

"Why?" said Izzy. "People bleed for all sorts of reasons. Maybe he had lung cancer or an embolism or something."

"I don't think he could see too well, or his goggles got clouded up."

"What does that have to do with anything?"

"There's broken bottles all over the bottom of the pool."

"Bottles?"

"Yeah, like you'd take a bottle and smash it and then put the bottom of the bottle on the bottom of the pool. I've got twenty-twenty vision and I could barely see them. There's hundreds of them. It looked like he was swimming and started walking up the deep end and got cut, badly. Not to mention this big long sliver of glass that's sticking out of his mouth. That was no accident."

Izzy took a sip of coffee and fished out his Zippo and his Marlboros. "A sliver of glass?"

Kenny nodded, somber. "About a foot long, like a dagger. Looks to've cut his tongue just about in half."

Izzy snapped open the Zippo, fired up his Marlboro and took a deep drag. He stared down at his breakfast plate. He felt a bubble of gas moving painfully through his system. He should have had something simple, maybe just the oysters. He sighed again and let out a cloud of smoke.

"Well, you're right there, Kenny boy. A foot-long piece of glass sticking out of an old man's mouth sure doesn't sound like an accident, even in Gulf Shores." He pushed himself away from the table and heaved himself upright. The gas bubble gurgled. "We better go take a look."

32

Finn Ryan pushed away from the computer in the Ex Libris office, pinched the bridge of her nose between her thumb and forefinger and squeezed her eyes shut. At her right hand there was a ragged pile of scribbled sheets from a yellow pad representing her efforts over the past few hours. She sat forward, yawned and tapped the pages together, trying to concentrate. Half her thoughts kept wandering back to the warm liquid feeling in the pit of her stomach and the faint iron memory of Michael as he'd slowly pushed into her, neither of them able to wait for the bed, her legs wrapped around his waist as she sprawled back over the table in the kitchen. Wonderful enough and enormously satisfying, but always with the feeling of distance and loneliness, of someone who could never quite give all of himself. A dark, cold anger that was as much the source of his sexuality as simple passion. Perhaps it was only the age

between them but she knew that whatever they
had together was not going to last for very long,
one way or the other.

"Fiona Katherine Ryan, you think too goddamn
much." She stared down at the yellow sheets in
her hand, focusing. Who else would start up an
intimate relationship with a man at least twenty
years older than her in the midst of investigating
a murder or two and trying not to get killed in
the process herself? And all because of a sheet
of parchment inked by the hand of a genius five
hundred years ago. It didn't seem quite real, but
then she remembered the copper tang of blood in
the air that signaled Peter's killing and the black
insect helmet of the homicidal bicycle freak as he
spun through the air to his death. Very real.

She'd started her research by looking for a
Greyfriars Web site. For some reason she'd been
a little surprised to find that it was slick, graphic-
based and very sophisticated. She'd been expecting something a little plainer, an austere page
in Times New Roman with a crest in the corner.
The crest was there, the faintly sinister image of
a shield split by a bar running left to right with
three thistles on the right and a black swan with
two Maltese crosses on the left. The word Greyfriars and the Latin motto *Mens Agitat Molem* sat
over the shield. A scroll ran below with a second
obscure verse in Latin: *Aut Inveniam Viam Aut Fa-
ciam.* The first motto meant: Mind Over Matter

and the second, roughly translated, meant: I Shall Find a Way or Make One.

According to the Web site's canned version of the school's history the Mind Over Matter motto fit the school's original purpose. Founded in 1895 by a Calvinist minister named George Haverford, the first principle of the school was to remove boys from the temptations of the opposite sex in an utterly isolated environment where they could turn their attentions to the Teddy Roosevelt concept of manliness in all things—particularly sports, military training and rigorous academics. Add cold showers and a hefty dose of hard-edged religious teaching and you had a school that every parent of the time could love. Reading between the lines it was the epitome of "Children should be seen and not heard"—and seen as rarely as possible. In every way that Finn could see it was the worst of everything she'd ever heard about English boarding schools.

Searching the Web and using Valentine's private and very complicated search engine, something called ISPY-XRAY, Finn found a variety of Web sites, some established by ex-Greyfriars students and others by run-of-the-mill information junkies that told a different story. Looked at a little closer it appeared that Greyfriars had a less illustrious background than the official Web site suggested. According to what she'd discovered, the "manliness" of the school had led to half of the alumni from the mid nineteen hundreds being slaughtered in the trenches of Belgium and France. An inordinate number had committed suicide. The hazing of lower form kids by their ''betters'' in the senior grades had led to at least one death and a series of lawsuits just before the Crash of 1929 that had nearly bankrupted the school. What the lawsuits didn't take, the Depression did, and the school foundered, buried under debt and bad publicity. In 1934 a group of alumni purchased the school, which by then was in receivership. At this point, Finn stumbled on her first real clue: a list of Greyfriars's new trustees. There were twelve names in all but it was the first six that caught her attention:

Alfred Andrew Wharton
Lauder J. Cornwall
Admiral Tobias Gatty
Jonas Hale Parker III
Orville Dupont Hale
Jerome C. Crawley

There was no room for coincidence; there couldn't be. A. A. Wharton was presumably the present headmaster's grandfather; Lauder Cornwall had to be related to James Cornwall, the late director of the Parker-Hale; Jonas Parker and Orville Hale were descendants of the museum's founder; Tobias Gatty was obviously connected to the colonel; and Jerome C. Crawley related to Alexander

Crawley. No coincidence, but no real connection either. What did six school trustees from the thirties have to do with a pair of present-day homicides and an errant page torn from a notebook half a millennia ago? Mysteries were mysteries but this was verging on the impossible.

Finn glanced up from her notes and looked around the room and its Sherlockian décor. She vaguely remembered something from a Sherlock Holmes story she'd read in first year English lit: "When you have eliminated the impossible, whatever remains, *however improbable*, must be the truth." So if the venerable detective was anything to go by, there was a connection; she just wasn't seeing it. The next two hours spent in front of the computer didn't make anything any clearer though; if anything, her research into the names and their associations only made things more confused.

Using the ISPY search engine, Google, and everything else she could think of, Finn ran not only the first six names but the rest as well, tracing them forward from 1934. Unlike schools such as Phillips Andover in Massachusetts—with alumni including everything from the creator of Tarzan to gay rights activists and assorted recent presidents of the United States—Greyfriars seemed to specialize in people just under the public radar. Of the twelve trustees who took over the school in the 1930s none was truly "A" material. Parker and Hale were only the inheritors of family fortunes and not their creators, like a Cornelius Vanderbilt or a John D. Rockefeller. Gatty was only a rear admiral and the ship eventually named after him was a Liberty cargo vessel, not a battleship or an aircraft carrier. Jerome Crawley, a lawyer, had worked with Bill Donovan, the man who headed up the OSS, precursor to the Central Intelligence Agency. All twelve trustees were like that: senators but not governors or presidents, secretary of the interior but not secretary of state, deputy directors of the CIA but never the head. In fact, when it came to government, the trustees and the sons who followed them were almost invariably non-political appointments: clerks to Supreme Court judges, but never the judges themselves. In business and every other facet of life it was the same—not quite famous, but never scandalized and never dropped. It was almost as though it had been planned that way, and after a while Finn began seeing a vague pattern: the trustees and their progeny weren't the movers and shakers, they were the bureaucrats and bean counters—the people who held the real power, and held it the longest. A president lasted four years, eight at best; a senator could go on for half a century if he was smart about it, quietly inserting himself or herself onto a dozen or more critical committees. A businessman could collect board memberships like matchbook covers, few people knowing who he was or the clout he wielded. Expediency over ego. Power by proxy. It could easily have been the real motto of the school.

The only other piece of information Finn managed to discover was the fact that all twelve of the trustees had purchased the school under the aegis of something called the Carduss Club. Carduss, she discovered, was the Latin word for "thistle," possibly in reference to the thistle on the school crest. It was also, obscurely, a pagan sect of Satanists. As far as she could tell, the Carduss Club had ceased to exist in 1945. She found no reference to it after that date. Checking the Web site again she found that everything on it was copyrighted to the Greyfriars Alumni Association LLC—which, she discovered, was actually a numbered trusteeship that had been incorporated in Delaware for some reason.

At that point Finn gave up for good. It was all too confusing. She checked her watch, discovered that most of the day had vanished and gathered up her papers. Maybe it would make more sense to Michael. She smiled at the thought. She thought of him as Michael now. A lover, an assault victim and a fugitive, all in seventy-two hours. She stood, stretched then threaded her way through the gloomy top-floor stacks of Ex Libris and went upstairs to the loft.

She rode up in the elevator, a thousand facts and feelings whirling around in her head. She reached the upper level of the building, waited until the elevator had thumped to a stop then pushed up the gate and opened the rumbling doorway. She stepped out into the brightly lit foyer that opened into the living room, the elevator door shutting automatically behind her. She paused, her heart beginning to thump wildly in her chest, her mind emptying of everything but a single, simple thought: when she'd gone down to the office hours before, the foyer light hadn't been turned on. Somewhere in the back of the loft she heard the sound of breaking glass.

33

Bobby Izzard smoked a cigarette and poked around in Carl Kressman's past, meandering through each room in the expensively decorated beach house, opening drawers and looking in cupboards. Maggie and her beefy assistants had zipped Kressman up and taken him away in the big Vandura coroner's van hours ago. Kenny Frizell was still outside by the pool, fishing for broken bottles with the skimmer net and methodically putting each deadly piece of glass into paper evidence bags, each one with its own little ID tag filled out scrupulously by the young detective. Izzy was alone in the empty house, the last of the light slanting in through the porch screens and the windows, filling the rooms with bars of dusty golden light. They'd done an initial ID by running the guy's plates. Year-rounder, no snowbird, no record, no violations, no nothing.

Kressman's house was a classic Gulf Coast "cottage'' of the old style, even though it was clearly very new. Covered and screened porches wrapped around the bottom floor, the second floor contained a master bedroom and a guest room and a spiral staircase led from the master bedroom to an eight-by-ten captain's walk on the peaked roof, fitted like the bell tower of a one-room schoolhouse.

The main floor had a living room and dining room that looked out onto the beach and the Gulf beyond. A kitchen led off from the dining room and behind that was a small bedroom facing the pool. Across the hall from the small bedroom was a large den. The bedroom, the den and the hall all had doors leading out to the pool area.

Even someone who had no idea of the victim's identity would have picked up on a couple of things as soon as they entered the front door, or maybe even before. The car outside in the garage was a top-of-the-line S-class Mercedes and the furniture inside the house was mostly Edwardian, antique and expensive. Kressman had money. As well as the furniture, all of the art on the walls looked like the real McCoy, canvases thick with paint and framed with lots of gold. Izzy didn't know art from a horse's ass but most of it had the same rich feel as the butter-soft leather on the inside of the Benz.

Kressman had been no fool about it either. There was a class-A burglar alarm system and it was connected to the cop shop up on Clubhouse

Road, not some empty office in a strip mall and a tape that told everybody the cops had been called in a loud, bullshit voice. At the price the old man had paid for the setup in the cottage there'd have been a cruiser at his front door thirty seconds after anyone so much as breathed too hard on his precious paintings. Not only that, as it turned out the art was all lag-bolted into the wall.

Izzy looked through the kitchen, checking the refrigerator first. In the first place it was huge, and in the second place it was almost empty. Automatic ice maker and a frigid bottle of white label Flagman vodka. Pricey stuff.

Down below a few takeout cartons from local joints, the carefully wrapped remains of a salad and a good supply of beer, most of it in the form of stubby brown bottles of Schultheiss Berliner Weisse which probably cost more to mail order than a single glass would cost in Germany. If it was one thing Izzy knew it was his beer.

He didn't hesitate for a moment. He reached in, picked up one of the frosty bottles and snapped it open. He took a sip. Like old gold. The picture on the label showed women with parasols walking down a tree-lined boulevard. Even the guy's beer was old-fashioned. Izzy gave a contented little sigh, belched lightly and continued on his tour, careful to keep the bottle top in his jacket pocket.

He moved into the study. It was good-sized, maybe fifteen feet on a side, and there wasn't any sign of a woman's touch. The curtains were dark, the walls were paneled in bookshelves filled with books by the yard and he had one of those Queen Anne–style globes that slid open to reveal a well-stocked bar.

Maker's Mark, Hennessy Five Star, Jack Daniel's, Johnny Walker Blue Label and a couple of single malts with unpronounceable names. Izzy grinned and wondered what Maggie would find when she sliced up the old man's liver. He thought about the coroner's exquisite, firm little fanny for a moment, took another sip of beer and continued his investigation.

Collection of beer steins, collection of model cars, a ship in a bottle, an old-fashioned rolltop desk. It was locked. Earlier on, Kenny had found a set of keys on a bureau which Izzy now had in his pocket. The detective sergeant took out the ring and tried the keys one by one.

He hit it right third time around and he pushed the rolltop back. Everything neat as a pin, envelopes and this and that sorted into the various pigeonholes. Right up front was an Acer Ferrari laptop in flame red, fitted with a wireless net access modem, very futuristic. Izzy tapped the computer on and spent five minutes noodling around in the old man's files. Half of them were password protected.

He got up, went out onto the porch and called Kenny in to work his magic fingers on the machine, then went upstairs to the bedrooms. Nothing in the guest bedroom, nothing of real interest in the bathroom except an array of high blood pressure medications and dandruff shampoo. No Preparation H, so Kressman had been hemmie free. He went into the master bedroom and looked around. More big furniture including an ornate four-poster bed that reminded Izzy of that scene in the old black-and-white Scrooge movie where he wakes up and realizes it's Christmas morning.

An old-fashioned hanging lamp hung from the ceiling and there was a palm tree in one corner, so tall its fronds were bent at the ceiling. Little rugs scattered everywhere, no wall to wall carpeting for a change. Izzy's old man had worked house construction for forty years and Izzy'd spent his summers building crap all over New York and Jersey. He knew exactly the kind of shit you could hide under spackle ceilings and cheap broadloom. Not here: this was all top-grade stuff.

The walls were hung with more art. Like the paintings he'd seen downstairs, these looked like the real thing, and even a slob like him could almost recognize some of it. Even a slob like him could recognize the little dwarf guy's stuff, the one they'd made the movie about. Always wore a top hat and liked hookers—what was his name? Toulouse-Lautrec—yeah, that was it.

The painting in question hung over the head of the bed, big, showing a man and a woman, both of them ugly, standing in some kind of beer hall at the edge of a dance floor. There was another one by the same guy, the same ugly hooker standing with a busy bar behind her. She looked bored. So was Izzy. Paintings weren't high on his list for holiday giving.

He went over and gave the one of the old broad standing by herself a tug. Lag bolted like all the others. Ugly or not, this wasn't the kind of thing you picked up at the starving-artists sale down at the Holiday Inn. The burglar alarm and the lag bolts said big insurance policies. Too bad one of them hadn't been stolen, at least then he'd have a motive to work with, but to steal one you'd have to cut it out of the frame with a utility knife and that hadn't happened. He went over to a big chest of drawers. There was a big silver plate with personal goods in it.

Rolex Daytona, money clip with half a dozen twenties and hundreds, loose change, pinky ring with a big green stone in it, a wallet and a cell phone. Izzy didn't know art, but he knew watches. The last time he'd looked at a Daytona they'd been ten or eleven grand. He stared at it, shook his head and sighed. Lovely but he'd never be able to explain it in a million years. Whatever, it hadn't been a robbery. Someone had whacked the guy for something other than money.

Izzy flipped open the wallet. Alabama driver's license in the name of Carl Kressman, showing a birth date that made the corpse seventy-five years old. The issue date was five years ago with this address, which meant he'd been here for at least that long. He flipped open the other flap and went through five major credit cards, social security card and a laminated Gulf Shores Library card. There was a single lambskin condom tucked into one of the interior pockets and something behind it. He pulled. A New York State driver's license in the name of Karel Kress. What was the guy doing with two names and two driver's licenses? Weird, but at least it was getting a little more interesting than just another dead old man. He went downstairs and checked in on Kenny, who was bent over the Acer laptop in the study, pecking away.

"Find anything?"

"The guy was rich."

"Figured that out for myself."

"He collected art."

"That too," Izzy answered, glancing around the room. Paintings everywhere . . .

"He got them all from someplace in New York, the Hoffman Gallery."

"Yeah?"

"Yeah, and he paid lots of money for them, look." The younger man leaned back and Izzy leaned forward. There was a row of names and figures on the screen.

Boucher, Francois/fstra	*2,870,000*
Cézanne, Paul/fvort	*9,430,000*
Fragonard, Jean-Honoré/wsmhb	*1,670,000*

Gogh, Vincent van/fvwyb	11,625,000
Manet, Édouard/liaoc	2,800,000
Toulouse-Lautrec/lgwhp	10,000,000
Toulouse-Lautrec/tbdm	4,000,000

The list continued on for half a dozen pages.
There were at least two hundred paintings, far
more than were in the cottage. Most carried a
price tag well over a million. Kenny demonstrated
the depth of the program by randomly picking a
name on the list by clicking the cursor on the odd,
underlined letter code:

Renoir, Pierre-Auguste/awlohe 750,000

Almost instantly the computer jumped to a digi-
tized photograph of a painting showing a woman
leaning on her hand with some sort of multicol-
ored background, perhaps flowers.

The title underneath read:

Algerian Woman Leaning on Her Elbow
1881
Height: 41.3 cm (16.26 in.), Width: 32.2 cm (12.68 in.)
Hoffman Gallery New York 1995
Deaccessioned: Park-Hale Museum of Art 1993
Grange Foundation bequest 1957

"I don't get any of this shit."

"It's a list of paintings."

"You really must think I'm some kind of an

asshole. I got that, Kenny, even though I didn't go to college."

"The list is keyed into these records through the letter code."

"The letter code being the name of the painting, yeah, I got that too, Ken."

"The other stuff is what we call 'provenance.' "

"We?"

"It's the name for where the picture came from, its background and sales history."

"And?"

"And so far they all ran through the same provenance. The same history. The Grange Foundation gives it to the Parker-Hale, who gets rid of it by selling it to the Hoffman Gallery, who then flogs it to private citizens like Kressman."

"Who winds up being sliced to ribbons in his swimming pool."

"You think the two things have anything to do with each other?"

"Lot of money."

"But nothing's been stolen."

"Any way you can add up all the figures on those sheets?"

"I think so." Kenny played with the computer for a few minutes. The figure appeared:

$273,570,000

"To one guy?" said Kenny. "Christ on a crutch!"

"I think we're out of our depth here, Kenny," said Izzy. "In deep water, you might say." And then he laughed. Kenny didn't think it was funny at all.

34

Eric Taschen's apartment on Fifth Avenue was on the top floor of a mid-1940s building, facing Central Park with a spectacular view out over the Sheep Meadow and the Ramble. From what Valentine could tell the apartment itself was modest enough, five or six rooms, one bedroom with a study, but the location, the view and the art on the walls were definitely high end. A Warhol John Wayne silkscreen in the foyer, a Roy Lichtenstein taking up almost an entire wall in the living room and a crockery-plastered Julian Schnabel facing it. There were no obvious clues to his domestic situation, no telltale feminine touch, nothing that spoke overtly about a male presence either. At a guess, Taschen lived alone.

Taschen himself was slim, well-dressed in a white-on-white open-collared silk shirt and tailored jeans, his feet pushed into a pair of expensive loafers, no socks. The watch on his wrist was plain stainless steel; he wore no other jewelry. The man appeared to be in his fifties, dark-haired with a smear of gray at each temple. He was clean shaven, his face unlined. When he met Valentine at the door he was wearing red-framed reading glasses and holding a section of the *New York Times.* He led Valentine into the living room, sat him down on a butter-leather, not quite new sofa and dropped into a matching armchair with a glass-topped coffee table between them.

"You collect sixties and seventies," said Valentine, looking over Taschen's shoulder at the huge Lichtenstein. The canvas showed a sofa and a chair not unlike the one the man was sitting in. Some kind of small joke; an art collector's pun. Taschen shrugged, then cleared his throat.

> *"She left the web, she left the loom,*
> *She made three paces thro' the room,*
> *She saw the water-lily bloom,*
> *She saw the helmet and the plume,*
> *She look'd down to Camelot.*
> *Out flew the web and floated wide;*
> *The mirror crack'd from side to side;*
> *'The curse is come upon me,' cried*
> *The Lady of Shalott."*

He grinned. "You live with William Holman Hunt, Burne-Jones and all the rest for the better part of ten years, you want to put anything else but on the walls."

You still work as a curator?"

"Still?" said Taschen. "Is that some reference to the Parker-Hale?"

"Peter called you?"

"I wouldn't have seen you otherwise. I've dealt with the Newman Gallery for a long time. He told me you were interested in stolen art—war plunder."

"Not exactly."

"Then what?"

"George Gatty."

"It amounts to the same thing. Gatty bought and sold stolen art; everyone knew that."

"What's the relationship to the Parker-Hale, or is there one?"

"Sandy bought and sold from Gatty."

"Sandy—meaning Alexander Crawley?"

"Yes."

"You were colleagues."

"Contemporaries, yes."

"As I understand it you were in line for Cornwall's post, but Crawley finessed you."

"Finesse isn't a word I'd use. Slander is more like it."

"You resigned."

"It was the classic case of resign before you're fired."

"On what grounds?"

"None. Fabricated. According to Sandy my relationship with James Cornwall was . . . unsavory."

"So he was slandering Cornwall as well?"

"Something like that. Most people knew James was gay but no one really cared. On the other hand, having a sexual relationship with the director was seen as too delicate, for public relations reasons."

"This was Crawley's reasoning?"

"The reasoning he used with the board of directors."

"Was it true?"

"Does it matter?"

"Not to me, but as the lawyers say, It goes to motive."

"Whose?"

"Whoever killed him." Valentine paused. "I assume the police saw you as a suspect."

"Sure." Taschen smiled. He got up and went to a small, black-lacquered, Art Deco–style wet bar at the far end of the room. "Get you something?"

"No, thanks," answered Valentine. Taschen mixed himself a Scotch on the rocks and came back to his seat. He sipped the drink slowly, not speaking, looking out through the large window that faced the park. The set of his jaw was tense and Valentine could see the strain showing around his eyes. A lot of restrained anger.

"I had an alibi," said the man. He smiled tightly. "I was in Prague on a buying trip."

"Buying trip?"

"I work as a private consultant for collectors, corporations, foundations, that sort of thing. There's a lot of interest now in eastern European avant-garde art from between the wars. Alois Bilek, Karel Teige, Capek's set designs—he's the man who invented the term 'robot'—people like that. Collectible but not prohibitively expensive."

"A long way from Burne-Jones and the Lady of Shalott."

"People change. So do tastes."

"And circumstances."

"Peter Newman told me who you are, Mr. Valentine, or should I call you Doctor? You've got more than one PhD, as I understand it. You know that the art on my walls is outside the means of most people, as is this apartment. I didn't need the job at the Parker-Hale but I wanted it, and I deserved it. Being born wealthy doesn't make you ineligible for academic scholarship." Taschen frowned. "I'm no trust-fund dilettante."

"I wasn't suggesting that you were."

"Then what were you suggesting?"

"Nothing. But I would like to know the reason for Crawley's evident dislike of you."

"It wasn't personal. There was no reason for it to be. Sandy was part of a ring; James Cornwall knew it and wouldn't have suggested Sandy for the job of director for all the tea in China."

"That still doesn't explain why he went after you like that."

"Sandy was making money from deaccessioning particular works from the permanent collection and giving particular dealers first crack at them. Kickbacks. A lot of galleries do it, but they're usually more discreet. I had proof of what Sandy was up to. By discrediting me he discredited anything I had to say against him."

"As I understand the timeline of events, Cornwall appointed Crawley while you were still at the gallery. Why?"

Taschen shrugged simply. "Because Sandy was blackmailing him."

"You sound awfully sure of yourself."

"I am. James told me. He showed me a letter Sandy had sent him stating the situation. He was left without any choice."

"So who do you think killed Crawley?"

"I have no idea. He had some unsavory friends. I know that much."

"Anyone in particular?"

"Deiter Trost at the Hoffman Gallery for one. Mark Taggart at the Grange Foundation for another. You've already mentioned George Gatty—a man James Cornwall loathed, by the way."

"Why?"

"I'm not entirely sure other than the fact that the colonel is a particularly odious human being without a shred of morality. I think there was some connection to the war."

"Gatty worked for G2 in Switzerland. Intelligence."

"So did James Cornwall. Not in Switzerland, but he was in the Monuments, Fine Arts and Archives division of the OSS. The art-looting people."

"A tangled web," said Valentine. "But it still doesn't explain why Cornwall appointed Crawley to succeed him. You said you saw a letter."

"That's right."

"Saying what?"

"Saying that Sandy was aware of James's involvement in some sort of secret club and if he wasn't appointed to the director's position he'd have no choice but to go to the press."

"And you assumed it had something to do with Cornwall's sexual history?"

"It must have. What else could it have been?"

"Cornwall didn't tell you?"

"No. And I didn't ask."

"Did this club have a name?"

"Yes. The Carduss Club."

Valentine frowned. "Latin for thistle."

"I know," said Taschen. "Strange name for a gay sex club. Sounded more like a college frat."

"Did he tell you anything about the group?"

"Not a word," Taschen answered, shaking his head. "Not a single word."

A telephone purred somewhere in the back of the apartment. Taschen took a last swallow from his drink, put the glass down on the coffee table and rose to his feet. He left the room, not in any hurry, and disappeared. The ringing stopped and Valentine was vaguely aware of the sound of the art consultant's muffled voice.

Valentine stood up and went to examine the crusty Schnabel on the wall. It showed a vaguely

Ethiopian figure against a mountain background with a skull off to one side. The bottom half of the painting was full of broken crockery. He'd never much liked Schnabel's work and this piece wasn't changing his opinion very much. The broken plates always reminded him of Zorba the Greek. On the other hand, the artist had made his reputation on the basis of the idiotic potsherds. Obscurity as art.

He turned as Taschen came back into the room. "That was Peter Newman."

"Yes?"

"He knew you were coming here. He thought you should know. He just heard it on the news."

"Heard what?"

Taschen let out a long breath. "George Gatty. He's been murdered. Someone ran him through with a Nazi ceremonial sword."

35

Lieutenant Vincent Delaney of the chief's Special Action Squad stood in the middle of Colonel George Gatty's living room staring at the body, spitted like a side of beef on the brown leather couch. Whoever'd done the ugly old man in had really outdone himself. According to Assistant M.E. Bandar Singh, twenty-three inches of cold steel had been shoved down the old man's throat, the point poking through his perineum, which meant it had come out somewhere between his withered old nuts and his puckered asshole.

Putkin the criminalist said that accounted for the smell; on the way through the razor sharp sword had sliced through half a dozen major organs, the stomach wall and both intestines. They knew it was a Nazi sword because of the big swastika between the talons of the silver eagle that made up the hilt. The worst part of it was that everything was there to see. Gatty had been murdered in his dressing gown and every inch of his old wizened body was splayed out in public. Flashbulbs popped as Putkin and his cronies measured and tested. A fucking Hollywood premiere for the dead.

Billy Boyd came rolling up to him, notebook clutched in his beefy hand. "So I guess this fits with the other one?"

"And the call we got from Deputy Dawg in Alabama." Delaney shook his head. "I never knew Alabama even had a coastline."

"Me neither," said Boyd. "I thought it was, you know, landlocked."

"Not that it has anything to do with the dead guy."

"This one?"

"The one in Alabama."

"But there's got to be a connection, right?" Boyd didn't seem too sure.

"Art creep gets a knife shoved down his throat on Fifth Avenue, the guy in Alabama is some kind of big-time art collector and gets stabbed with an Absolut bottle and the colonel here gets taken out by some kind of Nazi Vlad the Impaler? Yeah, Billy, I'd say there's just the tiniest chance of a connection."

"Who's Vlad the Impaler?"

"A guy on Wide World of Wrestling." Delaney sighed. "Go talk to Singh, Billy. Get me a time of death if you can."

"Sure, Loo."

Delaney didn't really need the confirmation. From the way he was dressed it was obvious he'd been in bed or on his way when he'd been killed, which made the TOD sometime last night. The man's butler, a man named Bertram Throens had an apartment in the basement with his wife, the colonel's cook, and neither one of them had heard anything out of line.

Like with Crawley, the guy from the museum, there were going to be lots of suspects. In the museum guy's case there were about five hundred of them at the reception being held on the main floor and by the looks of things here the colonel's late-night caller had probably come with the supposed intention of selling the old man the sword that was used to kill him.

They'd already found the leather-bound, silk-lined presentation case in the front hall. Delaney knew about as much German as he did Gaelic but the names Rommel and Adolf Hitler had jumped out at him. At a guess, the detective assumed there would have been real money involved, and real interest on the part of the colonel. By the look of the house he was a serious collector, so maybe seeing people late at night in his bathrobe wouldn't have been that much out of the ordinary. Interviewing the Swiss butler had led him to the same conclusion: the colonel often had late-night visitors.

Delaney sighed and tried not to breathe too deeply as the meat wagon boys lifted the body onto a snap-down morgue gurney. The real question nibbling away at the edge of his thoughts was the strange connection between all of this and the beautiful redhead that seemed to be at the center of events. And that led to the even bigger question—Just what had happened to Fiona Ryan, and where exactly was she?

36

They began moving out of the camp with the last of the night. The moon had set long ago and tattered clouds shifted from the north, fading the dim light from the stars. Most of the men except Reid and the sergeant were city boys; the depth of the darkness still spooked them. That velvet night was like something otherworldly, too close to the shadow of death that always hung looming in the back of their thoughts each and every moment of each and every day.

They moved through the woods quietly, keeping to the paths, pausing at the small depressed clearing that marked the fork of the trails. The men split into two groups there. Winetka, Bosnic, Biearsto and Terhune, armed with the bazooka and the two-inch mortar, took the south path leading to the road by the sniper's tower. The rest, with the sergeant bird dogging the artsy officer types, headed for the burnt-out old tank at the top of the rise.

The plan the sergeant had put to Cornwall was a simple one. Their raggedy little group was made from the remains of a 2nd Ranger Battalion from the Normandy invasion. They'd inherited most of a company's worth of ordnance. Terhune and Biearsto would take out the sniper and his tower with the bazooka while Winetka and Bosnic would use the two-inch mortar to lay down covering fire over the main entrance. When the sergeant heard the first bazooka round being laid down he'd open up with the twin 7.92mm machine guns, softening the flank for the squad made up of Patterson, Dorm, Teitelbaum and Pixie Mortimer, led by Reid and followed by the three officers. If necessary, the sergeant could also provide covering fire if they had to retreat, which he doubted would happen. As well as the bazooka and the two-inch mortar, Teitelbaum and Dorm made up gunner and assistant for the Browning Automatic Rifle. The others carried an assortment of relatively heavy weapons including a couple of Thompsons, a Johnson light machine gun, an M3 grease gun and Patterson's beloved Pah-pah-shah 71-round Russian machine gun: more ordnance by far than the Krauts in the farmhouse were likely to have.

The sergeant led his group north through the thinning trees, stopping finally within sight of the ditch. Taking Reid with him again, he scrabbled out to the old Panzer for a final reconnaissance of the farm. It was false dawn, a bare sheen of dull lightness on the eastern horizon. There was no light at all from the farmhouse or any of the outbuildings. Swinging his binoculars around to the abbey tower he looked for the slightest flicker from the sniper's position. The sergeant gauged the distance between the tower and his own position. A good five football fields, but nothing for a talented rifleman with one of those zs4 scopes on a Krag or even a 43. He figured it would take them the better part of two minutes for his bunch to get down to the side wall of the farmhouse with no real cover in between except a few depressions and one big boulder. Jeez, the sniper could take them all out with ease.

"You better take the cocksucker like I told you," muttered the sergeant.

"You say something?" Reid asked.

"No. What about Cornwall and his pals?"

"They know enough to stay back until we open things up."

"Good. I figure two minutes to get down to the wall. See the boulder?"

"Yeah."

"Keep everybody left of that on the way down. I won't traverse the guns on the tank any farther than that."

"Gotcha."

"I'll stop firing when you reach the wall. Hit it with a couple of those potato mashers you took off that Jerry a few days ago. Open up a hole."

"We take the place?"

"Not unless Terhune and the others have softened them up, and not until you're sure the sniper's out of it. He's the key. He manages to get out of the tower and find some other spot we are uck-fayed. Understand?"

"Sure."

"All right. I'm going to load the belts into the gun now. At six on the dot—that's ten minutes—we should hear Terhune and Winetka opening up. When you go in send Teitelbaum and Dorm on point with the BAR, maybe get them in one of those depressions. Then Patterson with that Russian gun of his, then you and the rest. The loos still got their Thompsons?"

"Cornwall's got a great gun."

"Probably blow you all away the first time they fire. Christ. Who came up with the idea of giving officers weapons?"

"Not me."

"Get going."

"Right."

Reid slipped away into the darkness and the sergeant snaked his way up to the open turret of the abandoned German tank and slithered inside. Trying to be as quiet as possible, he began feeding the long belts of ammunition into the twin machine guns. The rounds had different colored tips, so they were probably a mixture of tracer, ball and incendiary, just like their American counterparts, but it would have been nice to know which was which. It took him less than two minutes to load both guns with 250-round belts. He peeked out through the gradually brightening slot in the turret. He glanced at his watch; all hell was going to break loose out there in about five minutes. He grinned. The sergeant could hardly wait.

37

Michael Valentine moved through the rooms of the top floor of the Ex Libris building methodically. Every area of the apartment had been torn apart; no drawer was left unopened, every cupboard had been searched. The intruder had come in through an airshaft vent and exited through a small unalarmed bathroom window. Following behind Valentine, Finn Ryan was horrified by the damage. Valentine ended his survey in the kitchen.

Valentine sat down at the yellow Formica table. "What did you do when you heard the glass breaking?"

"I thought the thing to do would be to investigate."

"And then you thought again." Valentine smiled.

"It wasn't like in the movies. The girl goes out onto the moonless dock to look for her boyfriend and a hand comes out of the water and grabs her ankle. I'm not that stupid."

"The real thing."

"After Peter . . ."

"The glass breaks and . . ." Michael prompted.

"I turned around, got back into the elevator and went back to the office. I phoned the cell number you gave me."

"So he never made it down to the office, never got to the computer."

"No. I was there most of the day."

"It looks like he did a fair amount of damage, but nothing irreplaceable."

"What if he comes back?"

"I don't think that's going to happen. If he was really looking for something he would have come down to the office."

"He was trying to scare us?" asked Finn.

"I think so."

"Why?"

"We're getting too close to something. We've been doing a lot of digging. There could be, probably are, alarm bells ringing."

"Did you find out anything when you went to your dealer friend?"

"Lots," said Valentine, and then he told her about what Peter Newman had said and about his visit to Eric Taschen. In turn she told him about her efforts on the computer.

"So what does it all mean?"

"It means that there's more than one thing

going on. The murders of Crawley and Gatty are connected, and so is the third guy I told you about—the one my connection at One Police Plaza told me about, Kressman I think his name was. So far there's no real evidence but it looks as though they were all involved in some sort of deal to put stolen and looted art onto the open market. I don't think that particular set of killings has anything to do with you at all. The whole thing with the Michelangelo drawing was just bad timing. I think Crawley would have died anyway."

"Peter wasn't bad timing."

"No, which means that one of Crawley's partners in crime was worried about what you'd found. Whoever that was hired Peter's killer and the Vietnam gang member on the courier bike."

"So there're two killers out there?"

"Yes. One wants you and that drawing wiped off the slate. The other is interested in the group that Gatty, Crawley and this Kress were involved in—the ring that both Newman and Eric Taschen mentioned."

"They have to be connected."

"Yes. Presumably the art is the common factor."

"The stolen art market?"

"From what you told me about the history of Greyfriars it has to go deeper than that. This Carduss Club is obviously some kind of secret society, like Skull and Bones at Yale, except a little less obvious."

"According to what I found out they disappeared in 1945 or something."

"So did Skull and Bones, except they didn't disappear at all—they just changed their name. Your Delaware-numbered company—they have the least restrictive incorporation laws in the world; that's why the CIA always uses them for their proprietary companies, like Air America."

"You don't think this is some kind of spy thing, do you?" She looked at him carefully, trying not to think too much about what he really was or what his real relationship had been with her father. Maybe that could come later but there was no time for it now.

Valentine's expression darkened. "No. It's big, though. The man they just found murdered in Alabama was dealing in hundreds of millions of dollars." He shrugged. "It's not hard to get into big money when you're dealing in Michelangelos."

"So what do we do now? Detective Delaney must have figured out I wasn't part of any plot to kill Peter by now. Why don't we go to the police?"

"It's not just your boyfriend. Now it's Crawley, Gatty and Kressman as well. That's four murders in as many days and millions of dollars' worth of stolen paintings. Enough motive to keep you in jail for a long time; enough motive to have you killed. Somehow you've stumbled on a conspiracy involving a lot of big-time people—people with things to hide and the ability to keep them hidden at all costs. Until we know exactly who those people are and how far the conspiracy goes we stay away from the cops."

"None of it makes any sense. From what I read, these people were already rich. Why did they want more?"

"I don't think it has anything to do with money at all."

"Then what?"

"Power. I've got a thousand volumes down in the stacks about groups from the Knights Templar and the so-called Illuminati all the way through to the Shriners. It's never really about money. Power and how to hold on to it. Good old-fashioned Yankee xenophobia. People are afraid of change and they group together and try to stop it. China tried to ignore the rest of the world for a thousand years, but even they had to start changing things in the end."

"This isn't the first time you've dealt with this kind of thing, is it?" Finn asked.

"We're all dealing with it. All the time," answered Valentine. "The battle between the old and the new has been going on since time began. This is just another version."

"There were a dozen names on that list of trustees. I only tracked down a few of them. How are we going to know which one is next on our killers list?"

"There's no way of knowing. We don't even know if there's only been the three murders—

Crawley, Gatty and Kressman. Peter Newman seemed to think that Crawley's boss, James Cornwall, had died of natural causes. Maybe he was wrong."

Finn reached out and wrapped her fingers around Valentine's hand, squeezing hard. "Okay, like I said before, what's next?"

"We dig a little deeper. We need to know what kind of stakes we're playing for, and just exactly who the players are." He paused. "We'll have to see my hacker friend."

"Hacker?"

"Computer freak. His name is Barrie Kornitzer. We went to school together, way back when."

38

He stared down at the tiny figures on the page, ranged through the trees, drawn and inked and colored so carefully like miniature signposts indicating the spinning out of time from the single frozen moment they represented: here they were safe and alive, without the knowledge that some of them would soon be dead, as carefully erased as they had once been drawn. He stared at them and at the bloody page and suddenly he was in another world, one that had never really been and if it had existed, it existed in a time that had long since vanished.

At six a.m. the attack began. Dawn was a faint purple line and the men moved like dark insubstantial ghosts through the slow, seething mist that rose up off the dew-wet fields. Watching through the gunnery slot of the ruined Panzer, the sergeant saw the blossoming of the first bazooka round and a few seconds later heard the heavy thump of its projectile. Almost instantly the air was full of sound. The first round from the bazooka took out a large section of the abbey tower, but not enough to silence the sniper. The sergeant could hear the flat sound of the high-powered rifle as it searched for a target in the thick screen of trees on the far side of the road. Then the bazooka announced itself again, this time shattering the upper section of the tower, spraying crumbling masonry and roofing tiles in all directions. The tower must have been built of wood originally, wood that was now tinder-dry after centuries of curing. A moment after the second shot from the bazooka, it was a blazing torch. So much for the sniper.

Following the second round from the bazooka, the sergeant could now hear the steady, rhythmic pounding of the mortar as it lobbed its two pound bombs into the entranceway. He pulled back the cranks on both machine guns, manhandled the traverse so the guns both lined up roughly with the barely visible roof of the granary and the main house and opened fire, hot shell casings spewing down around his ankles as the belts emptied in time to his ragged bursts of fire. Every few seconds he paused, traversed the guns a little and then fired again, watching the movements of Reid's five-man squad as they spread out to flank the farmyard enclosure.

Reid and Pixie Mortimer moved first, slipping out of the woods and running across the dark

road at the first shot from Terhune's bazooka.
From the far side ditch they managed to get to
the big boulder halfway down the sloping field.
The other three, Patterson, Dorm and Teitelbaum,
followed on their heels, dropping down into the
first of the shallow depressions that looked as
though they might once have been drainage
ditches or perhaps the ancient remains of some
sort of weeping tile bed for sewage.

Not for the first time the sergeant found himself
almost dumbfounded by the amount of crap the
ordinary foot soldier was supposed to carry.
Teitelbaum, the BAR gunner, for instance, carried
the gun, sling, cleaning kit, twelve twenty-round
mags in a webbing belt, a trench knife, frag gre-
nade, hatchet, sidearm, regulation boots and cloth-
ing, plus personal gear amounting to almost
exactly a hundred pounds. Even a lily-white officer like Cornwall carried the same as a grunt and
more: ammo pouches, clips, binoculars, map case
and anything else specific to the mission. In addition to that Cornwall and his arty pals were carrying Thompson submachine guns and the
requisite loads for them. It was a wonder any of
them could move at all.

Teitelbaum and Dorm set up the BAR on the
edge of the ditch, Patterson covering them with
booming rounds from his Russkie 71. So far the
sergeant had only seen small movements in the
front yard of the farm below, but by the time the
abbey tower was alight there was a full range of

fire from the house and outbuildings. Pausing to listen, the sergeant heard nothing but rifle fire and scattered bursts from some sort of light machine gun, probably an MP43 or the larger M34. With Terhune and the others pounding it in from the front it looked as though it was going to be easy pickings unless the Krauts had some kind of secret weapon in those trucks.

With covering fire from the BAR, Reid and Mortimer moved out from behind the boulder. There was a burst of fire from the upper floor of the farmhouse and suddenly Pixie was down, his legs cut out from beneath him as though he'd stumbled over a wire, his chest torn open by a stitch of rounds, half of his forehead and most of his brain demolished by a second firecracker string of shots from somewhere else. Reid didn't pause even for a second. As Mortimer went down the Indian threw himself forward into the grass and rolled his way under the old battered farmhouse wall. The BAR swept over the upper floor of the house and the sergeant could see Reid pulling out a boxlike Russian M28 mine and smashing down the arming fuse. He scuttled away to the left, keeping to the wall but putting as much distance between himself and the demolition charge as he could. There was a heavy crumping noise, a blast of dirty brown smoke and masonry from the wall and then a hole the size of a pair of barn doors appeared.

The sergeant pulled back on the traverse handles of the twin machine guns and watched as the smoke cleared. Through the newly exploded opening he could see into the farmyard, the trucks visible and unharmed in the shadow of the main barn and the winter livestock shelter beside it. To the right of the shelter there was a wagon shed and from the dark doorway he could see bursts of fire. Three, maybe four men in Wehrmacht uniforms went running across the cobbled courtyard, trying to reach the safety of the house. There was the chattering roar of the BAR, the Russian 71 and the Pah-pah-shah in unison and the Germans went down in a sliding heap like someone running a scythe through wheat. From somewhere closer in there was the sound of Terhune's bazooka and the crack of the two-inch mortar, rounds going into the roof of the livestock shelter and the wagon shed. The sound of cracking timber, fire and exploding glass was added to the general thunder. The sergeant could feel the taut flesh of his cheeks, pulled back into a deathly smile. Letting the barrels of the twin machine guns cool for a moment he glanced down at the radium dial of his Grana Dienstuhr service watch, taken off the wrist of a dead Kraut on D-day in the town of Courseulles-sur-Mer. It wasn't quite five past. The whole thing had taken less than four minutes. As the sounds of the fighting faded the sergeant could hear the faint sighing in the branches of the trees off to his left. A last round from the mortar went off and something rattled deep in the guts of the old dead tank. Distantly he could hear the sound of someone weeping. It was done. The sergeant boosted himself out of the tank, sat on the edge of the turret and lit a cigarette. There was a little pause as people gathered themselves together and then a man wearing a distinctive black SS uniform stepped out into the gap in the wall carrying a scrap of white rag on the end of a splintered stick of wood. The man hesitated and began walking forward. Cornwall and Taggart, the tall skinny officer who served as Cornwall's second-in-command, came out from behind the boulder and began walking down the hill toward the German.

The sergeant thought about things for a moment, then dropped down off the tank and headed toward the SS man, cutting off Cornwall's approach and meeting the man first, the Colt automatic heavy in his hand. The German was short, pale, and wore steel-rimmed glasses. There was a smear of ash on his cheek. The holster on his belt was unsnapped and empty. He was wearing the single oak leaf collar tabs and three green stripes of a Standartenfuhrer, a colonel. He looked more like a bank clerk.

"You speak English?"

"Yes."

"What's in the trucks?"

"They are paintings there. Artworks of value."

"Who are you?"

"My name is Dr. Eduard Ploetzsch. I am an art curator."

"No."

"What, please?"

"You're nothing. You're dead." The sergeant raised his automatic and shot him in the face for no real reason at all.

39

The false priest sat in the dusty basement of St. Joseph's Church in Greenwich Village, sorting through the material brought to him by a put-upon volunteer with the martyred expression of someone who carries the weight of the world around on their shoulders. The middle-aged woman had been digging around through the ancient records for hours now and had a different sigh for each string-wrapped bundle of yellowed manila folders.

This wasn't the unconfirmed fuzzy-logic trail created by an ethereal trip through the data banks imprinted on the servers of a thousand search engines, it was the faded ink-on-paper truth of real history on documents old enough to crumble in your hands. Going through the files, the priest could almost feel the ghosts of a thousand clerks like the one serving him now and hear the echoed clacking of typewriters and the faint earnest scratching of pens. Boring perhaps, but in the end it was easy enough to find the trail of Frederico Botte through the formative years of his life.

The child, whoever he was and whatever his interest to the red-hats in the Holy City, had arrived in New York City on the Gdynia-America Line ship *Batory* on June 11, 1946, traveling from the Polish city of Gdansk. There was a slip from the Ellis Island Immigration authorities showing that Frederico was seven years old and traveling with his guardian, Fraulein Ilse Kurovsky, a German national. Frederico's place of birth was listed as La Grazie, Italy, where he had been under the care of the sisters of the convent of San Giovanni All' Orfenio. There was no birth mother listed in the appropriate space on the registration form but there was a faintly penciled name in the margin: Katerina Annunzio. Although it wasn't clearly stated, the false priest could read between the lines: Frederico was a bastard, raised by the nuns at the convent, and then given into the care of the German woman with the Polish name.

After arriving in America, it appeared that Frederico had been placed in the care of St. Luke's Orphanage for two years, then transferred to St. Joseph's School in Greenwich Village, where he was enrolled as a "scholarship" student. His reports from the school were uniformly excellent, especially in the arts and languages. It was assumed that he would finish at St. Joseph's and then be enrolled in one of the local seminaries where he would train for the priesthood. However, his records with the parish ended in 1952 when he was adopted by Sergeant and Mrs. Brian Thorpe of Barrow Street in Hoboken, New Jersey. Interestingly, the lawyers who had provided legal services for the private adoption was the firm of Topping, Halliwell & Whiting, the same ghostly firm of nonexistent people who had established the mysterious Grange Foundation. It was also interesting, although probably coincidental, that the Grange Foundation was now located on St. Luke's Place—the same name as the orphanage where Frederico Botte had lived, now presumably transformed into plain old Fred Thorpe.

The false priest felt a familiar tightening in his chest. The circle was closing; it was almost the end now. The clerk reappeared, carrying more files. The man from Rome gave the woman his best priestly smile and asked if she had the New York telephone directory around anywhere.

"Which borough?" she said, and sighed once again.

40

Barrie Kornitzer's office at Columbia University was located in an obscure late 1880s building tucked in behind the Low Memorial Library. The office was lavish by Columbia standards, with built-in oak bookcases, Persian carpets and several early American paintings—including an early version of Ralph Earl's *Looking East from Denny Hill*, a still life by Charles V. Bond and an Edward Hicks farmscape. The desk in the main office was a William IV Rosewood flat top double pedestal partner's desk with an inlaid black leather writing surface. There was a rumor that the desk had once belonged to the fifth president of the university, Benjamin Moore. It was also rumored that the desk had been loaned to Kornitzer because the University was scared of him. Kornitzer was perhaps the foremost authority on computer hacking in the world, owned the patents and other licensing for the best encryption programs on the planet and was a confidential advisor to several presidents of the United States and Bill Gates. He had also gone to high school with Michael Valentine and was a longtime friend.

After graduating from high school the two young men had parted ways. Kornitzer spent several years hitchhiking around the United States and Europe, taught English to the Iranian air force, herded sheep in Scotland and then went to Seattle where he worked for some time in a comic book store. He then went to Stanford, selling his comic book collection, which included Superman Number One, to pay his tuition. During most of his time he lived in a parked car in one of the school's parking structures. He graduated with a degree in classics, turned down a number of prestigious job offers including a teaching position at Oxford, then went back to school. He got his law degree several years later, then passed the California Bar exams, although he never practiced. In the mid-seventies he joined Bill Gates's Lakeside Programming Group back in Seattle, helping Microsoft in its early days. Eventually he went off on his own again to pursue personal interests, which included breaking into every major computer database in the world.

On his way to a federal jail for life in the mid-nineties he was rescued by his old friend Michael and eventually wound up at Columbia in a nominally legal job. Like a number of early hackers he turned legitimate by "consulting" with the very organizations he had once preyed upon, including AT&T, the FBI, the CIA, Chase Bank, Bank of America and his favorite—Wal-Mart. According to Kornitzer, Wal-Mart was fundamentally the most dangerous company in the world, dedicated to its founder, Sam Walton's, idea of taking over the world through retail sales.

In 1983, innovative as ever, Wal-Mart spent tremendous amounts of capital on a private satellite system that could track delivery trucks, speed credit card transactions and transmit audio and video signals as well as sales data. By 1990 it was the biggest purchaser of manufactured goods in America, and by 2002 it was expanding into China before China could expand into America. Kornitzer said that Steven Spielberg's *Pinky and the Brain* was taken from the Sam Walton prototype. A lot of people thought Barrie Kornitzer was completely out of his mind. On the other hand a lot of people thought quite the opposite: Barrie was utterly sane and a socioeconomic-technological visionary.

Kornitzer was rich, bald, edging from pudginess toward real fat and wore brown corduroy suits and paisley ties. The only computer in his office was a lowly Dell but it was linked to a Bull Nova-Scale 9000 computer being used in the Computer Systems Lab at Columbia, a few blocks away on the other side of Low Memorial Library. The Bull, according to Kornitzer, was one of the most powerful in the world. Barrie Kornitzer was unmarried and, as far as Michael Valentine knew, had never had sex with anyone on the planet—male, female, animal, vegetable or mineral. Valentine knew for a fact that his friend had eaten nothing but canned baked beans for the last decade, refusing to eat anything that had even the slightest possibility of sentient life. He might be sane, but he was extremely weird.

"So what exactly is your problem?" Kornitzer asked, seated behind his desk, one hand gently sliding back and forth over his keyboard, the other smoothing his left eyebrow.

"A lot of disjointed facts."

"Nothing linking them?"

"Several things, nothing very specific."

"Such as?" He began making notes on a yellow pad. Finn noticed that even as he wrote with one hand, the other continued to caress the keyboard. It was as though the hands were ruled by separate entities, as though someone had split the man's brain with a sword. She remembered a book she'd seen in her mother's office back in Columbus: *The Origin of Consciousness in the Breakdown of the Bicameral Mind* by a man named Julian Jaynes. She'd loved the windy title but she'd never read the book. Maybe that's what Kornitzer had—a bicameral mind. He had a face like a Neanderthal but he was oddly attractive nevertheless.

"Art."

"Any kind in particular?"

"Stolen. Plundered. Second World War."

"Anything else?"

"Names. People. Murdered people."

"That's interesting. Give me the names."

Valentine listed them. Finn added the few that he'd left out. Kornitzer stared down at his pad. He began to doodle in the margins, his other hand still working on the keyboard.

"Huh," said Kornitzer. He leaned back in his leather executive chair and stared at the landscape on the wall behind Finn's head. "You're beautiful," he said, smiling.

"Pardon?" said Finn.

"You're beautiful," Kornitzer repeated. Finn looked a little flustered. She glanced over at Valentine, who was no help at all. He just smiled. Finn was on her own. "It's not really a compliment. I'm just stating a fact. You don't mind, do you? It helps when I'm trying to think something through."

"Oh."

"I don't get to meet a lot of beautiful women. They don't seem to be attracted to this kind of work." He paused. "Which is strange, because historically of course, women have always made the best cryptanalysts."

"I didn't know that," said Finn.

"It's true." Kornitzer nodded. He glanced at Valentine and smiled. He looked like a child. "I never lie, do I, Michael?"

"Not that I'm aware of."

The pudgy man blinked as though coming out

of some sort of trance. He stared up at the ceiling. "Anything else you can tell me?"

"Not really," Valentine answered. "Except that it seems as though there's at least two lines of events, two vectors, and they don't seem to have anything at all to do with each other. We've got this Carduss Club or Society or whatever on the one hand, linked to Greyfriars Academy, and the stolen art on the other hand. If you look at it purely from the factual side the only linking factor seems to be James Cornwall. From everything we can find out he seems to have died from natural causes."

Kornitzer shrugged. "We'll run it through MAGIC and see what happens."

"MAGIC?" asked Finn.

"Multiple Arc-Generated Intelligence Comparison," Kornitzer explained. "It was software originally developed by insurance companies to help their actuaries and risk analysts predict problems. It compares information, analyzes percentages of comparison—like to like, unlike to unlike, then shuffles them all together to give you a clearer picture of what's going on. It can go through a couple of billion entries in a search engine like Google and give you an analysis in a few seconds. Going through all the engines—including the off-line private and government ones—takes about five minutes."

"I see," said Finn, who didn't see at all.

"I adapted it for the people over at Fort Meade

to use for comparing telephone-call content, the frequency of certain phrases or words over a given period of time to track down terrorists."

"Like an intelligence sifter," put in Valentine.

"Something like that." Kornitzer nodded, smiling benignly from the opposite side of the desk. He clasped his hands comfortably across his belly. Finn laughed. He looked like the caterpillar in Walt Disney's *Alice in Wonderland.*

"It really doesn't sound like magic," she said.

Kornitzer's smile widened. "I wish there were more people around like you," he said thoughtfully. "Everyone thinks of computers as being cold. Black and white. They're not, you know. Perhaps the hardware is but the software inevitably shows the hand of man within it. Sometimes there's even whimsy to be found." Finn wasn't sure but she thought she could hear the faint sound of a British accent.

"Deus ex machina." Valentine laughed.

"God as the machine." Kornitzer smiled.

"You're both nuts," said Finn.

"Thank you," said Kornitzer. "I like to be appreciated for my madness sometimes." He looked at Valentine for a second. "Most people are too frightened to tell me I'm completely insane." His eyes twinkled behind the thick lenses of his glasses. "They think I'll steal all the money from their bank accounts or tell their spouses who they're committing adultery with."

"You've done both in your time," said Valentine.

"True," said Kornitzer, "but I've never been spiteful about it. All in a day's work, as the superheroes say." He shook his head sadly and turned to look out his window. The view was of a sea of university buildings. "Sometimes I wish I was back in the old days. Superman, Lois Lane, Batman and Robin." He sighed. "Green Arrow was my favorite. I used to dream about making my own fancy arrows that could do all sorts of things, bringing down villains. I wish I could remember his real name."

"Oliver Queen," murmured Michael Valentine. "His sidekick's name was Speedy."

"I didn't know you were a fan."

"I'm not. I run a bookstore, remember?"

"I'd hardly call it that," Kornitzer said with a laugh.

Finn interrupted. "It's great to have you two old fogies reminiscing. Next you'll be talking about Woodstock, but we've got these murders to look into, so . . ."

"Why don't you both go for a walk around the campus?" said Kornitzer. "There's a Starbucks at One fourteenth and Broadway. Buy me a cappuccino, double shot, low-fat, artificial sweetener. I should have something for you in half an hour or so. It'll take me that long to input the material."

"All right." Valentine nodded and stood up.

"Cappuccino, low-fat, artificial sweetener, half an hour."

"Double shot."

"Double shot."

"Got to be exact in this business." Kornitzer smiled at his friend then turned his attention to the flat screen and the keyboard.

41

The sergeant stood in the huge summer kitchen of the farmhouse, a fire blazing in the massive stone fireplace to take off the chill. There had been seventeen survivors of the attack, nine of them clearly civilians, two of them women, one a small child. Most of the Americans were outside guarding the few remaining German soldiers, or checking through the outbuildings, securing the perimeter. The sergeant, Cornwall, Taggart and McPhail were the only ones in the farmhouse. The only one armed was the sergeant, keeping the peace with a machine pistol he'd taken off one of the dead Krauts they'd found in the ruins of the abbey tower.

Cornwall was making a list.

"State your names and positions."

"Franz Ebert, director of the Linz Museum." A small man with glasses wearing a dark coat and army boots.

"Wolfgang Kress, Einzatstab Rosenberg, Paris division." A heavyset, florid-faced man in his early thirties. A bureaucrat.

"Kurt Behr, also of the ERR."

"Anna Tomford, from the Linz Museum also, please." Dark-haired, young, frightened.

"Hans Wirth, ERR in Amsterdam."

"Dr. Martin Zeiss, Dresden Museum." A portly man with a beard. Sixty or so, looking sick and pale, his face mottled like old cheese. *A walking heart attack*, thought the sergeant.

"Who is the child?" Cornwall asked. The boy was about seven or eight. So far he hadn't said a word. He was tall for his age, hair very dark, almost black, his eyes large and slightly almond-shaped, his skin olive, his nose large and patrician, more Italian-looking than German. The woman with him started to speak but the Linz Museum director, Ebert, interrupted her.

"He is an orphan, of no account. Fraulein Kurovsky cares for him."

"Kurovsky. Polish?" Cornwall asked.

The woman shook her head. "*Nein.* Sudetenland, Bohemia, close to Poland. My family is German."

"Where is the child from?"

"We found him north of Munich," put in Ebert. "We decided to take him along with us."

"Magnanimous," said Cornwall.

"I do not understand," Ebert responded.

"*Edelmutig . . . hochherzig*," said the sergeant.

"Ah." Ebert nodded.

Cornwall glanced at the sergeant. "I'm impressed."

The sergeant shrugged. "My grandmother was German—we spoke it in the house."

"I'm impressed that you knew the word in English," said Cornwall dryly.

"You might be surprised," said the sergeant.

"I'm sure," said Cornwall.

"It was not so . . . magnanimous as you say," said Ebert. "It was simply something that had to be done. He would have starved otherwise, yes?" He looked across at the woman and the child.

"He speaks no English, I suppose."

"He doesn't speak at all," said the woman.

Cornwall looked down at the packet of documents spread out on the pale beechwood table in front of him. "These documents all have Vatican stamps on them. Laissez-passers from the papal secretary of state's office in Berlin."

"That is correct," nodded Ebert.

"Seems a little odd."

"Perhaps to you." Ebert shrugged. "I care nothing for the politics of things, I care only that the works under my care be safeguarded."

"Works belonging to the German government."

"No. Works belonging to various German museums, works belonging to the German people as a whole."

"Six trucks."

"Yes."

"Heading for the Swiss border."

"Yes."

"With Vatican seals."

"Yes."

"Why don't I believe you?" said Cornwall.

"I don't care if you believe me or not," said Ebert crossly. "It is the truth."

"Why did you have an SS escort?" McPhail asked, speaking for the first time. McPhail was a graduate of Bowdoin and had been a junior curator at the Fogg Museum in Boston before joining the OSS and the art unit. You could tell he thought he was hot shit and rated higher than Cornwall. Personally the sergeant thought he was a weak little twerp and probably a fairy to boot. The guy smoked a pipe and whistled Broadway tunes for cryin' out loud! Nothing magnanimous about him—that was for sure. McPhail sniffed. "I was under the impression that the SS would have more important things to do than guard *Volkskultur*." He drew the word out into a sneering drawl.

Kress, the heavyset man, spoke, his sneer just as obvious. "Perhaps you are not aware that the Einzatstab Rosenberg is by definition a part of the SS, and therefore that it is entirely logical that we should have just such an escort."

"With Feldgendarmerie pennants?" said the sergeant.

"I didn't think you were part of this interrogation, Sergeant," McPhail said, ice in his tone.

"Just ask him the damn question . . . Lieutenant."

McPhail gave him a stony look.

"Well?" Cornwall asked, speaking to Kress. The man was silent.

"What are you trying to say?" McPhail asked.

"I'm trying to say that none of it makes sense. These aren't SS types. The soldiers outside are wearing SS uniforms, but I checked a couple of the bodies and they don't have blood group tattoos on their armpits. The SS doesn't have anything to do with the military police, the Feldgendarmerie. The trucks are wrong too—where the hell did they get gasoline? The Krauts haven't had any gasoline since the Bulge—they've only got diesel and not much of that. I don't know beans about art but I know about Krauts. They're wrong."

"Give your weapon to Lieutenant McPhail, Sergeant," said Cornwall suddenly, standing up. "Then come outside with me for a smoke."

"Sure." The sergeant gave McPhail the machine pistol then followed Cornwall out into the early morning sunlight. The lieutenant squinted behind his glasses and pulled a package of German Jasmatsis out of the pocket of his blouse and offered them to the sergeant. The sergeant shook off the offer and lit one of his own Luckies instead.

"What's happening here, Sergeant?"

"Don't have a clue, sir."

"Sure you do."

"They're wrong."

"What does that mean?"

"Like I said, it doesn't add up."

"So how does it add up?"

"You're asking my opinion?"

"Yes."

"They're crooks."

"Crooks?"

"Sure. The trucks are full of stuff that was already looted. These guys knew it was stolen, no records, no nothing. So they stole it again. I mean, who's going to report them?"

"Interesting."

"The trucks are a hide. Not for us, but for their own people. How do you get through German roadblocks? Military police and the SS put the fear of God into most Krauts, even now. Not people to screw with, you know?"

"What about the kid?"

"They're lying about him—that's for sure."

"Why?"

"Maybe he's somebody important."

"The Vatican seals?"

"Forged maybe. Or someone in Rome's got a piece of the action. Wouldn't be the first mackerel-snapper to have his hand caught in the cookie jar."

"Do you dislike everyone, Sergeant?"

"It's not a matter of liking or disliking, sir. It's a matter of knowing what I know. We've got a lot of stolen art in those trucks across the yard, and the Krauts don't know anything and your people don't know anything and my people wouldn't give a damn even if they did know."

"What are you saying, Sergeant?"

"I'm saying what you're already thinking."

"You're a mind reader?"

"It's been a long war. You get to see things, after a while, you learn how to read people."

"And what do you read here, Sergeant?"

"The chance of a fucking lifetime . . . sir."

42

When it came, the answer came quickly. Barrie Kornitzer used the edge of his thumb to wipe away the foamy mustache above his upper lip, gazing at the computer screen in front of him.

"Interesting stuff," he said, blinking.

"Don't keep us in suspense," said Valentine.

"Where would you like to start?"

"The beginning would be good."

"That would make it the so-called Carduss Club at Greyfriars Academy."

"Okay."

"It originated in 1895, the year the school was founded. That was back in the days when clubs and secret societies were actually encouraged in schools. The name comes from the thistles on the school crest, which in turn relates to the school's Scots-Calvinist origins." He grinned at Valentine. "Sort of like the school you and I went to, Michael, remember?"

"Vividly."

"Carduss means thistle, as in Scotland," said Finn.

"That's it. At any rate, the Carduss members based their club on the English Order of the Garter, which has the thistle as its emblem. Twelve knights as in the twelve disciples. Twelve members in their club."

"But it grew into something else."

"Yes. By the early nineteen hundreds with the first graduating class, it turned into a benevolent society, like Skull and Bones at Yale. If you were a banker, you lent money to a fellow member in real estate. If you were in government, you passed laws that would help a member expand his business."

"An early form of good-old-boys networking," said Finn.

"Something like that." Kornitzer paused. "In the end it was the twelve members of the original club who bought the school out of bankruptcy during the Depression. For some reason they decided to go underground just after World War Two—that's your Delaware corporation. They used the firm of their lawyers to buy up a shell company that also owned an entity called the McSkimming Art Trust in Chicago. They changed the name to the Grange Foundation, which has offices here in New York. St. Luke's Place in Greenwich Village."

"What do they do?"

"Nothing, apparently. They have no legal mandate: It's a private trust. It doesn't have to make any kind of report except to the IRS. According to their tax records they're a nonprofit organization that facilitates museum and gallery research into particular works of art and artists. What they really are is an art agency. As far as MAGIC can tell they have several major clients, in particular the archdiocese of New York and the Parker-Hale Museum of Art. From what MAGIC tells me, nearly every transaction has been handled commercially by the Hoffman Gallery, which has its head office in Berne, Switzerland."

"We're getting closer."

"Closer still. Your James Cornwall was a member in good standing of Carduss before the war. So was Gatty, so was a man named McPhail. Cornwall and McPhail were officers in G5, which in turn was a division of the OSS, the Office of Strategic Services. They were part of a group of art specialists attached to the Monuments, Fine Arts and Archives unit in Germany at the end of the war."

"And Gatty was the OSS liaison in Switzerland, working for Dulles."

"It gets better. According to MAGIC there's a clear line of documentation in OSS records that shows that Gatty organized the movement of Cornwall and his men through the so-called Vatican 'ratline.' He also got them transportation out of Italy through the port of Sestri Ponente just outside of Genoa. The *Bacinin Padre,* which was renamed the USS *Swivel.* You can trace them all the way to an address on Hudson Street and a company called American Mercantile."

"This is getting very strange," said Finn.

"American Mercantile went belly-up in 1934. They made work clothes. The building was empty from then on. The real estate company leased it out as warehouse space." He grinned. "Ask me the address on Hudson Street."

"I'll bite. What was the address?"

"Four twenty-one. It's a condo building now, but it's right across the street from James J. Walker Park. Eight-story Italianate. Fancy for a commercial building. Built in the 1800s."

"I don't get it," said Finn. "Why is that important?"

"Because the street that looks into the park from the south side is St. Luke's Place—home of the Grange Foundation. It can't be a coincidence," said Valentine.

"It's not," said Kornitzer. He punched a key and stared at the computer screen. "The United States Quartermaster Department Archives show that the shipment underwritten by Gatty turned up at 421 Hudson and was stored on the main floor of the building, sealed and under guard for eighteen days from July 27 to August 15, 1945. On August 16, 1945 the guards were removed. There's no record of the shipment after that." He paused again. "Whatever Gatty had shipped for Cornwall just vanished."

"How big was the shipment?"

"Two hundred twenty-seven tons. Assorted crates and boxes."

"Two hundred twenty-seven tons of what?" asked Finn.

"It doesn't say." The pudgy hacker shrugged. "The records of the group passing through the Vatican ratlines mentions six sealed trucks traveling through Switzerland into Italy, then down the coast to Genoa, that's all."

"It's the Gold Train," Valentine murmured.

"What's that?" Finn asked.

"It's one of those World War Two stories nobody quite believes," he explained. "A book came out about it a couple of years ago. According to the book a shipment of looted treasure was put onto a train out of Budapest right at the end of the war by a man named Arpad Toldi, the SS Commissioner of Jewish Affairs in Hungary. He made sure there was no inventory made of the material on the train—three or four billion dollars' worth of gold—and sent the train off to Germany. It never got there. It fell into the hands of the U.S. Army."

"Then what happened?" Finn asked.

"It disappeared," said Valentine. "Just like Cornwall's six truckloads. It's all part of that

World War Two Nazi-treasure mythology. Nothing's ever been proven."

"There's more," said Kornitzer.

"Tell me."

"You remember the name Licio Gelli?"

"The man who was involved in the Vatican Bank scandal. Some kind of backroom boy."

Kornitzer checked the screen, chewing on the end of a pencil now. "His name's all over the Vatican documentation. A direct link with Dulles as well. Something called Operation 'Left Behind.' Among other things Gelli was helping Nazis get out of town back in 1945. The later stuff relates to something called Propaganda Due, P2, some kind of neo-fascist group in the Vatican. It fits."

After World War II, the race was on between the Soviet and western blocs to apprehend Nazi war criminals, or recruit intelligence and other assets. The Vatican used its resources to provide passports, money and other support for church-run underground railroads that transported former Nazis and supporters out of Europe to safer havens in the Middle East, Britain, Canada, Australia, New Zealand, the United States and South America. Organizations like ODESSA (Organization of Former Officers of the SS) and Der Spinne, "The Spider," took advantage of this service. By some accounts the Vatican ratline provided support to as many as 30,000 Nazis. Among the beneficiaries of the Holy See's largesse were former

Gestapo operative Klaus Barbie; Adolph Eichmann; Dr. Joseph Mengele, the "White Angel" or "Angel of Death" of the Auschwitz death camp; Gustav Wagner, deputy commander of the Sobibor camp; and Franz Stangl of the Treblinka extermination facility. Members of the Waffen SS "Galician Division" were resettled as well.

"Where's Gelli now?"

"He died in jail. Heart attack. A lot of people say he was killed by an overdose of digitalis, just like Pope John."

"It sounds like we're moving into Dan Brown territory here: weird cults, Catholic conspiracies, Leonardo da Vinci painting in code. Sounds like a lot of white supremacist David Duke twaddle to me."

"Call it what you want, but there's something running all through this information like a thread you can't quite see, that even MAGIC can't cut through, and that's saying something, believe me."

"Give me your best guess."

"I don't have one. There's not enough to go on except for this strange kind of itch, the kind you can't quite get at. Something else going on, something *underneath* all the other stuff."

"It's the killer," said Finn, suddenly seeing it all. The whys and the wherefores could sort themselves out later, but beyond a shadow of a doubt she knew that Kornitzer's itch, the thread running through everything they'd uncovered was the identity of the killer.

"Explain that," said Valentine.

"I can't, not really. But I'll bet if you looked hard enough, looked at the names of all these people, you'd find more deaths, killings. Somehow he knew about the Michelangelo, knew about Crawley firing me, knew that it might start a chain of events that would lead to his being discovered, and that's why Peter died. It was supposed to be me."

"That doesn't make any sense," said Kornitzer. "He kills your boyfriend, but he hires someone to kill you—that Asian kid on the bicycle you mentioned?"

"It would make sense if there was more than one killer," Valentine said slowly.

"I deal in hard-line mathematics. That just doesn't compute."

"Of course it doesn't, not mathematically, but I've seen enough killing to know that like attracts like," said Valentine. "What if Finn is right? What if Killer Number One has been murdering people long before Crawley. We've had four deaths so far, four murders—Crawley, Finn's boyfriend, Peter, Gatty, and Kressman in Alabama, all connected by art—looted art. The death of Finn's boyfriend is like shooting up a flare, a signal that something's out of kilter, the killer making himself known. That brings on Killer Number Two, who tries to cover things up by dealing with Gatty and Kressman, probably to shut them up. If this all goes back to that shipment, or maybe something even worse, there's a lot at stake. Certainly enough motive to kill for."

"Nice hypothesis but I'm not buying it," said Kornitzer, shaking his head. "Too much coincidence."

"Is there any way we can find out if other people on that list of names died unnaturally?" Finn asked.

Kornitzer lifted his shoulders. "I could probably figure out a way to do it. Take me more than half an hour though."

"Start figuring it out," said Valentine. "We're running out of time."

43

Woodside, still occasionally called Suicide's Paradise for its wealth of third rails and speeding subway trains, is a New York neighborhood wedged between two cemeteries in northern Queens—St. Michael's to the north and Calvary Cemetery to the south. La Guardia Airport is only a mile from the neighborhood's northern edge and the entire area is crisscrossed by elevated commuter and subway lines. Once predominantly Irish Catholic, it now has an astoundingly diverse population of Koreans, South Asians, Mexicans, Dominicans and Ecuadorians. There are pubs everywhere, the majority still selling quantities of Cork Dry Gin, Jameson's, Guinness and Harp in the broad flat accents of Derry, Dublin and Donegal.

The priest drove his rental car into Queens and eventually found St. Sebastian's, a huge, windowless tomb of yellowing brick in the dour basilica style of County Cork churches. The deacon there, a man named Wibberley who'd volunteered there for so long he thought he owned the place, took the man from Rome through the old records. Neither they nor his own memory could recall anything of Frederico Botte or his adoptive parents, Sergeant and Mrs. Thorpe. Young Freddie had not been an altar boy, communicant or even a member of the church's famous basketball team. The only place Wibberley could think of that might know more was the funeral home a few blocks south along 58th Street, a Woodside institution since the early 1900s, when the area was still virtually rural.

The funeral home had indeed buried a Mr. Brian Thorpe on March 18, 1963. A few questions and lunch in an Irish greasy spoon called the Stop Inn Diner by the Long Island Rail Road elevated tracks on Roosevelt Avenue sent him to Sunnyside and the archives of the *Woodside Herald,* a Queens community newspaper that had been in operation since the second world war. According to the microfilmed copies of the paper for the week of March 20, 1963, Brian Thorpe, a member of the American Legion, a decorated veteran and the owner of the D and D hardware store, was accosted and killed on his way home from a late night at Donovan's on Roosevelt Avenue. The police report stated that he was stabbed repeatedly. No weapon was found at the scene. He was survived by his wife Annalise and his son Frederick.

An address for his wife was listed on Woodside Avenue.

He checked the Queens phone book but there was nothing for Anna or Annalise Thorpe. With no alternative he drove back into the neighborhood and discovered that the address in the *Woodside Herald* was for an apartment above the Chez Diamond Styling Hair Salon. The name on the scarred, grimy door was for A. Kurovsky. Finally, the circle closed: Annalise Kurovsky, the woman who had taken Frederico Botte out of Germany and to the United States on the *Batory*, married a man who had been murdered—stabbed, like all the others. He rang the doorbell. Almost immediately there was an answering buzz, as though he had been expected. He pushed his way through the door and went up the long, dark flight of stairs to the apartment above.

Whatever she had been before, Annalise Kurovsky had become a very dry stick. In her eighties her flesh had shrunk in on itself until it was no more than a wrinkled parchment shroud for ancient bone and sinew. Her face was sagged and wattled, marked in places by sun blotches and reddened areas. Out of it all burned a pair of dark, angry eyes, glaring with intelligence and some deep bitterness. The road she had traveled to find herself above a hair salon in Queens had clearly been a long and very difficult one.

The woman's living room was dark and cluttered. A row of mismatched bookcases stood against one wall, crammed with knickknacks and photographs. More photos hung on the stippled plaster walls along with decorative plates and several official-looking plaques. In the middle of it all, bizarrely, was an oil painting over the mantel of a gas fireplace. The painting, large and ornately framed, showed a young Mary stooping over a cradle holding the infant Christ while several angels watched from the upper left corner. The painting, and the artist who painted it, were instantly recognizable.

"Do you know what that is?" the priest asked.

"Certainly," the woman snapped, her voice as dry as her thin skin. "It is a Rembrandt. A study for the *Holy Family*, painted in 1645. The fully realized painting hangs in the Hermitage Museum in St. Petersburg."

"Where did you get it?"

"My husband gave it to me."

"Where did he get it?"

"I can't see that it is any of your business."

"No, perhaps not."

"You didn't come to speak to me of paintings anyway. You came to ask me about my son Frederico, yes?"

"Perhaps."

"Don't be coy." The old woman smiled. She sat down on a worn couch under the window. The priest chose a seat where he could see the startling presence of the Rembrandt.

"Yes, I came about the boy."

"I have been expecting you for a long time."

"Expecting me?"

"Of course. With all this talk of making Pacelli a saint."

"You know a great deal."

"I know everything," said the woman. "The whole story. It is a story that must be told, and I am the one to tell it."

"The priest smiled. "Not you, and not now."

"Who will stop me?" she asked, her voice snapping like twigs. "I have a duty to my son!"

"I will stop you," said the priest quietly. "And your duty is done."

The man from Rome had thought about using his gun but instead he rose to his feet, went around the cluttered coffee table that separated them, then leaned down, driving the palm of his hand under her chin, snapping her head back and breaking her withered neck. He let her fall face forward, breaking her nose on the coffee table. He checked her carotid pulse, found nothing and began to search the apartment.

44

Finn Ryan sat on the bench directly across from 11 St. Luke's Place in Greenwich Village and decided that Michael had been right: knocking on the Grange Foundation's door to get a better idea of what they were dealing with was really stupid. Not only that, it was potentially dangerous, maybe even fatally so. On the other hand, Barrie Kornitzer's MAGIC program could take them only so far. In fact it was MAGIC's limitations that made places like Ex Libris so important: in the end, the Internet was nothing more than a seething, almost infinite cauldron of half truths, opinions, outright lies and lunacy. It wasn't the Wild West of communications and information gathering; it was the twilight zone. Sometimes—and, in fact, more often than not—you had to go to the source.

And there it was, right next to the Huxtable house of the *Cosby Show*, one of a score of three-story brownstones on a pleasant tree-lined street that looked into Hudson Park. A block west was Hudson Street and 421, once a warehouse, now a renovated yellow brick condo building. Beside it another red brick industrial building, this one with a forest of huge satellite dishes on the roof. There was a restaurant on the corner of Hudson and St. Luke's but other than that the street was residential. Two blocks south she could hear the sounds of Houston Street. She was willing to bet there were fifty places within spitting distance where you could buy a five-dollar cup of coffee.

Eleven St. Luke's Place was much like its neighbors: black-edged windows, black wrought iron fence around the well leading to the basement floor, an outside central air unit and a brass knocker beneath the classic stone pediment over the front door. In the case of number 11 there was also a small brass plaque, blindingly polished. Even from here she could see the iron grilles over the basement window. The cars in front of the building included a dark green Lexus, a silver Mercedes and a black Jag coupe.

She'd been sitting there for half an hour now, staring at the house and second-guessing herself. Too much longer and someone was going to look out the window and spot her there. She took a deep breath, let it out and stood up. She straightened her short black skirt, tucked her plain white blouse in at the back and adjusted the leather bag on her shoulder. She felt as though she was wearing a parochial school uniform. She spent a few seconds putting her hair back with a covered elastic, stuffed the unruly ponytail through the back of a blue-and-gray LA Dodgers cap and crossed St. Luke's Place. She swallowed, cleared her throat and headed up the steep flight of steps and paused. The brass plaque said:

**The Grange Foundation
McSkimming Art Trust
PRIVATE**

Despite the unmistakable notice, Finn ignored the knocker on the door and turned the knob. Nothing happened. She noticed a large flat plate screwed to the door, painted black to blend with the wood. Up in the corner by the pediment she spotted a small closed-circuit camera. It appeared that entering without knocking was not an option. She lifted the black iron ring clamped in the mouth of the black iron lion and hammered it down three times. There was a ten-second pause and then a crackling voice came out of nowhere and asked her business.

"On Time."

"I beg your pardon."

"On Time. Courier. I'm supposed to make a pickup." This was the plan she and Valentine had concocted the night before. It didn't seem to be working too well. There was a long pause, then the voice buzzed out of the ozone again.

"We don't have anything for you."

This was the clincher. "Topping, Halliwell & Whiting." The firm of lawyers in Chicago that had provided the original shell for the Grange Foundation.

"Excuse me?"

"That's the name they gave me."

"*Who* gave you?"

"Dispatch." She let out a long-suffering sigh. "Look, I just go where they tell me to—there's no pickup, it's no skin off my whatever. I'll see you." She waggled the fingers of one hand up at the video camera. "Bye now." She turned to leave, holding her breath as she turned. She had her foot down one step when the electronic voice came again.

"Wait."

Bingo.

"I'll have to check. Wait."

"I'm not going to stand around out here."

Another pause and finally a sharp *click* from behind the plate on the door.

"Come in."

"Thanks a bunch." Finn turned the knob and pushed in through the heavy door, trying to keep the bored, faintly annoyed look on her face.

Once inside she found herself in a plain, narrow foyer with a second door directly in front of her. As the first door clicked shut behind her there was a faint sound from the second door and it popped open slightly. A second closed-circuit camera looked down on her from the doorframe. The foyer was an airlock, trapping anyone they considered a risk.

Finn went through the second door and stepped into a large reception room furnished in Arts and Crafts–style with what appeared to be a genuine Stickley desk and office chair set, a pair of armchairs and a long wooden "settle" complete with leather-covered pillows. The floors were dark cherry. On the cream-colored wall behind the middle-aged male receptionist's head there was a framed oil that looked a lot like one of Monet's *Garden at Giverny* series. If it was genuine, it was probably worth in the neighborhood of twenty million dollars.

Nice neighborhood.

The receptionist had dark thinning hair, broad shoulders, a white shirt with a blue-on-blue silk tie and what appeared to be a Hugo Boss suit that didn't quite disguise the heavy-looking bulge under his left shoulder or the broad, pale leather rig that held it in place. A gun. Which made sense if the Monet was real. Finn was in too deep to back out now: the bluff was on.

"Wait here," said Hugo Boss with the obvious shoulder holster.

Finn did as she was told, slowly turning in a full circle, taking in the entire room. Beyond the expensive furniture and the Monet it could have been the office of any tasteful professional in Manhattan—lawyer, accountant, upscale consultant. There were two doors at the end of the room, one folding, a closet, the other leading deeper into the building. Somewhere behind it Finn could hear the flat thumping of a photocopier and the *whirr-click-hum* of an office-sized laser printer. She looked carefully. The phone on the receptionist's desk had half a dozen lines, four of which were lit. Once again, nothing out of the ordinary.

Hugo Boss returned. "There's nothing here for you. And we don't use any courier company called On Time. When we use couriers we use Citywide."

"That's right," said Finn, trying to go with it. "Only when Citywide is overbooked they give the slush to us."

"Slush?"

"Overflow. And like I said, I just pick up and deliver. You say there's nothing here, then there's nothing here. No problem." She pulled the Dodgers hat more firmly down on her head and turned to go. At the last second she paused and gave Hugo her brightest eager-beaver "I'm just a shy country girl in the big city" look. "Uh, can I ask you a favor?"

"What?"

"I've really got to pee." Which was true enough; Hugo and the gun he was wearing were scaring the hell out of her.

"We don't have a public toilet."

"I'll only be a second, promise. You can check out that pickup for me again."

Hugo Boss paused and then frowned. Finn turned up the wattage on her pleading look, the same one she'd used in high school when she hadn't done her homework.

"All right," said Hugo. "Through there. First door on the right." He pointed. Finn trotted down to the far end of the room, watching from the corner of her eye as Hugo picked up the phone on his desk. She went through the door and shut it behind her. She was in a short hall between the front and rear of the house. To the left was a copy room, the source of the photocopier noise. To her right was a plain door with a sign that said WASH-ROOM. Straight ahead was an archway leading into an inner office. Two women and a man were sitting at computer work stations in a brightly lit windowless room. A flight of narrow stairs led up to the second floor. Yet another door led even farther back into the building, probably into what had once been the kitchen. No one was paying attention, so Finn ignored the toilet for the moment and ducked into the copy room. There was a big floor-standing Canon digital copier, an office fax machine and an industrial-sized scanner as well as a shelf full of coffee-making equipment and a row of coat hooks. Someone had left a bunch of keys beside the photocopier and without thinking Finn scooped them up and slipped them into her shoulder bag. She left the room, slipped into the bathroom and sat down, breathing hard. She gave herself a few seconds to calm down, flushed the toilet, ran the water and then hurried out to the front office again.

"Anything?" she said to Hugo, knowing what the answer would be.

The receptionist was on the phone. He shook his head briefly.

"Thanks for the bathroom," Finn whispered gratefully, giving the man a smile. She added a brief wave, then fled. A few minutes later she was on Hudson Street, looking for somewhere to get keys cut.

45

Michael Valentine moved through the stacks of Ex Libris, following his own arcane system of notation that was about as far from the Dewey Decimal System as you could get. He'd been working for most of the morning and part of the afternoon, consulting a dozen different encyclopedias of New York, old insurance plat books, ancient subway blueprints, the church records of half a dozen parishes and a complex sociological treatise on Greenwich Village from the 1930s that listed every single place of business and institution, street by street throughout the entire neighborhood. As Valentine made his way through the gloomy tiers of books and records he began to put together a picture of what the area around 421 Hudson Street had once been.

Originally of course it had been on the very edges of New York in the small rural village of Greenwich on the shores of the Hudson River. By the early 1800s the fields belonging to the Voorhis family had been sold to Trinity Church, who in turn leased the property to the St. Mary Magdalene Benevolent Society. By that time the two-block square of property bounded by Hudson Street, Clarkson, Morton and Varick was already being used as a burial ground for the Episcopal Church of St. Luke's in the Field a little to the north. In the 1820s a Roman Catholic Church, Holy Redeemer, was built on the property and a stark, redbrick convent and home for "disadvantaged" girls built across Hudson Street. It was at this time that Edgar Allan Poe lived in the area, and his dour, stooped figure was regularly seen plodding through the tombstones of the burial ground. As time went on the burial ground property was subdivided and the first town houses on what was to become St. Luke's Place were erected, the road being an extension of Le Roy Street to the west and running through to Varick. Holy Redeemer Church burned in 1865 and burials in the area were taken over by St. Paul's to the south and St. Luke's to the north. By the 1870s the first elevated trains were appearing, infringing on the property owned by the convent at 421. A fire in 1877 forced the closure of the building and the ruins were demolished in 1881 to make way for the eight-story warehouse building that presently occupied the site. By 1900 there was no trace of the convent, the church or the cemetery. The graveyard was a park, St. Luke's Place was home

to the Mayor of New York and streetcars and
horse-drawn trolleys rumbled up and down Hudson Street.

Nothing about the building containing American Mercantile seemed to be special in any way
but there had to be a reason Cornwall and his
cohorts from the Grange Foundation had chosen
it as the storage facility for their shipment. Clearly
it had something to do with the foundation's
choice of an office but according to the plat books
and Valentine's ancient, dusty collection of Manhattan reverse directories the foundation hadn't
moved into the old brownstone on St. Luke's Place
until long after the shipment had disappeared.

After carrying a half dozen reference books back
to his office, he dropped down into his chair and
closed his eyes, trying to see the problem in some
kind of rational order. What did Cornwall know
about the location that wasn't immediately obvious to someone browsing through the history
books, or more directly through the thousands of
volumes and books of records surrounding him
now? Irritated by his inability to figure it out for
himself, he turned to his computer, booted up the
ISPY program Barrie had custom-built for him and
punched in Cornwall's name. A brief biography
appeared almost immediately.

Name: Cornwall, James Cosburn
Date of Birth: 1904
Place of Birth: Baltimore, Maryland

Date of Death: 2001
Place of Death: New York, NY

HDescrip: Cornwall was born to Martin and Lois Cornwall, the latter a prominent interior designer and teacher at the Baltimore School of Art. The young Cornwall attended private schools, where he was especially interested in monastic and church architecture. He studied in Europe before college for two years at the École Sebastien in Paris. In 1922 he returned to the United States, attending Yale University the following year. He graduated cum laude from Yale in 1927 and joined the Parker-Hale Museum the same year as an assistant in the department of decorative arts. He was assistant curator 1929–32 before being advanced to associate curator. Beginning in 1930, he worked with Parker-Hale director Joseph Teague (1885–1933) in planning the new medieval extension to the museum. Cornwall was named assistant curator of medieval art in 1934 after Teague's death. He was named curator of the medieval department the same year. He married Katherine Metcalfe in 1942. In 1943 he joined the army and quickly rose to an appointment as lieutenant in the Monuments, Fine Arts and Archives section of the Seventh United States Army, Western Military District. His chief responsibilities were the discovery and preservation of art treasures hidden by the Nazis. Cornwall was responsible for seizing the looted collections of Goer-

ing, Goebbels and Alfred Rosenberg, among others. Returning to the Parker-Hale, he was made director in 1955. In June of 2001 he suffered a fatal heart attack after a particularly contentious board meeting and was succeeded by his protégé, Alexander Crawley (q.v.).

The biography didn't tell him very much he didn't already know but a notation in the bibliography of Cornwall's published works leapt out at him. A reference to his PhD thesis at Yale: "Giovanni Battista de Rossi and the Catacombs of San Callisto: A Biographical and Architectural Evaluation."

Using that as a starting point Valentine skittered around through the Internet putting the pieces together. Cornwall's interest in the subterranean world hadn't ended with his doctorate. Over the years he'd published a dozen articles on the subject, edited and compiled several scholarly works and had even been an advisor on a series of History Channel programs about crypts, mausoleums, cemeteries and catacombs all over the world. The last program in the series was called "New York Dead."

Within an hour the pieces had all fallen into place and he had the answer. He searched through the sociological history of Greenwich Village to confirm his theory.

"My God," he whispered, as the reason for Cornwall's choice of the Hudson Street warehouse became blindingly clear.

What was now a park where young children played had once hidden the underground crypt of Holy Redeemer Church, connected to the convent on the other side of the road by a "priest's hole" tunnel so the nuns and "disadvantaged" girls would not be seen in daylight as they made their way to prayer. Cornwall and his fellow conspirators, along with two hundred twenty-seven tons of crates and boxes—six truckloads of looted booty—had vanished under the streets of New York.

And it was still there.

46

The false priest moved through the cluttered rooms of the dank, verminous-looking apartment on Ludlow Street, far below the trendy stores and salons that lined the narrow one-lane thorough-fare above Delancey. As he examined the pitiful rooms, he carried the Beretta at his side. Rooting through the old woman's apartment in Queens had led him here, but the place was empty. There were only terrible ghosts and memories left be-hind. The floor was covered with stained and cracked linoleum that might have been blue once. The ceiling sagged in seams and lumps, threaten-ing to split open like overripe fruit. With each step, shining roaches scuttled greasily toward the open baseboards and silverfish fled under the scraps of old carpeting that lay here and there.

It was, without a doubt, the horrible den of a madman. The crumbling plaster and ancient floral wallpaper were covered with newspaper clip-

pings, drawings, pictures from magazines, anno-
tated maps, scrawled letters in script so small it
could barely be read, reproductions of paintings
and here and there the broken pieces of plaster or
plastic saints and angels, glued, tacked, nailed or
simply placed in niches dug with spoons into the
soft spongy walls themselves. It was a museum
dedicated to the insane meanderings of an ob-
sessed heart, the obsession impossible to penetrate
or analyze except that it concerned the old war
and people who had taken part in it, artists, art
and the deaths of a hundred nobodies in a score
of countries and most of all the life and times of
a single hawk-nosed man in steel spectacles wearing the robes and mitred headpiece of a pope. The
man from Rome had lost his faith long ago and
sometimes found himself agreeing with the cynics
that man had been placed on the earth to do no
more than eat, fornicate and excrete but being here
he knew there was something else: this man had
been created to prove that hell existed. This place
was a petri dish meant to provide a culture of
the damned.

There were more rooms than he would have
expected, as though perhaps two or maybe even
three of the decrepit tenement apartments had
been joined together. The only thing new in the
place was the metal-clad front door and the locks
that guarded it, easily picked. The kitchen lay in
the middle of the apartment in the old-fashioned
style with a pass-through into the small, dark par-

lor beyond. It was a horror, the chipped enamel sink resting on its own plumbing, open without cabinetry, stacked with crusted plastic plates and bowls and cups, a jar of grape jelly open and moldy on the counter along with a box of cornflakes, a soured pint carton of milk and a half-empty mug of coffee. A choked twist of old-fashioned flypaper hung from the overhead light fixture. Reaching up with thumb and forefinger the false priest tried the dangling pull cord but nothing happened.

He went into the parlor. An old rag rug, brown and curling at one side. A drawing in ink directly on the left wall: Christ on a cloud above a grotesque Calvary below and words beneath the triple crucifixion:

THOU WILT SHEW ME THE PATH OF LIFE
IN THY PRESENCE IS FULLNESS OF JOY
AT THY RIGHT HAND THERE ARE PLEASURES
FOR EVERMORE

A closer look and the man saw that the figures on the crosses were women, bleeding from breasts and eyes and that there were strange inscriptions in faint winding circles above Christ's head, vague and indecipherable.

There was a short hall and then another door, old and scarred but painted bright, fresh, robin's egg blue. Inscribed on the door was a single word:

TSIDKEFNU

The Old Testament word for "Righteousness,"
one of the thousand names of God.

The man from Rome eased back the slide of the
Beretta with his free hand, took a breath and held
it. He pushed open the door and went into the
room beyond, the end of his journey. He reached
up to shade his eyes with one hand, almost
blinded by the light.

47

Behind them in James J. Walker Park Finn and Valentine could faintly hear the sound of children jumping rope, singing a counting song that became faster as they skipped.

> "I am the Baby Jesus,
> Marching to the cross.
> I am the Baby Jesus.
> My daddy is the Boss."

"Are you sure this is the right thing to do?" said Finn, sitting on the bench beside Valentine. Between his feet was a bag of equipment. They were both dressed casually in running gear. It was past seven and dusk was falling, the rush hour traffic on Hudson Street thinning.

"You're the one who went in there today and took the keys." Valentine smiled. "Besides, if we want to bring this thing to some kind of conclusion that will satisfy the authorities we have to have evidence. Right now everything's circumstantial, Internet paranoia and conspiracy theory."

"I just wanted to find out who killed Peter."

"We will," Valentine offered. "I promise you." He kept his eyes on the house on the far side of St. Luke's Place. The last lights went out and a moment later Hugo Boss appeared, locking the door behind him. The tiny Panasonic D-snap camera Finn had carried in her shoulder bag earlier in the day had given Valentine all the information he needed about the inside of the interior of the building including the name on the security panel just inside the front door. It appeared to be a relatively simple ADT system with a telephone line connection to a central security center. The system was almost ten years old and a single call to Barrie Kornitzer had given him the bypass code for the system within five minutes. Finn's theft of the key ring had simplified things even more; after copying them at a locksmith's shop on Carmine Street, she used the beeper on the ring of originals to find the car the keys belonged to, eventually finding a Toyota Camry on Varick Street that answered the call. She simply tossed the keys on the floor underneath the front seat and then manually relocked the car behind her. When the owner eventually discovered them he or she would assume the keys had been left behind when exiting the car earlier in the day.

"I am the Baby Jesus.
I see every single sin.
I am the Baby Jesus
And I always win."

Valentine checked his watch and then the darkened brownstone across the way. Nothing moved except the leaves in the trees. The traffic hummed a block away. Finn could faintly recall a few lines from an Edgar Allan Poe sonnet about some spooky dead love. She tried not to think about what lay beneath her, buried deep under the soil of the park. Old secrets. Older bones.

"Time to go."

"All right."

"I told Barrie most of what we know. If I haven't called him by midnight he'll let a friend of his in the Bureau know what we found."

"That's a comfort," said Finn with a hollow laugh. They both stood up and headed across the street. Behind them, lost in the gloom, the children skipped.

48

They stepped into the dark house. Ahead of them and to the right was the ADT panel. A small, angry red light pulsed. Valentine punched in a set of numbers. The red light reverted to green.

"That was easy enough," Finn whispered.

"This isn't some high-tech heist movie," Valentine answered. "After a while people get careless and they don't bother with the basics." He shrugged. "Besides, why would anyone break into a place like this? As far as anyone knows they're just a bunch of paper pushers."

"Maybe that's all they are," said Finn. "Maybe we're wrong."

"You said you thought your receptionist in the expensive suit was wearing a gun."

"I'm sure of it."

"Then we're not wrong. You don't need a gun to guard papers."

Valentine paused for a moment to examine the

painting behind the desk. "You do need a gun to guard something like that, however."

They moved quickly through the reception room and down the hallway into the open area at the center of the house. Finn dropped the equipment bag on one of the desks and slid open the zipper. Valentine took out a heavy flashlight and switched it on, panning the beam around the room. He saw nothing any different from what the camera had shown him: a large rectangular windowless room with a flight of stairs against the right-hand wall. There were three desks and a row of filing cabinets. A doorway at the end of the room led into a comfortable conference area with a long table and a half dozen chairs. There was a painting over the mantel of an old-fashioned fireplace to the left. It was too dark to see clearly; a muted landscape of some sort. Another door led to the rear of the house. It was locked. Finn stepped forward with her set of keys and tried them until she found one that fit. She turned it and the door popped open. They stepped through.

"Now this is interesting," Valentine murmured.

The room was completely empty. A window on the far wall had been bricked up and the original rear door had been replaced by something that looked vaguely like the sliding mechanism usually seen on garages. Instead of the cherry in the other rooms here it was wide oak planks, dark with age. It was the original floor.

"A loading bay," said Valentine. "The insurance plat books show an old court-style alley in the back with an entrance on the Varick Street end. That's where this must go."

"That doesn't make sense unless they've got something to load," said Finn.

"Look." Valentine pointed. In the center of the floor there was a square seam in the planks. He swung the light around the walls. Beside the operating mechanism for the heavy rear door there was a single large button, much like the elevator call at Ex Libris. "Hit it."

Finn crossed the room and slapped her palm down on it. There was a humming sound and a section of the floor six feet on a side pushed upward slowly. A large open cage appeared, finally thumping to a stop.

"What the hell is that?" said Finn.

Valentine played the beam of his light over the open cage. A stamped metal plate across the top beam read: OTIS BROTHERS YONKERS NY 1867.

"I couldn't find anything out about the original owners of the building but it could easily have been some kind of tavern or small hotel. This would be the freight elevator they used to bring up beer barrels and food from storage down below." Valentine stepped into the cage and swung the flashlight around. He spotted a switch on one of the cage uprights. "Looks safe enough."

Finn stared, horrified. "We're going down in that thing?"

"I don't see any other way." He waved her forward. Tentatively she stepped onto the old steel floor of the cage and Valentine tapped the button. The cage descended ponderously. By the time they reached the bottom they were smothered in darkness. They stepped off the elevator and Valentine swept the beam around. They appeared to be in a modern, concrete-walled basement filled with boxes and crates. Valentine found a light switch and flipped it on. Overhead fluorescents crackled into life.

The basement was as large as the entire house, a long narrow room with a well-outfitted packing facility complete with storage bins for lumber, saws, worktables and a large overhead setup for blowing in foam popcorn, and an area devoted to metal strapping. All very efficient. A dehumidifier hummed against one wall and the room was cool and dry. A half dozen medium-sized crates had been arranged close to the freight elevator, neatly labeled and bar-coded. They were all designated for various outlets of the Hoffman Gallery around the world and they each had a plastic pouch stapled to one side already packed with customs clearance papers. Off in one corner of the room was a metal desk with a computer and heavy-duty label printer. Valentine took a box cutter out of his bag and slashed one of the pouches open.

"Form 4457, Declaration of Goods only. One of the great assets of dealing in fine art and antiquities: no duty. It's like transporting millions of dollars across international borders without raising an eyebrow."

Valentine found a pry bar on one of the worktables and began pulling open one of the small crates. The top finally pulled free and he carefully lifted out the contents.

"Rembrandt. *The Raising of Lazarus.* It's been missing since 1942. It was stolen from a Jewish art dealer in Amsterdam."

"Is that enough evidence?"

"No. We have to find the rest."

"It's not here."

Valentine looked around the room. "First we have to establish exactly what the extent of 'here' is." He walked to the far end of the basement and stared at the wall. Like the rest of the long, narrow room it appeared to be made out of solid brick. There was nothing against the wall that might have disguised some sort of hidden entrance.

"It's got to be here. We're facing the park." He looked left and right. "These are adjoining walls to the buildings next door and the back wall is facing in the wrong direction." He checked the floor carefully, looking for signs that something had recently been brought out from behind the wall but there was nothing.

Valentine dropped down on his knees, carefully checking the join between the front wall and the floor. Finn turned and looked back the way they had come, remembering the office at Ex Libris and Sherlock Holmes. When the possible has been eliminated . . .

The whole back wall was taken up by a series of metal shelving units full of packing supplies. Leaving Valentine to his study of the floor she walked back to the north facing wall and stared. Six shelving units filling up the whole wall and rising to within an inch of the ceiling. They were lifted half an inch off the floor by stumpy little angle iron feet. The units were painted an institutional green and looked old. Finn turned again. The old-fashioned freight elevator was twelve or fifteen feet away. There were more shelving units against the left adjoining wall but none against the right, which was hung with a large piece of pegboard for holding tools instead. She continued to stare, frowning, knowing that something was wrong. Then she saw.

"Michael," she called. He stood and turned in her direction.

"What?"

"I think I've found something."

"Where?" He headed down the low-ceilinged basement room toward her.

"Look," she said, pointing as he joined her. "The pegboard."

"What about it? That's an adjoining wall."

"There's nothing on it."

"I don't get it."

"All the tools are on shelves over there, none

of them are hanging up so what do you need the pegboard for?"

Valentine was silent for a moment. He stepped forward and checked the pegboard, tapping at it with his knuckles, then checked the place where the adjoining wall and the rear wall formed a junction. After a moment he grabbed the center shelf of the nearest wall unit and tugged hard. At first nothing happened and then, smoothly and almost silently two of the units closest to the adjoining wall rumbled forward until the double-wide shelves stood two feet out from the back wall. They clicked decisively to a stop like a cork in a bottle. Changing his grip slightly Valentine pulled the shelf unit to the left, away from the adjoining wall finally revealing the dark, hidden entrance.

He grabbed his flashlight and headed down a wide concrete ramp that led down to a circular antechamber. The walls of the chamber were quarried, Pound Ridge granite, the ancient bedrock on which the skyscrapers of New York had been built. Valentine put his hand out and let it rest on the rough-hewn rock. Cool and dry, a perfect place to bury the city's favorite sons of history and keep her later secrets from prying eyes. Edgar Allan Poe.

"Lo! Death has reared himself a throne
In a strange city lying alone
Far down within the dim West

Where the good and the bad and the worst
  and the best
Have gone to their eternal rest."

"Sometimes you can be downright spooky, Michael," Finn muttered. She followed the beam of the flashlight. Two metal rails like a miniature railway line led through a narrow, pitch-black cavern to the left. There was a switch box bolted onto the near wall and a line of heavy insulated conduit led into the hole. Valentine flicked the switch and a line of industrial bulbs came on, dimly illuminating the tunnel ahead. He switched off the flashlight. The opening was seven or eight feet high and little more than that across. The walls had been constructed on the same stone as the round antechamber and the floor was overlaid with a thick absorbent pea gravel.

"I wonder where this goes?" Valentine said quietly. He headed into the tunnel.

"I'm not so sure I want to find out," said Finn, but she followed him anyway.

The tunnel turned and twisted half a dozen times as they moved forward. Here and there narrow niches had been cut into the walls, bodies interred and then bricked over, but the crumbling brick had long since vanished and the old interment sites were empty. The rails at their feet seemed strangely out of place in this dead place, the low lightbulbs overhead in their metal screen safety baskets even more so. Finn tried not to think of the weight of the earth directly above her head; tried to breathe evenly in the oppressive, gloomy passage. She'd never been particularly claustrophobic but this was something on a completely different order of magnitude. Hell wasn't hot, it was just like this—empty and buried underground. Buried alive.

They moved through the passage for a lifetime and then finally came to another widened antechamber. The rails ran across it to a heavy iron door set on massive hinges bolted into the wall. The door was some kind of dark heavy wood, the strap hinges as old as the stone walls they were attached to. A pair of obelisks had been neatly carved in half relief into the stone on either side of the door, then picked out in whitewash and some dark, ancient stain. Words had been neatly hammered into the rock over the entrance, picked out in black and white the same way as the obelisks.

"Silence, Mortals, you are entering the Empire of the Dead," Finn read out aloud. "Nice." She looked at the door and then at Valentine. "Are we going in?"

"I think we've come too far to back out now," he answered. He tapped the rail with the toe of his boot. "They're not using these to transport old bodies. This is a warehouse, not a crypt." He stepped forward and grabbed the wrought iron handle. He pulled open the door and stepped through.

There was a deep, guttural moan like the sound of some wounded animal, and then the lights went out. Finn screamed, the terrible scent of fresh-spilled blood suddenly in the air around her. She screamed again, feeling the air rush from her lungs as the stony floor of the tunnel rushed up to greet her. In the distance, echoing, came the flat hard sound of a shot being fired.

49

For a single terrible instant Finn felt consciousness failing her and a sudden vision of the last instant she had seen Peter's face appeared before her. Heart pounding, she got to her hands and knees then pushed herself to her feet. Screaming Valentine's name she stumbled forward, arms outstretched, fingers clawing at the empty air. She lurched to one side as something struck her hip with a grunt and she felt her cheek smack hard into the rough wooden surface of the door. She lost her balance and twisted away, smelling blood and the thick reek of some kind of cheap men's cologne or aftershave. It touched some kind of vague sense memory on the edge of conscious thought and then vanished. Close beside her she could hear the sound of ragged breathing and the dull hard sound of a bunched fist smashing into softer flesh. She fell to her knees again, realizing that the floor beneath her was smooth concrete now, not gravel. Bizarrely, filtered down from above her head she could hear the children playing in the park.

> "I am the Baby Jesus.
> I never, ever lie.
> I am the Baby Jesus,
> And if you don't believe me,
> You will surely fry."

The children's voices were coming through the old ventilation system that brought fresh air down to the crypt, still somehow connected to the surface. Pushing to her feet a second time, arms outstretched again, Finn reached a smooth wall in the darkness and edged along it, feeling desperately for a light switch. The smell of blood had been replaced by something else: the heavy pungent odor of spilled gasoline. There was a horrible sighing sound and then the sound of something heavy crashing to the ground. She felt a plastic switch plate underneath her hand and flipped it upward. The lights came on again and she saw where she was.

The bunker was arch-roofed and enormous, at least a hundred feet on a side, stacked with aisles and rows of crates and wooden boxes, old suitcases, trunks and huge strapped sheet metal steamer chests that reached up to the ceiling, twenty feet overhead, interspersed with steel support beams installed to keep the old stonework from collapsing. A tall crate nearby was open and a Dutch master portrait by Franz Hals leaned against it. The label on the crate was clear, if faded, and had the distinct lightning bolt runes of the Nazi SS. A steamer trunk was open beside it, filled almost to overflowing with thousands of old-fashioned spectacle rims, solid gold, lenses gone. Over everything was the reek of gasoline and out of the corner of her eye Finn saw the familiar red shape of a plastic five-gallon container. The twin narrow-gauge rails that ran into the room ended at a buffer made from a heavy slab of oak beam. A flat pallet dolly rested against the wood: a simple way of transporting plunder from the vault to the loading bay beneath the house on St. Luke's Place.

"Michael!"

"Here!"

The sound came from behind the large crate. Leading to it she saw a bright trail of fresh blood. She ran forward, pushing the crate out of the way. Valentine was pushing himself upright, grabbing at a pile of flat crates for support. At his feet lay the body of a man, still alive, clutching his belly, groaning, hands clasped around the haft of a long, bone-handled hunting knife. He was gray-haired, in his sixties and wearing some kind of olive drab–colored uniform—the uniform of a World War Two infantry sergeant, much too large on the small man's frame. Finn recognized him instantly.

"It's Fred!"

Valentine grunted painfully, finally standing erect. There was a large bloody slash across the shoulder of his heavy sweatshirt. "Who?"

"From the museum. He was a security guard," she answered faintly. "I used to say hello to him. Just a shy old man." She stared at Valentine's shoulder. "Are you all right?"

"Just a graze. I'll live." He bent over the man on the floor. "I'm not so sure about him."

"What was he doing here—how did he know about this place?"

"Presumably he figured it out just like we did. From the looks of things, he was about to torch it all," answered Valentine. "God only knows why, and God knows who he thought he was." He looked at the uniform. There was a faded patch at the shoulder. A gold-and-red stepped pyramid on a blue background. Seventh Army. Cornwall's unit. He glanced out across the enormous vault and shook his head, then reached out with a bloody hand and touched his fingers to the side of the man's neck. "Faint," he said. "If we want any answers we'd better get him some help." Valentine stood again, weaving slightly, leaning against the crates at his side for support. "You go. Phone 911. Get the cops and an ambulance." He looked out across the room again. "We've got the evidence we need now. It all adds up: The Foundation, Cornwall, Crawley, Gatty, all the other names. All part of keeping this a secret. The more people who see this the better."

"You sure you'll be okay?"

"I'll be fine. Go."

Finn turned and ran.

50

Finn ran through the twisting passageway, her breath coming in hard gasps, her mind whirling with a thousand different thoughts and images as she tried to concentrate on the matter at hand. It didn't work and as she made her way back to the basement of the Grange Foundation all she could think about was the drawn, pale face of the dying man on the floor of the bunker, the knife sticking out of the upper end of his gut, the thick, blood-black gout of color spreading across the front of his white shirt, his slim, piano player's fingers clutching at the blade's bony handle.

She reached the end of the tunnel and stumbled out into the circular chamber behind the hidden doorway in the basement of the house on St. Luke's Place. She stopped, rearing back, eyes wide. Lieutenant Vincent Delaney of the New York Police Department was squatting over the figure of a man slumped against the stone wall of the room. A man with half of his face blown into a bloody pulp, disfigured beyond recognition except for the white circlet of a Roman collar, bloody around his neck. A priest. A priest with the flat black shape of an automatic pistol in his hand. As Finn stopped, gasping for breath, the policeman rose and turned, the Glock that had killed the man still in his hand—the sound of the shot she'd heard half a lifetime ago at the other end of the tunnel.

"Miss Ryan," he said slowly, "I knew you'd turn up eventually. Still with your new friend, Valentine?"

"How did you know about that?"

"I know more than you think."

"Why are you here?" She stared at the shrunken form of the dead priest. "What's going on?"

"Is Valentine with you?"

"What is a priest doing here?"

"He's not a priest. He's a hired killer. An assassin."

"He killed Peter?" Her head was beginning to spin, the connections she'd been making disintegrating and flying in all directions, sense and logic vanishing.

"No. Peter was an accident. It was meant to be you."

"Why?"

"Because you stumbled onto the drawing. If you'd pursued it, you would eventually have made your way here. You had to be stopped."

He paused. "I asked you a question. Is Valentine with you?"

"Yes."

"The child?"

"What child?" This was insane.

"Botte. Frederico. An old man now."

"Fred? The security guard?"

"He's always been referred to as the child. Every man was once a child. This one has been dangerous from the moment of his conception."

"You're out of your mind," Finn whispered. "What are you talking about? There's a vault full of stolen, looted art back there! Billions of dollars! People have been murdered to cover up the fact of its existence. What does an old man have to do with it? For that matter, what do you have to do with it?" She looked down at the corpse huddled against the wall. "Or him?"

"I'm more than just a policeman, Miss Ryan," said Delaney quietly. "And the people I work for have secrets to keep—old secrets. It's never been about the art. It's always been about the child. We thought we had him and then we lost him. He'd started to kill again. If the wrong people catch him, the truth will come out. That can't be allowed to happen. The Church is in enough trouble as it is. This would be the end." He nodded in the direction of the dead man. "He worked for another faction who believed that your death would be enough, who craved power more than protection. To reach your hoard of looted art and steal it back, they would have risked everything."

"He was trying to destroy it," whispered Finn. "A thousand years of priceless beauty and he was going to burn it all." She paused, bewildered, staring at the policeman. "Who is he?"

"Eugenio Pacelli's son. The bastard child of a pope, held ransom by the Nazis for blackmail, for services rendered, for your looted treasure until they ran into James Cornwall and his own group of thieves, his own band of Nazis: American ones."

"Carduss. Greyfriars. The Grange Foundation."

"If you wish. Much more than that now."

"How did you find this place?"

"I followed the priest. I knew he'd eventually lead me to the child. He found out where the freak had been living but he was already gone."

"The freak, as you call him, is dead," said Valentine, stepping out of the tunnel. Startled, Delaney turned, the Glock in his hand coming up, its aim centering on Valentine's chest. "It's over."

"Not quite," said Delaney. "Just a little bit of housekeeping."

"We're housekeeping?" said Finn.

"He means murder," explained Valentine. "He can't leave us alive. He knows none of this can be made public. He's right. Eugenio Pacelli, Pius XII, is about to be canonized. It's bad enough he's been called Hitler's Pope, but fathering a child? Vatican spies and assassins—real ones, not just imaginary ones of some paranoid Hollywood script— wouldn't look good on the front page of the *New York Times*." Valentine took half a step forward, turning his body slightly, offering Delaney a fractionally smaller target.

"Something like that."

In that moment Finn knew exactly what was going to happen. Any second now, Valentine, sublimely and with idiot chivalry, was going to make his move, distracting the policeman and giving her at least the faint possibility of escape. What was that silly thing her mother used to say? *Faint heart ne'er won fair lady?* Sometimes she wondered how the world had continued to exist in the face of that kind of thinking, Helen of Troy being a prime example.

Not today, she thought to herself. Not today and not on my account. She realized that she had the bunch of duplicate keys in her hand and gently she eased the long jagged door key for the Toyota into her fist, end pointing out. She hesitated for a second, swallowing, her eyes flickering to Valentine, knowing desperately that she didn't have what it took, the courage or the foolishness, the anger or even the basic instinct for self-preservation. Jesus! She was from Ohio! This kind of thing didn't happen! She was a girl!

"Bullshit!" she whispered. Delaney turned, his eyes on her again, widening as she danced toward him, a single blinding image of Michaelangelo's dissection drawing of the woman in her mind. Valentine moved as she did, and for a fatal instant the policeman froze, unable to decide.

Finn's balled fist struck him in the neck and the gun went off, shattering the light over his head and throwing Finn into darkness for the second time, shards of glass scattering everywhere. She felt the length of the newly cut car key tear into Delaney's flesh, the rough burrs of the stabbing metal shaft ripping through his external carotid artery, blood suddenly pumping up and splashing across Finn's cheek. The Glock fired a second time, the bullet tearing past her ear, the muzzle flash lighting up the gouge she'd torn with the key and Delaney staggering back, free hand clapped to the spurting wound. He dropped to his knees in front of the body of the man from Rome, life draining away in measured pulses as he fell and darkness furled inward once again.

51

She sat on the front steps of the elegant old house on St. Luke's Place and looked out through the rustling trees to the park beyond. The children were still skipping as darkness fell. The lights of the night city were blossoming everywhere. She could hear Valentine on the reception phone, calling everyone he could think of in the press. The police were on their way, as were the FBI. He'd called Barrie Kornitzer as well, who would now get busy spreading the story across the World Wide Web. Notoriety would keep them safe enough, at least for the time being.

The next hours and days were going to be a nightmare, but at least the killing was over, and slowly, very slowly, the pent-up fear was fading. In a little while she'd figure out some way of getting in touch with her mother and begin to tell her at least some of what had happened, perhaps even a little bit about Michael Valentine and the drawing she'd discovered from Michelangelo's notebook. But not yet. All she really wanted now was to rest. She listened to the invisible children, chanting:

"Matthew, Mark, Luke and John,
Once they were, but now they're gone.
Judas, Andrew, they're both dead.
Then came Paul, who lost his head."

Finally, she dropped her head down onto her folded arms. In the distance the first sirens began to wail. It was over now, but she knew that really it had just begun. Behind her, through the open door she could hear the quiet sounds of Valentine on the telephone. In the park, beyond the trees, the children's voices faded like a dark dream.

"Simon he was simple.
Andrew came to grief.
Thomas was a doubter.
Judas was a thief."

Finn smiled to herself and closed her eyes, and then, for a moment at least, she slept.

Author's Note

Much of the information contained in *Michelangelo's Notebook* is true. Eugenio Pacelli, later Pope Pius XII, is known to have had an intimate relationship with his niece, Katherine Annunzio, while he was both Papal Nuncio in Berlin and later as Vatican secretary of state, a post he held until 1939, when he was elected pope. It is also known that his niece was confined in a convent in northern Italy and committed suicide shortly after the birth of her son. There is no conclusive evidence as to the fate of the child although some Vatican historians have speculated that Pacelli's close friend, Archbishop Francis Joseph, Cardinal Spellman of New York, may have helped in the child's relocation to the United States. Spellman, as chaplain to the United States Army, was in Rome during the closing days of the second world war.

It is also known that there was a direct relationship between Pacelli and the disappearance of the so-called Gold Train, as well as six truckloads of looted art hijacked by associates of Gerhard Utikal, Paris director of the ERR unit directing the theft of art from France, Belgium and Holland. Utikal's fate, at least officially, is still a mystery although there is some evidence that he escaped to South America through the so-called Vatican ratlines.

A large amount of looted art, including a startling quantity of ecclesiastical works, has recently been showing up in the United States. The largest amount of this art, commonly referred to as the Quedlingburg Treasure has now been returned to its rightful owners.

The annual world market for stolen, looted and otherwise misappropriated artwork and antiquities, including that held by museums and public galleries, exceeds five billion dollars. The vast majority of art looted during Hitler's Third Reich has never been found. The looted artworks mentioned in the story, such as the painting by Juan Gris and Rembrandt's *Raising of Lazarus*, are all real.

There really was a convent/maternity home occupying the site of 421 Hudson Street in New York, and the children's playground directly across the street really was once a large burial ground occupying two city blocks of Greenwich Village, including the churchyard once favored by Edgar Allan Poe on his midnight rambles. There is no Number 11 St. Luke's Place, but the exterior of Number 10 was used as the facade of the Hux-table residence on the Bill Cosby show of the 1980s.

The notebook known to have been used by Michelangelo for his human anatomy drawings has never been found.